D0201126

how elizabeth barrett browning saved my life

Also by Mameve Medwed

Mail

Host Family

The End of an Error

wm
WILLIAM MORROW
An Imprint of HarperCollins*Publishers*

how elizabeth barrett browning saved my life

MAMEVE MEDWED

Grateful acknowledgment is made to reprint excerpts from the following:

"the Cambridge ladies who live in furnished souls." Copyright 1923, 1951, © 1991 by the Trustees for the E. E. Cummings Trust. Copyright © 1976 by George James Firmage, from *Complete Poems: 1904–1962* by E. E. Cummings, edited by George J. Firmage. Used by permission of Liveright Publishing Corporation.

"Who's Sorry Now." Music by Ted Snyder, words by Bert Kalmar and Harry Ruby. Copyright 1925 (renewed 1951) by EMI Mills Music, Inc. All rights controlled by EMI Mills Music, Inc. (publishing) and Alfred Publishing Co., Inc. (printing). All rights reserved. Used by permission.

FIRST EDITION

Designed by Sarah Maya Gubkin

Printed on acid-free paper

Library of Congress Cataloging-in-Publication Data

Medwed, Mameve.
How Elizabeth Barrett Browning saved my life / Mameve Medwed.—1st ed.
p. cm.
ISBN-13: 978-0-06-083119-6
ISBN-10: 0-06-083119-7
1. Browning, Elizabeth Barrett, 1806–1861—Relics—Fiction. 2. Antiques roadshow (Television program: U.S.)—Fiction. 3. Collectors and collecting—Fiction. 4. Antique dealers—Fiction. 5. Boston (Mass.)—Fiction. 6. Single women—Fiction. 7. Chamber pots—Fiction. I. Title.

PS3563.E275H66 2006
813'.54—dc22 2005049611

06 07 08 09 10 WBC/QWF 10 9 8 7 6 5 4 3 2 1

For Howard

Let me count the ways. . . .

the Cambridge ladies who live in furnished souls

the Cambridge ladies who live in furnished souls
are unbeautiful and have comfortable minds
(also, with the church's protestant blessings
daughters, unscented shapeless spirited)
they believe in Christ and Longfellow, both dead,
are invariably interested in so many things—
at the present writing one still finds
delighted fingers knitting for the is it Poles?
perhaps. While permanent faces coyly bandy
scandal of Mrs. N and Professor D
. . . the Cambridge ladies do not care, above
Cambridge if sometimes in its box of
sky lavender and cornerless, the
moon rattles like a fragment of angry candy

—E. E. Cummings, May 1922

I

It's midafternoon on a Monday, too quiet here at Objects of Desire. And too gloomy. Those cruel calendar pages have flipped to January. Short days. Endless dark nights. After months of ho-ho-ho to assault a bah-humbug soul. The fluorescent tubes ringing my booth flicker and buzz. The shepherd and shepherdess lamps that flank the faux mantel—$129 a pair, nineteenth-century English, a real bargain—lack bulbs. Their wiring is faulty. Clyde promised to fix it. He promised a lot of things. I look at the sign—A&C ECLECTIBLES. I should have painted over the *C* when Clyde ran off with that woman whose goods he appraised a month ago. But A ECLECTIBLES offends my grammarian's soul.

I pick up the *New York Times* crossword puzzle. Four-letter lake in

Africa. Starts with *M.* Clyde was good at geography. He collected old maps. I toss the paper in the coal shuttle—solid brass, eighteenth century—which serves as wastebasket. *You never finish anything,* I can hear Clyde say.

Not true, I'd protest. It's just that I don't like putting periods on the ends of sentences; I prefer to keep things open. Have many experiences. A lack of focus, my father would diagnose. My mother would have said I was finding myself. She'd found herself in her fifties when she left my father, the world-renowned R. Griffin Randolph, the holder of the Epworth chair in humanities at Harvard. She ran off with Henrietta Potter, the wife of Bickford Potter, the Harvard economist, near Nobel laureate. Henrietta had been her roommate at Smith. *You go on finding yourself until you die,* my mother said.

It comforts me to remember that my mother, having found herself, also found happiness before she and Henrietta died last year in that earthquake in India. You saw the photos in the newspaper. Tattered, soot-showered children buried under the rubble. Sari-wrapped keening mothers. Cows and goats flattened by collapsed walls. In such a landscape, who could ever picture my tidy mother and no-nonsense Henrietta with their scrubbed rosy faces, their neat gray pageboys, their sensible Birkenstocks, their money belts and multipocketed safari vests ordered from the Travelers' Catalogue? Their natural self-effacement struck an incongruous note against such high drama. But when a postcard came a month later, *Sunset over the Taj Mahal,* I realized the niche I'd put my mother in couldn't contain her. *I have at last discovered true joy. Pure ecstasy,* my mother had written.

Now that my mother's not around to defend me, or Clyde to defend myself against, I have to admit that Clyde had a point about my not finishing things. I'd quit Harvard four credits short of my B.A. I joined the Peace Corps and dropped out before the posting at Rwanda. I headed for a banking internship on Wall Street but turned back at Hartford.

At thirty-three, though, I figured I was starting to settle into a career as a partner in A&C Eclectibles. The *A* for Abigail. The *C* for . . . Well, it doesn't take a Harvard degree to figure that out. In spite of my starts and stops, I'd always liked everybody's leavings, the discarded and dented bits and pieces of other people's lives. Even as a kid, I'd look forward to trash-collection mornings the way my lower-school mates anticipated opening day at Fenway Park. The old books, chipped china, frayed lamp shades I'd rescued from Brattle Street barrels threatened to turn my room into a Collyer Brothers annex. *Our Abigail's a pack rat,* my father would opine as I'd tiptoe past his study with yet another box of salvage. *Everything's a learning experience,* my mother would soothe.

My mother took me to flea markets and auctions before I could walk. She scored the Lincoln portrait in my father's study while I was in utero. When I was seven, I bid on a yarn-haired, gingham-pinafored doll at a farmhouse auction in Maine, where we rented a lakeside cottage. I'd squirreled away five crisp birthday dollars. All the other bidders dropped off when they saw my grubby hand shoot up in ten-cent increments. All except a burly man sporting a billed trucker's cap who raised me a dollar to my every dime. *Let the little girl have it,* chimed an angry chorus, the summer people and locals for once in accord. *A great big bruiser like you,* somebody scolded, shame slapping him down into his seat.

The victory of that moment trumped my successes to date: winning the neighborhood scavenger hunt and guessing, within twenty, the number of jelly beans in a mayonnaise jar. I was hooked.

I met Clyde two years ago at the Brimfield flea market when our hands grabbed at the same time for a copper bed warmer stamped PLYMOUTH, MASS and on sale for a song. He tugged; I tugged. He wouldn't let go; neither would I.

"Ladies first," I said, a feminist not opposed to using nonfeminist wiles. My grip tightened on the splintered wood.

"All's fair in love and war." He yanked.

"This isn't either," I said, though I could hear the roaring of far-off tanks. "And may I point out that I won the badge for arm wrestling in Girl Scout camp."

"Not to one-up you," he one-upped, "but I myself have wrestled steers to the ground in a rodeo." He smiled. His eyes crinkled. Just as I was thinking, He's cute, he said, "Though let me add, I've never wrestled someone quite so cute."

I felt my grip loosening. I couldn't help myself.

He pulled. I held on. "Do you ever read those wedding columns in the *New York Times* about how people met?" he asked.

"Not really," I lied. I who ignore the news, flip past Sports and Business, and turn to the Styles section the second the Sunday papers hit my front door.

"Well, there was one recently about this couple who met at the Chelsea flea market while fighting over a pink pasta canister."

"Oh," I said, feigning the indifference of someone who'd just heard East Asia's weather report. I remembered that column; I'd memorized the groom's toast to his bride: *Who knew in looking to furnish my apartment I ended up furnishing my heart and soul.* "So?" I asked.

He ducked his chin. "Not that I'd dare presume. Not that it would ever happen to us."

"Of course not." I was about to add that such things don't happen in real life. According to the *Times*, however, they did. Who could dispute the authenticity of all the news that's fit to print? I stroked the dented copper of the warming pan. I admired the patina that guaranteed age.

"Why don't we see if the dealer will put this aside for an hour to let us settle ownership issues over a drink."

We squeezed onto the end of a picnic bench next to two fanny-packed collectors on one side; on the other, their just-purchased spinning wheel and four-foot-tall Elvis made out of beer cans. Clyde bought lemonade and fried dough. By the time our fingers were shiny with grease and powdered with confectioners' sugar, I'd learned this: He'd just moved to Cambridge. He had a room at the Y while looking for a place he could afford.

"What a coincidence!" I exclaimed. I who'd lived my whole life in a Cambridge Victorian on Brattle Street had just rented a needs-work walk-up in Inman Square a few blocks from the Y. For reasons I won't go into, I was lonely. I was miserable.

Well, as you already know, this is no reader-I-married-him scenario. No met-cute-and-now-keeping-the-copper-polished-for-our-grandchildren bit of nostalgia. But as you must have guessed, we rushed back to the booth and bought that bed warmer together. Split it right down the middle with Clyde supplying the extra penny for the tax.

Within a month, that bed warmer was warming the wall in my Inman Square apartment over our shared Sealy Posturepedic the way other couples might hang those kissing lovers in Chagall's *Birthday*. Until we sold it for double what we paid for it. We rented the booth together at Objects of Desire. Spent weekends and mornings trawling for treasure at flea markets and auctions and junk stores. Clyde, a graduate of an aggie college in the Midwest who grew up with Barcaloungers and dinettes and fifties bad taste before it was fashionable, had an inordinate reverence for earlier centuries and for all things New England, especially my parents' separate effects, their rooms full of Chippendale, their minor Hudson River painters, their leather-bound first editions, their silver grape shears, their China trade demitasse sets. *Her father holds the Epworth chair,* he used to say when introducing me. I guess I—Abigail her-father-holds-the-Epworth-chair Randolph—was the vanishing perspective point in the big picture. Even so, I must confess we got as far as discussing theoretical wedding plans. We were keen on the subjunctive. "If I were to get married, I'd pick a rocky beach in Maine," I said.

"If I were ever to tie the knot, it would have to be the Harvard Faculty Club," he said.

I'd taken him there once when the line for Mr. Bartley's Burger Cottage snaked down the sidewalk and onto the steps of the Harvard Bookstore. The only benefit was no cash changed hands; I could sign my father's name. "If you remember, we both agreed the food stinks. If I were to choose, I'd like a clambake. With corn on the cob cooked in its husk. And blueberry pie."

"If it were up to me, I'd go for the Faculty Club's *saumon en croûte*," he said. "The perfect wedding dish." He hesitated. "If there were a wedding," he hastened to add.

I'd had the *saumon en croûte* at Lavinia Potter's nonsubjunctive first wedding. It was a soggy mess. Like her marriage. But I didn't say so. What I said was, "How about Brimfield? That patch of grass next to the concession that makes fried dough. If one were looking for a sentimental setting . . ."

He was not touched. He was not amused. Not even theoretically. "It needs to look good. Appearance matters," he instructed.

This turned out to be the truth. You can't say I wasn't warned when he ran off with that woman whose silver he appraised. "What chair does *her* father hold? Louis Quatorze?" I asked Clyde when he dropped the news.

"It was not that she was sexier or more accomplished," I told my friends, who loyally claimed they had never liked Clyde anyway—too eager to please, too quick to laugh at their jokes, to compliment their Cambridge jeans and vintage Bakelite bracelets. "It was that her stuff had better hallmarks than mine."

I don't even miss *him* that much, I remind myself. I miss our treasure hunts, our mutual love of distressed pine and foxed lithographs and flaking mercury glass and crazed porcelain. Can I confess that our mutual exhilaration over a bargain turned out to be more of an earthmover than our near-mutual orgasms. Not that the sex wasn't fine, too. As was the simple comfort of another body to warm my cold toes on a gloomy night, to attack the cockroaches in the silverware drawer.

It would be nice to replace that body with a spare held in reserve like the backup roll of paper towels under the sink. No such luck. There aren't many prospects in my business. They're either gay, or antique themselves, or pudgy, tracksuit-wearing, comic-book-collecting husbands married to pudgy, tracksuit-wearing, Hummel-collecting wives. Or, worse, men so slick you want to slide right away from them. My neighborhood doesn't offer many possibilities either; Portuguese family men and beer-swilling off-duty cops. Most of my friends who haven't already nabbed significant others spend their nights in bars looking for them, then want to fix me up with their discards. "It's not that you're that fussy, Abby," my former college roommate once pointed out. "Look at Clyde."

"Clyde had his charms," I protested. But she and I both knew my argument was weak.

These days I'm trying to resign myself to the possibility of all-out spinsterdom. Even though I'm considered acceptable in the looks department, even though I long got over my fears of inheriting my mother's midlife proclivities once I realized I wasn't the only one at Girl Scout camp to fall in love with Miss Garnett. (I was a mere spear-carrier in the mass crush on our exercise instructor, who had danced with Martha Graham and was recovering from a nervous breakdown when she came to test the restorative waters by leading us in jumping jacks.) Don't get the wrong impression. While mine's hardly a *Sex and the City* life (we Cantabridgians frown on that—who could wear such shoes on New England cobblestones?), I've had my share of romance. I've slept more than adequately with four men; one I thought I loved. But better not bring *that* up. Besides, I've completely gotten over him.

Still, it's on low consumer Mondays like these that the quiet and the loneliness take their toll. I shift sideways to avoid the lumpy spring in the Victorian chair of ripped tapestry and arms that end in dragon's heads. FIFTY PERCENT REDUCED declares a yellow tag that hangs from a twist of mahogany flame shooting from the dragon's mouth. If I don't sell this soon, it will be reduced to the price of a subway pass and will end up in my doll-sized Inman Square apartment squeezed next to other misguided purchases, stools made of antler's horns and vases you couldn't stuff a tulip's stem in—my own personal *salon des refusées*. Whatever I inherited from my mother, after I wrestled a few items from Henrietta's kids, my ex-friend Lavinia in particular, went directly to those big storage vaults out near Alewife.

Boy, did Clyde want to stick his hands on my mother's stuff. While pretty much everything was of a higher quality than our cut-above junk, it's their sentimental value I treasure. I will never sell them, I promise myself. Even if starvation looms. At Clyde's urging—an amicus brief on behalf of shabby chic—I did bring in a couple of Henrietta's chipped bowls and a cracked platter with a drawing of Eliot House that my mother and Henrietta used to serve cheese and crackers on. Lavinia didn't want these, although it was her father who had been master of Eliot House. And I can understand why Ned, her brother, didn't even bother to put in a claim.

After Clyde left, after we split the stock, I had to bring in a few bits and pieces to fill the holes. A half-empty booth is never inviting, especially one that looks like it's been excavated in the aftermath of a heavy-duty division of spoils attendant on a divorce. But these were things—pots and plates and platters—no one would buy.

Now I lean over to take a year-old mint from a battered pewter plate and catch my sleeve on a slivered shard of wood. Clyde and I had discussed getting the chair refinished and reupholstered; the springs tied. We'd discussed, subjunctively again, recaning a stool, regilding the chips of a gold-leafed frame. Around us, other booths were set up like living rooms, polished and primped, smelling of beeswax and bowls of potpourri; magazines fanned out on coffee tables, pillows plumped. If we spiffed up our booth, maybe our sales would improve, was the theory we floated. But we were purists, we boasted. Shabby chic was coming back. And when it came down to it, we were cheap.

Now I hear some scraping, furniture being moved, a carpet shifted from the booth next to me. A partition separates us. Clyde and I painted our side white. We hung a few Currier & Ives lithographs on it. *Reproductions,* dismissed the Fogg Museum's curator of prints, who stuck his head in during a semi annual scouting mission. On Gus Robideau's side, called Les Antiquaires de Versailles, though he's Québécois, the walls are covered in brocade; anchored to them are gold sconces topped by fat cavorting cupids whose dimpled fists clutch arrows. The sconces sell like hotcakes. Anointed "one of a kind," they are immediately replenished from an unending supply. *People go big for cupids and cats and dogs,* Gus has pointed out more times than I can count. *You need to know your customers.*

There's not a cupid or cat in all of A&C Eclectibles, though I once thought I could make out a rubbed-away sketch of a dog on one of my mother's pots. My problem, I guess, is that I *don't* know my customers. Unlike Clyde, who got to know one of them a little too well.

"No customers?" Gus now feels the need to state the obvious. "How you doing, Abby?" He saunters into my booth. He leans his considerable weight against the faux mantel, but I don't say anything. If it cracks, it'll just give it more age. He's wearing a suit with vest and foulard tie. His mustache is waxed to curl up at the ends. And his glasses are antique pince-nez refitted. I can see the bifocal line. I'm in jeans and an old Gap T with a stretched-out neck. His brow is knitted with concern. The kind of look you'd give someone slumped on a Victorian chaise like an invalid with a wasting disease.

"Always slow on Mondays," I say.

"Not always," he corrects. "An hour ago I sold a set of girandoles for three times what I paid for 'em. One of those decorators," he adds.

I nod. The decorators are usually blondes with lacquered pageboys secured behind one ear by a tortoiseshell barrette, French manicures, chic bouclé suits, and needle heels that pockmark the planked wood floors like acne scars. We all pretend to disdain them, those who want to match a painting to a sofa, to buy books that look well read for clients who will never open them—but without these ladies, well, we might not be able to afford the occasional jug of wine to go with our day-old loaf of bread.

Gus points. "How about moving that pot around so the design's in the front," he suggests. Before I can answer, he leans over and turns an inch of rim against the wall. He straightens the fake fern I have put inside it. I'm embarrassed. The fern is not to my taste. Or Clyde's. We hated fake flowers, plastic plants, silk begonias. But because the booth is an interior one, no windows, no natural light, the pot looked forlorn without the hint of greenery, however man-made.

"What have we here?" Gus asks. Gus bends lower; he pulls out a stemmed champagne flute from the Styrofoam moss and pebbles that nobody would mistake for soil. "Must be from the party last night." He chuckles.

I sit up. "What party?" I ask.

He has the good sense to blush. He blots his forehead with a matched-to-tie foulard handkerchief. "Well, it *was* last-minute," he explains. "Rankin had a case of champagne. He finally unloaded that Biedermeier sideboard. Buyer didn't even try to bargain. Paid full price."

I lean back into my chair. My wallflower's chair.

"I guess people figured you wouldn't be in the mood, considering Clyde and all," he goes on.

"It was a while ago. I'm over that."

"You may think you are."

"What does that mean?"

He doesn't answer. He turns away from me and pretends interest in my demoted Currier & Ives. He moves a few plates aside, taps a dented umbrella stand. "That son of a bitch who doesn't know a priceless object when he sees it," he insists with a good-walls-make-good-neighbors loyalty. "You're one hell of a fine-looking woman. And nice," he adds as an afterthought.

"Thanks." I lower my eyes. "Really."

"It's nada." He shoves his handkerchief back in his pocket. "For starters, let's take this hideous fern out of this perfectly saleable pot." He picks up the fern, scoops out the Styrofoam and pebble soil, and dumps it into the coal shuttle, first rescuing the page of the *Times* with the half-filled crossword puzzle. "What's this?" he asks.

"Four-letter lake in Africa. Starts with *M*."

He crumbles the paper. He rubs the inside of the pot. Looks closer. Then spits into it.

"Gus, this isn't a cuspidor."

He ignores me. He rubs again, harder. The paper squeaks.

"What are you doing? Trying to raise a genie?"

"Very funny. If you'd take time to clean your merchandise . . . a little spit and polish." He taps the bottom. "I mean, what's *this*?"

"It's a chamber pot," I say.

"I know that." Gus sighs like someone bravely bearing an insult. He turns the pot upside down.

"It was my mother's," I explain. "One of my mother's old things I brought in after Clyde left, to spiff up our inventory. Nothing special," I add.

"Its *provenance*?" Gus demands. He gives the word the theatrical French spin of an Hercule Poirot.

"Marked *Made in Portugal*. Which means, of course, it's not old."

"Don't be so sure." Gus is studying the chamber pot; he takes his pince-nez off; he puts them on. He turns the bowl over and around.

"Gus, you of all people know how things are 'antiqued' for the tourist trade."

"Hmmm," he says. He sticks his face all the way in. I shudder even though it's clean and its purpose long obliterated by decades of indoor plumbing. "There's some faint sketch of a dog here," Gus mumbles.

"I know. You can barely see it."

"A cocker spaniel, looks like. And a bit of writing. Seems to spell *Flush.*"

"A subsequent owner's idea of a joke," I say. "Whoever bought it must have added it. Rather anachronistic when you consider the function . . ."

He shakes his head. He flicks a couple of fingers against the side and makes a resounding ping.

"I could probably dig up a couple of drumsticks and a washboard," I joke. "We could have ourselves a party." I am thinking of the glass flute. Of the party in my own place of business that excluded me.

"If I weren't an honest dealer . . ." he begins.

"Come on." I remember when he showed me how to make new mirror glass black and smoky, to rub a table leg just so to exhibit age, to distress a clockface, to soak a white linen cloth in tea. Not to mention those "nineteenth-century" pairs of sconces, their cupids clutching arrows at the exact same angle while rolling off a twenty-first-century assembly line somewhere in the third world. Would I myself have been tempted to pass off the reproduction Currier & Ives as the real thing? No. Not Abigail Elizabeth Randolph, who, without a (metaphorical) pot to piss in, still has her integrity.

"If I didn't like you so much . . . Didn't feel sorry for you, that good-for-nothing just up and taking a powder with that decorator type . . ."

"Yes?" I ask. I've got all morning. I've got all day.

"Abby, this doesn't say *Made in Portugal.* It says *From the Portuguese*—and seems to be scribbled in by hand, not a china maker's mark . . ."

"So?"

"Come take a gander," he orders.

I push myself up out of my wallflower's chair. I follow his pink-tipped finger. Manicure? I trace my own ragged nails framed by bitten cuticles (it's hard being left for an object even if the leaver is not necessarily the object of your desire). Gus is right. The blue letters, smudged and faded, spell out *From the Portuguese*. The porcelain is discolored—from age and—well—you know from what; the design, blue and yellow flowers, seems sweet but uninteresting. Underneath the crude, faint drawing of a spaniel, I can indeed make out some scratched letters spelling *Flush*. Funny how I hadn't noticed that before. Funny how I hadn't noticed lots of things. "It's a mistake," I suggest. "Someone who didn't have the benefit of English as a second language must have mixed up *Made* with *From*. And later"—I stroke my chin in my best Sherlock Holmes impersonation—"probably a pet lover sketched his dog. No paper handy. Then scratched in *Flush* as a joke, being ironic. In place of the usual *Please keep me clean so I won't tell what I have seen*."

Gus shakes his head. He sets the chamber pot back on the floor with an unexpected tenderness.

"Take it from me," he says.

"Isn't it already mine?" I ask.

"I'm not joking," he says. "Let me give you a piece of advice."

I smile nicely, trying to hide my well-warranted distrust of Gus's advice. Even his restaurant and movie suggestions left a lot to be desired. Elaborate presentations that tasted lousy. Gorgeous settings with no story line. As for the mechanic he recommended, Tom and Ray themselves would have been at a loss for words over that "rebuilt" carburetor.

"If I were you, I'd take this little ole chamber pot onto *Antiques Roadshow*. I've got a connection to get you a ticket. I just have a feeling you might be harboring a treasure here."

2

I get to the Hynes Auditorium at 7 A.M. Gus has told me I'd be smart to arrive before dawn. The line starts forming even when it's still dark, he explained. I meant to take his advice, I really did. But, well, February mornings in Cambridge are—well, February mornings. The way my radiators were hissing and clanking with so much rah-rah-rah, only a masochist would crawl out from under the burrow of my three (nineteenth-century Amish) piled quilts.

At six-thirty, I took the T. I had sold my mother's car when I realized how much it would cost me to park it, to register it, to get the snow tires taken on and off. Besides, cars in the city make no sense. When I need to lug stuff or go out of town, I've got my choice of dozens of SAVE THE

WHALES–bannered station wagons from the Rent-A-Wreck around the corner. Otherwise, we have a broad public transportation system.

Which doesn't always act great, but this morning did. I got to the station just as the train pulled up. I snagged a seat right away, two, in fact, since the chamber pot is padded in so much Bubble Wrap it's more than double its size. Gus had devised a cat's cradle of rope with handles on each side so that when I got to the Hynes stop I could just about carry it up the steps. Surprise, surprise, the escalator was broken; it's never worked in my lifetime or anybody else's. Halfway up, I was out of breath and struggling (note to myself: Raid petty cash, join gym) when this guy behind me tapped my shoulder.

"Need help with that?" he asked.

I turned around. He looked about twenty, with pinchable cheeks and cowlicks you just wanted to reach out and tame.

I'd like to think he tapped me on the shoulder because he felt the same about me. But from the back, what could he tell? A woman, older, huffing and puffing because she didn't go to the gym, hefting this huge bundle in front of her stomach as if she were pregnant with twins. Should I accept his offer? I was pretty sure such gallantry came not from the automatic pilot for flirting turned on by the opposite sex, but from the imprinted good manners of someone who'd been taught to help little old ladies across the street. Little old ladies with unwieldy packages.

Still, looks deceive, as I've learned only too well. I clutched my package tighter. All I needed was this baby-faced Nelson sweet-talking me. You know the rest. The minute I put that bundle into his hands, he'd vault the frozen escalator with one jump of those well-muscled legs so sexily bursting his jeans. And that would mean the end of my maybe valuable, probably not, chamber pot.

"I can manage just fine," I lied.

"Whatever." He shrugged. "Excuse me." He brushed by, jostling my hip, and cleared those stairs like a gold medalist in the triathlon.

By the time I got to the top and struggled out the door and across two streets to the auditorium, I started to regret my lack of trust. Was it something innate? Behavior learned in my childhood? The old nature-versus-nurture conundrum. Maybe it was something formed by too many betrayals. Or by one in particular. God knows I could never do those exercises where you fall backward through space confident that your fellow camper will be there to catch you. I'd start to lean, then jerk upright like I'd received an electric shock. Even when I heard a voice assure me, "Let go, I'm right here," I still couldn't help it. It was downright Pavlovian.

When I finally make it inside the door, the line is so long and packed so tight the crowd would hold you up even if you wanted to fall.

I take my place at the end. Yellow police tape holds back the throngs. The din of a thousand voices chatting rises to the rafters. Across from the line, huge partitions mark off appraisal areas and production sets. Excitement sparks the air. By comparison, the hand-clapping, hip-swiveling, feet-stomping crowd at a Pearl Jam concert seems subdued. That time I went—lover number three—I was nearly flattened to death in the stampede of fans toward the stage just as Eddie Vedder grabbed the mike. But if there is this kind of fan base for collectibles, I can only congratulate myself (and thank Gus) on a smart career move.

"Sorry, miss." A man with a lopsided dolly bumps my shins. He is having trouble steering this two-wheeler, especially hampered by the enormous carousel horse strapped with bungee cords to its planked platform. "When I borrowed this here thingamajig, I didn't think I'd need a course in drivers' ed."

"It's okay," I say, though I can already sense the black-and-blue marks colonizing my legs. "Some horse," I add. It *is* impressive. Nearly my height with a spiral barber pole and lots of bright gold paint. A bit too bright, I think, but don't point that out. Carousel horses don't fall under my sphere of expertise.

"Isn't it a beaut? I found it at a flea market. A steal. I did the research off the Internet. Good ones can go for seventy thousand dollars and up."

Wow. Imagine what I could do with even seven thousand dollars. I think of my limited wardrobe, my needs-work apartment, my shabby booth. I think of the flea markets of Paris and Rome. I think of Sotheby's auction halls. I think of antiquing through the coastal towns of California, stopping for R & R in inns with hot tubs and Pacific views, signing up for wine-tasting trips to Napa in the company of laid-back wine-loving men. I think of Caribbean islands, piña coladas, bikinis in winter, the gym membership to fit those bikinis all four seasons of the year.

"So, what have you got there?" asks the man with the horse. He points to my globe of Bubble Wrap.

"A chamber pot."

He pinches his nose with fingers thick as fish sticks. "Pee-ew." He smirks. "You're kidding, right?"

I pat my package like it's an underachiever with Ivy League potential. "I was told on very good authority—an expert in the field—that it might be something quite valuable."

He guffaws. "What field might that be?" He snorts. "Water closets? Urinals? Toiletology?" He slaps his thigh. "Not worth a pot to piss in, if you pardon my French. See them by the dozens at Brimfield. Dealers can't get rid of them. Maybe a little old lady might buy one for her Boston fern. Some decorator to fill with magazines. If you ask me, you're wasting your time waiting in this crowd."

I look around. The line behind us now hits the door and curls back into a figure eight. People are carrying, pushing, lugging, dollying, trolleying, shopping-cart-wheeling, red-wagon-yanking the most amazing things. Toys, paintings, armoires, mirrors, stuffed animals. One man drags a fireplace mantel with trompe l'oeil marbling; another leans on a black potbellied stove. There's even a quilt hanging over someone's walker, and what must be a dozen Barbie dolls in their boxes crammed into an old-fashioned English perambulator.

"Thanks for the advice. Since I've invested this much time and effort, though, I might as well stay."

He shrugs.

"Plus you never know," I say, my voice with a brightness as faux as the marble on that mantelpiece.

"Suit yourself." He turns to the man beside him, who is carrying a box of polka-dotted Easter eggs.

I study the hall. People are talking to each other. Everyone but me, that is, now that my neighbor has found a better conversationalist. Me who didn't get asked to the party. Me who got left. Me with the dysfunctional family and dysfunctional social life. The people just in front of him, a family, mom and dad in GO SOX! scarves, are arguing with their two sullen teenage daughters in matching cargo pants. "Grandpa's pipes may pay for college," the mother placates.

"As if," one daughter says.

"This sucks," the other daughter chimes.

I am almost starting to agree when there's a big commotion. The hall goes quiet with a sudden communal intake of breath, then starts to buzz again. The line begins to move. At the same time, the partitions vibrate as important-looking people with name tags and clipboards come out from behind them and head toward us huddled masses inside our yellow-police-taped barricades. We could be an army of immigrants dragging, kicking, pulling, wheeling our goods and chattels forward waiting to be offered—what?—a job, a bunk in a displaced persons camp, a crust of bread from a soup kitchen? But at least we're not the downtrodden masses. We—some of us anyway—laugh, smile, chat. Full of high spirits, we reach for the brass ring, our Horatio Alger pot of gold, our American dream.

A dream that's instantly dashed for the man with the horse behind me. "Sorry," says a woman with a name tag—ERNESTINE EVERETT—clipped to her lapel and a magnifying glass hanging from a chain around her neck. "It's a rather inexpensive copy, not wood, but resin." She runs a crimson nail fashionably squared off over the ridged horse's tail. "Not real gold leaf either. Too bright. Too thick."

"Are you sure?"

She nods. She's got I-feel-your-pain eyes. She manages a chin-up smile. "I'm sure your children will enjoy it whether or not it's an antique."

"Don't have them," he grunts, then sideswipes my ankle as he rolls his rejected, cheap, resin, not-real-gold-leaf carousel horse out of the line of the happy possibles and into the sad, dashed-hopes trek home.

Meanwhile I am unwinding the Bubble Wrap shrouding my chamber pot. I'm thinking how my mother used to peel an orange, in one smooth graceful motion, producing at the end of her knife a single continuous spiraling rind. The sudden sharp stab of missing her comes at me sideways. Unprepared, I reel. The fact of her death hits at odd times, in unlikely places. How could she not be here? How could she die? My picture of her flashes like a hologram. Just as I start to see her face, she turns into Uncle Sam, then a logo for MasterCard. I can't grab hold of her. Everything I once thought fixed now shifts. I had a certain kind of Cambridge childhood. She was a certain kind of Cambridge academic wife. She should have died of old age in her mahogany four-poster attended by me and her creaky friends from her bluestocking lunch-and-earnest-conversation clubs. She should be lying in the family plot at Mount Auburn Cemetery surrounded by the headstones of Winslow Homer, Nathaniel Bowditch, and Fanny Farmer, not to mention her Brattle Street neighbor, Henry Wadsworth Longfellow.

How could someone so sensible, so competent, so conventionally Cambridge fall so dramatically and unconventionally in love? And at such an unlikely age? How could she have died so unnaturally? So far away from home? So far away from me? What of her is in me? Not her competence, I realize now, as I wrangle with an inert piece of plastic. Her romanticism, her passion, lay just under the surface, unseen by me, unnoticed by my brilliant Epworth-chair-holding father, a man who can excavate from the densest text the most deeply buried splinter of clarity but for whom family members tiptoeing past his study, those seen-not-heard souls at his dinner table, remain an enigma hardly worth deciphering. Who would have thought that the real beating heart of Emily Granby Randolph would be heard only by mousy-haired, quiet Henrietta Potter—the last person on earth you'd ever imagine sharing the sunset over the Taj Mahal with.

Love can be dangerous, I know that. Friends betray you. Family members die or disappoint you because you disappoint them. Misunderstandings turn poisonous. You have to be careful. I've had my moments. I've scaled ecstasy only to plummet to despair. And I don't mean Clyde. Look at my mother—would she have died if she hadn't given all for love? Would she have traipsed across continents to a country where the seismic activity means you're never on solid ground? Without such love, she'd still be here, on good old Brattle Street terra firma, serving bouillon in translucent china cups, writing letters to the editor, composing exquisite thank-you notes.

My mother's delicacy and grace in all things, like her competence, seems not to have come down in my DNA. I'm making a mess of unpacking this chamber pot. There was an article in yesterday's *Globe* about an artist whose medium was Bubble Wrap. He videotaped himself popping six hundred square feet of it in sixteen hours, then hung the spent warp on the walls of a gallery at the Boston Center for the Arts. Such obsessions help bring order to a chaotic world, the art critic wrote. Wrestling with this wadded tangle, I know the critic got it wrong. But if I'm not good at unwrapping, I'm a master at unraveling. Give me a little plastic, and I can add chaos to an already chaotic world. I'm ripping; I'm pulling. Bubbles are sticking to the layers of bubbles underneath like dovetailed LEGO blocks.

"While these are quite charming," the woman is explaining to the family now in front of me who have set out their pipes on a gray flannel cloth, "they are of limited value, too new, made, alas, for the tourist trade."

"I like them anyway," the father says. His voice is defensive, almost belligerent.

"But Daddy kept them in his safety deposit box!" his wife exclaims. She sounds close to tears. "At the Bank of Boston, which became the Fleet and is now the Bank of America," she persists, as if the constancy of those pipes sitting in the vault through three changes of management should accrue enough interest to mark them as authentic antiques.

"I realize it's hard," the woman says, "but their actual value hardly mitigates their sentimental appeal."

I'm thinking what a tough job she must have. Bursting hopes. Destroying dreams. Not to mention changing one's views of one's ancestors; their taste, their business acumen, the degrees of their generosity. Imagine counting on Grandpa's pipes for your college fund.

"Come on, Ma," urges one daughter. I don't think the daughters look like college material anyway; all that makeup and hair point to cosmetology school. But who am I to talk? I who looked like college material from the day she was born, who was born into college material, whose family exuded doctorates the way pores exude sweat, never got even the lowliest B.A.

"Let's hit Filene's Basement," the other daughter demands, "and forget about this shit."

The way things are going with this little corner of the line—bad luck comes in threes, I figure—I'll soon be heading to Filene's Basement myself. Not that I could justify even one of their seven-day bargain markdowns given my career to date. *Look to the right of you; look to the left of you,* an old professor used to gloat in the days before grade inflation handed even the class dunce a *laude* of some sort, *these particular classmates—not to mention you—are bound to flunk out.*

One, the horse. Two, the pipes. Three, my turn to get an F for a pot not worth pissing in.

"What have we here?" the woman asks. She circles that chamber pot. Her mouth falls open. She drops her clipboard to the floor. Her magnifying glass sways wildly against her chest. Then catches on her ERNESTINE EVERETT name tag. Her breath comes fast in little whistles and sighs. She hoists the pot with the strength of a karate black belt. Then cradles it with the gentleness of a Madonna soothing her newborn son. She turns it. Tilts it. She sticks her head inside. She grabs her magnifying glass. She peers through it to study the faint outline of the dog.

Heads turn our way. In our immediate vicinity, conversation stops. I feel myself, like my offering, an object of sudden interest. A person of worth. I straighten my shoulders. I raise my chin. I tuck in my stomach. More people are staring now. I smile at them. I'm a benevolent monarch awarding her subjects the briefest acknowledgment. Let me ask you, how many people can attribute their rising self-image to the rising value of a chamber pot?

Things happen fast. Smiling people with VOLUNTEER pasted on their shoulders lead me behind partitions. I wait in lines with other smiling people in front of tables where more smiling people examine my chamber pot and—well—smile at me. I smile back. At ceramic experts. At Victoriana experts. At antiquarian book experts. Smiling even wider, I sign papers and release forms. Smiling appraisers, teeth bared in Cheshire cat grins, hand out their business cards. I put them in my pocketbook. I notice how shabby my pocketbook is. Its stitching's undone, its leather corners nearly white with wear. The lining is ripped; there's a stain the shape of South America from beer spilled at a Harvard Square bar that went out of business five years ago. Maybe I will go to Filene's Basement when I get out of here. I nod at another beaming face. Oh God. Maybe I'll skip the basement and buy something full price *upstairs*.

Though it takes a while, my chamber pot and I clear every obstacle in this particular Olympiad. We're heading for the awards ceremony. I can practically hear the *Oh, say, can you see* as we are steered toward the

Green Room. We are going to be taped for TV. My chamber pot will find out what it's worth. It and I will, in a month's time, be shown on every PBS station—and in continual reruns—across the land. It and I will be in your living rooms, your kitchens, your dens, on your bedside tables, in your gas station offices, and at your reception desks. My heart swells. Someone lugs a mirror fit for Versailles past me. I glance at it. My heart shrinks. My hair falls over one eye. I am wearing ragged jeans and a once-black ribbed turtleneck that has developed gray blotches from too many mixed-dark-and-whites cycles at the corner Laundromat. I'm going to be on TV!!

I stop smiling. I turn to the impeccably groomed, pressed, color-coordinated *Vogue*-modelish volunteer who is now pointing out the entrance to the Green Room, which I gather is neither green nor a room but a curtained-off area across the hall. "I'm not dressed for TV," I plead.

"You look fine," she says. And belies this statement when she adds: "We like our people to look real. Ordinary. Not like stars."

She should talk, I decide. Sure, her suit is Chanel, her shoes the sort fashionistas would pawn their silver serving trays for just to slip their pedicured feet into those torture-rack toes. I need to tell her I don't want to look ordinary. I want to look like a star. She should know certain things about me: that I was second runner-up for Queen of the May. That on more than one occasion my mother swore I'd grow into my looks. With better clothes, a decent haircut, some makeup . . .

"You'll be made-up," she says. Her lips are two perfect ellipses of cherry red. Her cheeks are two apples brushed with bronze. Iridescent shadow of a hue somewhere between blue and green glitters from her two lids. She points to the chamber pot, which I am now wheeling on a trolley, its railing padded like a baby's crib to prevent bumps or falls. "Even so, you don't want to outshine the real star."

That's life. A competition even with inanimate objects. But I don't say anything. I don't expect anything, mind you. Compared with how

I started out my day, what has happened so far is nothing short of a miracle. I don't expect to be one of those people who pay a quarter for a painting at a yard sale that turns out to be a long-lost Rembrandt. I understand that objects might be chosen for historical interest, quirkiness, best in show. Not a single one of the smiling minions will give me any numerical sense of my pot's worth. "In due course," confides the antiquarian bookseller, who sports a Harry Potter necktie and gold cuff links marked *Vol. I* and *Vol. II*. "No diagnosis until the results of all the experts are in," cautions a woman my age who must have been premed. Frankly, I'm not counting on much. Unlike actors up for Oscars, I *really* mean it when I say I'm just happy to be nominated.

Though I'm not exactly happy with what the makeup "artist" is now doing to my face. I'm in the "Green Room," by the way. Let me reassure you, it's nothing that *Architectural Digest* would be rushing in to photograph. Black curtains. A bank of TVs. Donuts and coffee. Seltzer and apples. A hunk of cheddar in a wreath of broken saltines. People scattered in semicomfortable makeshift chairs stroking the objects on their laps like pets in need of quieting. At the far end, in a small photography studio, my chamber pot glows on a white-draped turntable against a silver backdrop. Lights shine on it. Assistants adjust it. A photographer takes photos of it from all angles. People gather round. They watch. *Hmmm,* they offer. *Ahhh,* they marvel. A man in a plaid suit turns to the Howdy Doody doll on his knee. He pats its head. "Never you mind," he consoles.

I am shunted off to one side in a high wooden chair. Carol, filling in for Louise who's "out sick, poor thing," has painted a layer of gunk on my face and is now working with sponges and brushes, pencils and tubes that she plucks from an apron pocketed like a carpenter's. I admire the tattooed fish on Carol's left bicep.

"My sign," she says. "Pisces," she adds in case I need enlightenment. "What's yours?"

"Sagittarius."

"I would have guessed." She dips a powder puff in a shallow round box. A cloud gusts above my head like the halo of dirt hovering over Pigpen in the *Peanuts* cartoon. "You're loyal. Generous. An original thinker. Optimistic even when your hopes are dashed."

"You can tell all that?"

She lays her hands on my temples. She rubs. "I can feel your energy."

"Through all this makeup?"

"Nothing can get in the way of a person's energy."

I remember a graduate student of my father's who'd fled the dinner table in tears. When she mentioned she earned an extra bit of income from making astrological charts, my father had banged the table so hard the silverware had scattered to the floor. "That's for idiots," he'd yelled. When I'd come to her defense, explaining in my most reasonable voice that a lot of people were interested in such things these days, people of my age, Harvard students even, he'd called me an idiot too. "How can you, daughter of mine, entertain such stupid ideas?"

"And what about love?" I ask now, still, years later, entertaining such stupid ideas.

"When you find a compatible partner, hidden, deep passions will surface. And, then, well, watch out."

I want to ask watch out for what. But before I can, Carol says, "I have a business on the side doing charts. If you want, I can do yours. I'm good at the love stuff."

"Maybe if I hit the jackpot with my chamber pot. I'm bad at the love stuff."

She laughs. "Sagittarians have quite a sense of humor." She rubs rouge onto my cheeks. I look like the Kewpie dolls sold behind my booth in the collectibles room. "Plus they also are modest and often religious with a strong sense of morality, though they tend to overemphasize the ethical codes they follow."

"I'm afraid that doesn't fit me." I stop. "Though I don't want you to get the wrong idea." I need especially to make this point because I'm in the antiques business, a petri dish for fraud and scams. I catch her eye in the mirror, her head sits just above mine like the top figure on a totem pole. "I *am* ethical. But I'm an atheist."

She raises a penciled brow. "They say there are no atheists in foxholes."

"Let's hope I'm never put in that situation. Even metaphorically," I amend.

"Fingers crossed." She nods. "Will you do me a favor?" she whispers. Her head swivels to take in the activity behind us. No one glances our way. She moves her lips closer to my ear. I smell garlic and vinegar. "Please don't mention our astrology talk."

"Mum's the word," I pledge. "Mind if I ask why?"

She points a rainbow-colored fingernail to the bank of TVs. The man with the Howdy Doody doll has left the Green Room; he now fills the screen. His mouth is stretched into an astonished O. His eyes roll in their sockets. The expert, who looks like Howdy Doody himself—a shock of red hair, freckles, a goofy grin—is pumping the owner's hand. The caption underneath reads *Howdy Doody Doll in Box—$1,000–$1,200.*

"Astrology may be big on *Oprah*. But this is PBS."

I see my father's pounding fist. "I understand completely," I agree.

With sisterly affection, she cups my chin and studies my face. "Good bones," she pronounces. "Good structure."

Are good bones a part of my sign? I wonder. I'm pleased. You have to figure people in TV and antiques have a sense for the visual. Still, how can anyone appreciate my structure considering the layers of foundation she's slapping on my face like a sculptor kneading thick rolls of clay onto the flimsiest of armatures. Beyond the crook of her ministering elbow, over the top of her ministering shoulder, above the tattooed fish, between her ministering fingers, I can see in the small mirror hooked to the curtain a face unrecognizable, a face belonging to a geisha maybe, or a Las Vegas drag queen.

"The camera bleaches out color. It kind of blunts your features. Which is why I need to play them up."

My eyelashes are as spiked as the Statue of Liberty's crown. My eyebrows could be Groucho's. I'll have to take her word for it. The word of an astrologer. Of a professional. Which leads me to hidden deep passions ready to surface with the right man. As if. Believe me, I know exactly what happens when those deep passions get mucked about by a right man turned horribly wrong. They get so buried not even a million-horsepower backhoe could dig them up. What a relief to have survived young love.

"It's nice to have a young'un to work on," she continues. "With the older types the makeup kind of settles into the cracks and jowls." She laughs. "Just like the dust in some of them antiques."

"Which makes it all the more valuable."

"In a *plate*." Carol takes off my bib, brushes powder away from my shoulders.

"I'm not exactly dressed for success," I say.

"You look great," she insists. "Besides, it's your antique that's stage center in this show."

"So tell me the story of this chamber pot," the ceramics expert says. "How did it come to be in your possession?" I have left the Green Room for the production set. Lights blaze. Cameras roll around on dollies. People in *Roadshow* T-shirts and headsets run back and forth checking, testing, adjusting mikes. I am sitting across the table from the ceramics expert. MORT GRINSPAN, STERNS AUCTION HOUSE, his name tag states. He has kind eyes behind trifocals. He has graceful hands. His teeth are blindingly white. He wears a pinkie ring with a coat of arms. His own? Or one he picked up in an antique booth? The chamber pot lies between us. Under its concentrated beam of light, on its lazy Susan altar, you can see its nicks and cracks, its faded flowers, its discolored surfaces, the tired lines and sags of use and age. It seems like a humble object, indeed, to be stage center, to be the focus of so much fuss.

I'm feeling humble myself. Or rather, humbled by stage fright. I clutch at the edge of the table with such force my tendons and knuckles are high ridges of white. "Well," I begin. I swallow hard. My throat closes up. I freeze. You're not under oath, I remind myself. You don't have to tell them everything. The divorce. Henrietta. The division of the spoils. Clyde. Your pathetic 1040 tax return and the refund you're hoping for.

"Well?" he repeats. Mort's used to us tough cases. His voice warms.

And melts mine. "Well," I repeat. "It was my mother's. When she died, I cleaned out her apartment and nobody else—none of the other heirs—wanted it."

"Do you know how she came into its possession?"

"She and . . . she . . . traveled a lot. She liked flea markets and antiques shops. She liked to bring souvenirs home. She said they reminded her of—well—good trips, nice times."

"Do you have any idea where your mother found this particular chamber pot?"

"I assumed Portugal."

"Yes, I can see how you'd think that." He turns the chamber pot over. He pushes it toward me. "Can you read this inscription?"

"I thought it said *Made in Portugal*. But a friend pointed out that it actually says—though it's very faint, no doubt an English-as-a-second language mistake—*From the Portuguese*."

"Yes indeed," agrees the expert. "Indeed," he repeats. "And that makes all the difference."

"It does?" I sense my mouth hanging open, unhinged like a Howdy Doody jaw. Still, I wouldn't mind looking as astonished as Howdy Doody's owner if only to see $1,000–$1,200 flash beneath my big O lips.

"Well, let me tell you about this pot," Mort confides. He's taking his time. Not giving anything away. He leans back. His chair creaks. "But first let me ask you something else. Did your mother, in all her travels, spend time in Italy?"

The guy must be psychic. "Why, yes. It was her favorite country. She and Henri—her friend, *friends*—spent months at a time there. In Florence particularly."

"Aha. Just as I thought."

"Does the chamber pot come from Florence?" I ask. "By way of Portugal?" I add. I try to remember European history. A freshman-year survey course. Did the Italians colonize the Portuguese? Did the Portuguese colonize Italy? Did I get that far in the syllabus?

"We-ell-ell-ell . . ." He stretches the word, then follows with an excruciating pause. The camera moves closer. I'm boiling. I tug at my turtleneck. Sweat beads my upper lip. Rivulets pour down my forehead. If we don't get this *Roadshow* on the road, I'll disappear into a puddle like the Wicked Witch of the West.

Which is starting to look pretty appealing. Why did I come here in the first place?

He leans toward me. "Tell me," he asks. "Did you ever hear of Elizabeth Barrett Browning?"

I flinch. My chair legs skip back. What a question to ask an educated person from an academic family in Cambridge. Even one who gets her Portugal and her Italy mixed up. "Of course," I say, indignant. "Nineteenth-century poet. Married Robert Browning. Against her father's wishes. Invalid. Lived on Wimpole Street," I recite. "Fled to Italy. Regained health. Had a child. Nicknamed Pen. Died in her husband's arms." How's that? I want to ask, show-off that I am. "And of course wrote *Sonnets from the Portuguese,*" I continue. I freeze. I gasp. *Fled to Italy*. *Wrote* Sonnets from the Portuguese.

"Eureka!" exclaims Mort. He actually claps. "Attagirl," he cheers.

I forget about the cameras. I forget that my makeup is sliding off my face. I forget the lugging and the climbing and the waiting-in-line. I forget my exhaustion. I forget my shame. I forget that I, a miz from way back, have been called a girl on national public television. My full attention is riveted on this man across from me. Despite the cast of thousands hustling about, we are the only two in this room. His eyes behind their trifocals hold mine. They are watery with—what? Emotion? Allergies? I lean forward so far into the table that the edge bruises my ribs. It's all I can do not to grab his wrists and pin him into a wrestler's hold. "Yes?" I demand.

"We-ell-ell-ell . . ." he multisyllables again.

"So?" I prompt.

"Your chamber pot belonged to Elizabeth Barrett Browning. There's actually a photo of it glimpsed in her bedroom—half hidden by a coverlet but unmistakable nevertheless—at Casa Guidi, where the Brownings made their Florence home."

"Wow!" I shout. "Yikes!" I yell.

"And there's more."

"More?" I am beside myself. Then puzzle over the meaning of *to be beside oneself*. How do you parse it? How do you define it in a literal sense? What a strange phrase. One I'll have to look up in my dictionary of American slang. Unless it's British. My mind spins out. What is the matter with me? I force my attention back to Mort. My eyes lock with his. I study the lines on his trifocals.

Mort Grinspan either has the patience of Job or a great sense of dramatic timing. He clears his throat. "This chamber pot is valuable for many reasons." He holds up his hand. The coat of arms on his pinkie ring gleams. When I look closer, I am disappointed to see it's not a coat of arms at all, no royal escutcheon, no clenched sheaves of wheat, no family name arched at the top. It's a Boston College shield, embossed with *Class of 1956*. No matter. Who knows better than I that a love of antiques, an appreciation for English poetry, can hardly be kept locked inside Ivy League gates. "Though it is not valuable in and of itself. Nineteenth-century ironstone. Italian. A dime a dozen. A lira a dozen, that is, or should I say euro." He chuckles. "Its value lies in the fact that"—he ticks his fingers—"one, it belonged to the Brownings—and we have the documentation, ergo a photo, to prove it. But that's not all."

I nod. It sounds enough to me. But then I'm not greedy. Or didn't think I was.

"Two, the bottom of this chamber pot bears the handwriting of Elizabeth herself, *From the Portuguese*. So what can we conclude from this?"

"You've got me." I shrug.

"That after a hard day of composing sonnets, she woke up in the middle of the night, had the idea for the title, and scratched it on the nearest item in hand."

"Which would have been the chamber pot," I fill in. I pause. "She didn't have any paper available?" I can't help myself.

"Irrelevant." He waves his hand the way you dismiss the dumbest student in your class.

Nevertheless, I don't go to the dunce's stool in the corner without a fight. "But how do you know it's Elizabeth Barrett Browning's actual handwriting?"

He gives me an incredulous, are-you-challenging-an-expert? look. Then sighs. "We have our ways of documenting such things." He waits for this to register.

It does. I nod.

"And what is even more exciting," he goes on—and his voice sinks into the kind of churchy whisper you might use in the presence of the Dalai Lama or a just-beatified saint—"is Flush."

"Flush?" I ask. Maybe I should quit the antiques business and hire myself out as a straight man at a comedy club.

"Flush was EBB's beloved dog. A cocker spaniel." He frowns at me. "You must have come across her enchanting poem, 'To Flush, My Dog'?"

I shake my head. Guess that's what we would have covered if I hadn't dropped out of college last semester of my senior year.

He pulls a sheaf of paper from his breast pocket. Adjusts his glasses. He takes a sip of water from a beaker resting on a stool at his right. " 'But of thee it shall be said, / This dog watched beside a bed, / Day and night unweary, / Watched within a curtained room, / Where no sunbeam brake the gloom, / Round the sick and dreary. / Roses, gathered for a vase, / In that chamber died apace, / Beam and breeze resigning; / This dog only, waited on, / Knowing that when light is gone, / Love remains for shining." His eyes tear up. From the same poem pocket, he digs out a handkerchief the size of a banquet napkin and blows into it.

What can I say? It's more treacly than Omar Khayyam. I who in the interest of full disclosure must confess my favorite poets are E. E. Cummings, Dorothy Parker, and Ogden Nash, not to mention a decided fondness for Allen Ginsberg's *Howl*. But I've got my eye on the prize. And on the TV cameras. "How beautiful," I lie.

"And, by the way, none other than Virginia Woolf herself wrote the biography of Flush."

Now he's got me. I've devoured *To the Lighthouse, Mrs. Dalloway, A Room of One's Own*. I've read the diaries, the letters. I went through my Bloomsbury phase. I've visited Charleston Farmhouse, walked the graveyard in West Firle. I've skipped stones across the river Ouse. How could I not know this? "What's it called? The book?" I ask.

"Flush: A Biography."

I hang my head in shame.

Mort Grinspan tips the chamber pot in my direction. All the better for me to see the scribbled dog inside.

"Take a closer peek at the drawing of the spaniel. That iconic dog, in the poetess's very hand. As you can see, at the bottom of his collar, she has written *Flush*."

And what a better name to grace the inside of a chamber pot, I want to point out—but the awed silence surrounding us clamps my lips shut.

"Now that we've described and verified this item, Miss Randolph, do you have any idea what it might be worth?" Mort Grinspan asks.

"Not the slightest clue."

"Care to hazard a guess?"

I think of Howdy Doody. I clench my jaw. I put my hands in my lap. I cross my fingers. Given the snugness of my boots, there's no room to cross my toes. I try anyway. I take a deep breath. "Fifteen hundred?" I manage to get out.

Mort Grinspan laughs. "With this provenance? With this *From the Portuguese*? With this drawing of Flush? My dear young lady, you are wildly off the mark. I'd stake my reputation on seventy-five."

"You're kidding! Seventy-five hundred?" I yell.

"Hardly, Miss Randolph. Seventy-five thousand at the very least."

3

The buzzer wakes me. I glance at the bedside clock. It's eleven in the morning. Even though it's Saturday, I can't help blushing with shame. Since I hired a Rindge and Latin High School sophomore to help out on the weekends, you couldn't say I've been rushing to get to my booth. Which has, I'm proud to admit, recently been receiving a glut of visitors. I've sold the dragon armchair. I've sold the glass-fronted bookcase. I've unloaded a cachepot and two silver-tipped walking sticks. A newlywed has put the coal shuttle on twenty-four-hour hold. She needs to check with her groom. "See what a little advertising can do," Gus crowed.

My *Antiques Roadshow* appearance aired two weeks ago. Though

I've got it on videotape, one viewing is more than enough. There I am, raccoon-ringed eyes, Kabuki-mask skin, Kewpie-doll lips opened in an astonished, clichéd O while running underneath, like the subtitles of a foreign film, is this: *Chamber Pot Belonging to Elizabeth Barrett Browning—$75,000.* During my fifteen minutes of fame, I blink fast. I pull at my hair. *Wow! Wow!* I exclaim. *You're kidding,* I add. *Gosh. Gosh.* Over and over like an old LP with a nick in its groove.

Now I throw on a bathrobe. I open the door a crack. The intercom has been broken ever since I moved in. "Who is it?" I call down three flights of stairs.

"Mailman. You've got a registered letter. You need to sign for it."

I slip on my boots, which, though it's March, lie just inside the door. I hurry down the stairs. Thank goodness no one's coming or leaving to witness my slovenliness.

Except the mailman, of course. Who, given the nature of his job, has no doubt seen worse. People out of the shower. Lovers out of bed. Couples in the middle of a fight. Roommates kicking each other's empty yogurt cartons into the corridor.

The mailman's wearing a cap with blue postal-issue flaps. His eyes stay on my boots. No wonder. My hair's a mess. I slathered my face with cream last night, and haven't wiped it off. He thrusts a letter at me. He props a clipboard under my nose with a stubby pen attached. I sign. "Have a good day," he says. His heart's not in it, I can tell.

I don't look at the envelope until I'm back inside my apartment. I flip the coffeepot on. I fall into my mother's armchair, upholstered in a faded chintz of cabbage roses and peonies. When I was a little girl, we'd sit here together before dinner, me curled into her lap, as she read from *Winnie the Pooh, A Child's Garden of Verses, Charlotte's Web.*

One arm of the chair shows the singed hole made when I was thirteen and sneaking cigarettes. The lumpy down cushions still give out the faint whiff of the lavender sachets she kept in her sweater drawer. I tuck my legs underneath me. My knees buttress the edge. Once, I fit here so easily.

The envelope is of thick ecru stock. *Snodgrass, Drinkwater & Crabbe,* Ten Court Square, Boston, Massachusetts 02110, is engraved on the upper left. I tear it open.

SNODGRASS, DRINKWATER & CRABBE LLP
COUNSELORS-AT-LAW
TEN COURT SQUARE
BOSTON, MASSACHUSETTS 02110-2811
TELEPHONE 617-555-8805 FACSIMILE 617-555-8818

James P. Snodgrass, Esquire
617-555-8825

Dear Ms. Randolph:

I have seen evidence which conclusively shows (1) that you appeared on *Antiques Roadshow* (program number 2036) with a certain ceramic vessel (hereinafter referred to as the "Chamber Pot") and (2) that you claimed to have inherited the Chamber Pot from your mother, Emily Granby Randolph, late of Cambridge, Massachusetts.

I represent Mrs. Lavinia Potter-Templeton of Concord, Massachusetts, and Mr. Edward Bickford Potter, of New York City, children of Henrietta E. Potter, late of Cambridge and longtime companion of Emily Randolph. Henrietta E. Potter died in possession of the Chamber Pot.

Emily Granby Randolph and Henrietta E. Potter, having died simultaneously or under circumstances such that it cannot be determined which of them survived, the Chamber Pot passed to my clients under Article Second of Henrietta

E. Potter's Last Will and Testament, which was duly admitted to probate.

My clients strenuously demand that you return the Chamber Pot forthwith. If you do not do so promptly, my clients intend to avail themselves of all appropriate civil and criminal remedies. By the time you receive this letter, a restraining order will have been issued enjoining you not to sell, assign, or transfer the Chamber Pot or to remove it from this Commonwealth.

Failure to obey this order will put you in contempt of court and may subject you to further penalties.

I look forward to your timely response in this matter.

Very truly yours,
James P. Snodgrass
James P. Snodgrass
JS/chs

4

Two backpacked students hold the door of the Harvard Bookstore open for me. I haven't been here for an age. The only B.A. I claim comes from my self-invented membership in Bookstores Anonymous. I avoid bookstores one day at a time. I don't read the *Globe* book section. On Sunday mornings I drop the *New York Times Book Review* in the recycle bin the minute I pick it up from my welcome mat. This must surprise you, considering where and how I grew up. Considering I've been a reader all my life. Now I reserve my books by phone from the Cambridge Public Library. That way I can put myself on the waiting list. When my name hits the top, they call me. In minutes I'm standing at the circulation desk and handing over my library card. For the few seconds such a transaction takes, I can leave one or another of my Rent-A-Wrecks running in the Do Not Park zone of the parking lot. There are a zillion choices, even if I'm no longer test-ready on current best sellers, pink-covered chic lits, embossed and foiled thrillers, and Pulitzer-winning literary lights.

Once I was. Before that slim volume that catapulted me to Bookstores Anonymous and into emotional decline. Bear with me. I know I'm getting to the point where I'll have to explain. For now, let's just say the Irish have the Troubles. I have the trouble. Lowercase but not lower in intensity.

Still, misery is misery, whatever the typescript.

I've checked in advance. The Harvard Bookstore has one copy of the paperback edition of *Flush: A Biography*. Given what is now going on in my life, I need full ownership rather than the library's temporary custody.

I'm not surprised to find my impatience punished. Just inside the front door, on the nearest wall, hangs the poster for the Book. I turn my back. It's two years old already. The paperback came out last June. Nevertheless, loyal to its Cambridge writers, the Harvard Bookstore still keeps a few on the center table, their Autographed by the Author stickers curling slightly at the edge. More paperbacks are ranged along the Local Authors shelf. Who says avoidance can't be the healthy choice? Who claims denial shouldn't be a way of life?

I go to the information desk. "Abby! Have you been away?" Kate calls out. Just my luck. I'd hoped for a new clerk, one of the many with piercings in their nostrils and a notebook of poems they work on when there's a lull.

"Just busy," I excuse.

"For a whole year?"

"It hasn't been that long." But it has. Longer. Ever since *that* book on *that* poster over there hit the stores and blindsided me.

"You've left a void," she says.

I can see how she'd think that. I used to drop in three or four times a week. After the movies. Before dinner. Killing an hour between appointments. Meeting a date. Trawling for a man. In fact, I met lover number two in the aisle between Psychology and Computer Sciences. I was a regular regular. More than once a customer would stop by the information desk to ask about a certain book. *A woman intern,* he might begin. I'd point to Fiction. *The Pursuit of Alice Thrift,* I'd supply before the clerk could turn on the computer to look it up.

"Anytime you want a job . . ." Sanj or Kate or Mary would joke.

"Don't be surprised if I take you up on that," I'd reply. "I spend so much time here I might as well get paid." After all, the Harvard Bookstore was my Café de Flore, my Harry's Bar, my Deux Magots, my City Lights. Until . . .

"Here's the book." Kate hands me *Flush* already in a bag, the sales slip already made out. "Unlike Woolf's others, there's not a big demand for this." She sorts my exact change into the cash register's pinging, slotted drawer. "But, funny enough, we sold one just yesterday."

I stop. I clutch the bag to my chest. I want to ask to whom. I think I can guess. "Is it . . . ?" I begin. I slam my mouth shut. How can I? I, who was one of the first customers to sign the Harvard Bookstore's petition against the Patriot Act.

"Don't be such a stranger," she says.

"Ciao." I wave. When she's once more pounding her computer keys, when the other browsers are hidden from view in Travel and in Mystery, I lean against the wall. I snake my arm behind my back. I spider my fingers up an inch. I grab an edge of paper. I rip the bottom half of the poster—*A Novel by Edward Bickford Potter*—clear off and straight across. I macerate it into spitball size. I lob it at the trash.

But before I get to Ned, I'll tell you about Lavinia. Not that *she*'s easy. Only that she's easier.

It's a long story, however. You'll need your own chintz-covered comfy chair and a mug of tea, though straight gin might be the preferred antidote. Instead, for the moment, why don't I keep you up to date on the chamber pot.

The minute I got that letter, I called my part-time help. *At Auction out of Town,* I had her post on my booth and lock it up. Then I jumped back in bed and stayed there for almost a week. Though I didn't starve—there are plenty of Inman Square restaurants with takeout menus and Lycra-clad bicycle messengers—I did shed enough tears on my pillow to clump the goose-feather filling and stain the (antique) Belgium linen hemstitched pillowcase.

On Monday, even though the Szechuan chicken wasn't due to be delivered for another hour, I made the mistake of answering my buzzer. It wasn't the most Herculean effort since I had already crawled out of bed for a two-minute bathroom break. What did I expect? A care package? A search party of concerned citizens? Social services? I guess I did because when a voice called up from three floors down, "Abigail Elizabeth Randolph?" I answered "Yes" with such a pathetic eagerness for human contact I must have sounded encouraging.

"Something for you," the voice replied.

"Bring it right up," I yelled.

He was huffing by the time he reached my door. A fat man in a cheap suit whose necktie bore the dregs of a breakfast of scrambled eggs and strawberry jam. But there was no basket with a bow tied to its handle, no tower of pears peeking out from its crackling cellophane, no artful mood-elevating bouquets, no meals-on-wheels for suffering shut-ins. "Abigail Elizabeth Randolph?" he repeated.

"Who wants to know?"

He held up a blank envelope. "I'm a constable."

"And I'm the queen of Romania."

He ignored this. He reached into his pocket. He fished out a badge. He stuck it in front of my face. A police shield as shiny as the ones in the cops-and-robber shows I used to watch as a kid.

I moved my eyes from the badge. I'm not the least impressed, I made my body language show.

He was not deterred. He kept holding out his envelope, motionless as the mime busking for quarters in Harvard Square on summer nights.

I stuck both my hands in the pockets of my bathrobe. I felt crumbs and a wadded Kleenex in one. The other had a hole so gaping my fist went right through it and down to my knee.

He stepped toward me. In the split second before I could slip away, he shoved the envelope up into my armpit, where it caught on a fold in my sleeve. He sighed. "According to regulations, the injunction has to have physical contact with the injunctee to count as delivered," he stated in the robotic way officers of the law read a suspect his Miranda rights. "You are served." Then he turned on his heel. "Have a nice day," he added.

Do you suppose the soldiers who dropped the atomic bomb waited for that mushroom-shaped cloud to sprout, then said, "Have a nice day"?

As soon as I heard him shut the front door, I opened my own particular bomb. *Temporary Restraining Order—Commonwealth of Massachusetts—You are enjoined neither to sell, remove* . . . blah blah blah . . . *premises. In ten days hence, Miss Abigail Elizabeth Randolph and said chamber pot are to show up in court. On penalty of* . . . blah blah blah. I pictured all the business cards from appraisers and dealers now tucked away in my desk. Money in the bank, I comforted myself. My retirement fund. "When you're ready to sell," "If you decide to put this on the market," one or the other advised with Uriah Heepish rubbing of palms and assurances of my best interest at heart. *Temporary Restraining Order!* I thought that was something confined to cases of domestic violence. Not that I couldn't declare myself a battered woman, at least metaphorically.

I did the only thing possible. I wept some more. I went back to bed.

By Wednesday, when I climbed out of my grubby hibernator's nest, I was mad. I stomped around my living room so hard that even the heavy-metal musicians by night/computer programmers by day downstairs complained. In my kitchen I threw a plate on the floor—not one I ever really liked, not an antique. In the bathroom, I kicked the wastepaper basket. It hit the tub and chipped the already-chipped porcelain. I punched a hole in the wallboard. I slammed a closet door with such force the hinges broke. By now I suppose you've decided I'm heading through the four stages of grief. You could be right, but only partially. Acceptance will never come. I swear. I'll take the oath on it.

As soon as I realized I was hurting only myself, and damaging my apartment in the process, I pulled off my pajamas, which were getting more than disgusting with the bad hygiene of angst, not to mention soy sauce and pizza grease. I took a bath in my chipped tub. I brushed my teeth. I combed my hair. I got dressed. I changed the sheets. I put gold hoops in my ears and called my lawyer.

She wasn't my lawyer until I called her, of course. Our family lawyer—my parents'—is a semiretired octogenarian—though age hasn't withered him enough to keep him from estate plans nor custom staled him sufficiently to avoid the dress-down Friday set. Now that my father's in La Jolla, his lawyer's firing those eighty-year-old synapses setting up trust funds for my half brothers. Did I mention that indecently soon after my mother left, my father married his graduate student Kiki, the very grad student who had once fled our dinner table in tears, ridiculed by the great professor for her part-time job making astrological charts? Within weeks, my father had moved West, not-so-young man, and sired three sons, each a year apart. You should read their Christmas letter. *Proud Dad goes to all their plays and games, he takes his turn at cooperative nursery school, he toilet-trained Atticus in one day, he signed up for father-and-son drum lessons with Julius, who has a spot of ADD,* Kiki reports. *He dotes on his family. He's a changed man.*

One certainly unrecognizable to me, the terrifying pater familias who ignored me as long as I showed good manners and whose wrath knew no fury the minute I acted teenage-appropriate. But this is not my father's story. What's more, he's pretty much out of the picture, emotionally and geographically.

Who's in the picture right now is my lawyer, Mary Agnes Finch. She lived on my hall freshman year. She went to Yale Law on full scholarship. She made law review, she clerked, did legal aid, serves on the board of the ACLU, is active in the Big Sister/Little Sister Association of the Greater Boston area.

And she's a shark.

I took a taxi to her office. Profligate, I confess. But then I had to lug the chamber pot. All seventy five thousand dollars' worth. "Bring it with you," she ordered. "I'll hold it in escrow. We'll keep it in my law firm's vault."

Frankly, I was relieved. My apartment's not secure, what with its broken intercom and flimsy front-door chain. A DVD player disappeared from the first floor; a computer from the three-decker across the street. You wouldn't expect the petty thieves and small drug dealers in my neighborhood to watch *Antiques Roadshow,* to recognize in a nondescript and downtrodden Cinderella of a pot a glass-slippered princess of an heirloom worth a princely sum. But you never know. Let's face it, even yours truly, in the business, never had the slightest clue there was anything more to this pot than its intended use or as a receptacle for phony flowers.

A secretary who introduced herself as "Ms. Finch's associate" led me to a corner office on a high floor.

Mary Agnes Finch was as put together now as the night back in Cabot Hall when she was the first person to file out onto the quad at the blast of the fire drill alarm. I can still see the camel's-hair coat neatly wrapped around her Snoopy pajamas, tops and bottoms matching, her bunny slippers unmatted and on the correct feet, highlighter clenched in her right fist, all the next day's homework tucked responsibly under her arm.

"Abigail!" Mary Agnes exclaimed. She leaned forward over a huge island of a desk swept clean of everything but a carefully centered blotter, pens and pencils lined up at right angles to it, and a small silver scales of justice that looked to my discerning eye like an antique, though it could have been a good reproduction, second period. And a single exquisite rose in a Waterford vase.

I felt bad about marring this perfect expanse with my oversize, messily rewrapped chamber pot. But I had to put it down to shake her hand.

Her hand was cool; her grasp firm. No wedding ring, I noted. Nails filed straight across, one coat of clear polish. She was as impeccably tailored as her office, in a gray suit with that simple cut that screams *Made in Italy*, pearl button earrings, the kind of glossily shined shoes that nuns at parochial schools warn young girls about.

I tucked my hands with their ragged bitten nails and inflamed cuticles under my skirt and sat in the client's chair. Her clients as a group must have been big-boned and long-limbed because my feet barely touched the floor. Behind her desk, high up in her even higher chair, Mary Agnes Finch cut an intimidating figure, although she was my age and I once snuck her toast and tea from the cafeteria when Andrew Peabody dumped her for Nancy Murphy.

Even so, I felt like the unruly child called into my father's study for keeping a great mind from important work. On his throne of a chair, behind his skyscraper desk, my father loomed like a giant while I shrank smaller and smaller down into my rabbit hole of shame. A blind date—unsuccessful—from the Harvard Business School once told me about his course on corporate psychology. Lesson number one, he instructed, was that any success-driven alpha male must fight for the corner office, the fortress of the biggest desk, the tallest chair, all the more quickly to get to yes.

Obviously Mary Agnes Finch had already got to yes. Now she got down to business. One thing you could say for her, she was not judgmental. Nothing registered across her face except neutral interest and bull's-eye attention.

I told her about my mother and Henrietta. Their life; their deaths; how they had shared everything. I recounted how Lavinia and I had divided up the spoils. How Ned had left it to his sister to act for him. I didn't go into why. I described word for word the way Lavinia had offered me the chamber pot. She hadn't wanted it. I explained that except for clothes and jewelry, and items that each of us could identify as having occupied certain rooms of our respective houses before my mother and Henrietta had set up their domestic partnership, all the other belongings were things they had bought together, things they had owned jointly. But the chamber pot was mine, I repeated. Lavinia had scorned it. It was only when it had turned out to have more than sentimental value that she, that she and Ned . . . My voice went hoarse. I stopped. My throat felt raw. Was I going to weep? I pointed at the object of our disputation, now flaunting its remonstrative bulk on my lawyer's desk. "The idea of being forced to take this pot into court . . ." I cried.

"Not so fast," Mary Agnes warned.

But my mind was spinning out dire scenarios. "Will it be passed through security? Will it be tagged exhibit A? Will it become a ward of the court?" I was on a roll now, gathering the moss of desperation at accelerating speed. "Will I have to go to trial? In . . ." I stared at Mary Agnes's Bauhaus calendar. "Oh God, it's already Tuesday—in eight more days?"

"You've been seeing too many *Law & Order*s," she diagnosed.

"Special Victims Unit." I managed a smile. "I'm a victim myself. I can identify."

"No need for panic yet."

I patted the chamber pot. A couple of the plastic bubbles popped in solidarity. "But it's mine. It's meant for me."

Her voice was soothing. "Let me call Jim Snodgrass," she said. "The chamber pot will be safe in my vault. It's not going anywhere. I'm sure he'll agree to letting the temporary restraining order lapse. No need for a preliminary injunction. We'll enter a stipulation without prejudice. These are two responsible, intelligent families we're dealing with here. I'm sure we can settle out of court. I'm certain we can come to an acceptable resolution."

"You don't know Lavinia," I started to wail.

5

I've procrastinated long enough. I owe Lavinia a chapter. I'll try to flip fast through the early years; what counts in this story is our more recent history. (Please note that I'm not lumping her brother here. He'll have pages all his own.) There's no need to pile on the facts for you to get the gist. Sharp and intense as wasabi, just a daub of her will flavor the whole meal. Unlike those of us who hope to change, to grow, those for whom the therapeutic hour counts as water to a plant, Lavinia's been the same since she was five. It's I who didn't see it until too late. But then that's one of my problems. I'm Miss Give-Her/Him-the-Benefit-of-the-Doubt. Miss People-Are-Really-Good-at-Heart. An attitude that didn't help Anne Frank, by the way, no matter how well it defined her character.

Still, to understand Lavinia and me, it's important to know the sociological context. I'm sure right now you're saying, Stick to the point, Abby. Deliver what you promised. I swear I will. But in order for you to have the 360-degree view of her, let me fill in some background.

My father always pronounced me thick as a board. When Princess Diana used the term to describe herself, I figured she'd swiped it from my father, who'd spent a sabbatical at the London School of Economics. As soon as I learned it was a common Anglicism, I saw how, in a monarchy, Princess Diana's heart, beauty, grace, and social conscience could more than compensate. In my own non-blue- but academically blooded family, no amount of charm could refute a phrase which we Americans would define as dumb. How could the only child of the Epworth chair holder turn out to be so limited? Of course R. Griffin Randolph was speaking grades and SATs, summa cums and valedictorian addresses. All the school reports that stressed my niceness, my plays-well-with-others qualities, my helpfulness, my sensitivity meant zilch measured against my lack of intellectual rigor and my alternative-style lust for sand castle making and Play-Doh modeling. My Miss Congeniality awards paled compared with the gavels wielded by class presidents, the torches waved by debating team captains.

For a long time I was pretty sure I'd been adopted. I'd even hoped that I'd been found swaddled on a church step or in a basket made of rushes floating down the Charles River. In any other family, any *normal* family, my accomplishments would have earned pasted-on stars and double scoops of Heath Bar Crunch. Here's a typical example of the upside-down nature of *Randolphus Familius Academicus* reproduced from my real life. Abigail Elizabeth Randolph: The (Later) Teenage Years.

ME: I made the honor roll at Shady Hill.

HE: Second tier.

ME: I got into Harvard.

HE: Faculty brat.

Maybe that's why he ran off to sire Atticus and Julius and Lucius. Second chances. New testing grounds. Does committed fatherhood transform *thick as a board* into *sharp as a tack*? Can perfect toilet training hike IQs up into the stratosphere?

My loyal mother, on the other hand, always admired my artistic soul, touted my fine character. Emotional intelligence, she called it. Though it was impossible to stand up to my father, she tried. I'm not blaming my mother for any of this, let me reassure you. Ours was a male-o-centric household. One male. One household. One center of everything. My mother and I deserved the shaved heads of collaborators. We were detainees on Brattle Street, prisoners of academe, whose wills were broken down with rules the Geneva Convention would never tolerate. *Darling, Abigail is so talented. She made the loveliest drawing, wrote the loveliest poem . . .* she'd begin. But to my father, my messy scribbles, my awkward rhymes, showed only that his ivied ivory tower harbored no Mary Cassatt, no Emily Dickinson.

No Elizabeth Barrett Browning either. At least in the poetry sense. Still, I once wrote several stanzas to my dog Jinx that, thanks to a rhyming dictionary, compared him to both a minx and a sphinx. This effort won an honorary-mention volume (paperback) of the collected E. E. Cummings. (The judge was a former student, my father felt obliged to enlighten me.) In fact, now that I think of it; Elizabeth and I turn out to have a lot in common. We've got not only our canine poetry but also our domineering-father issues; such a bond would unite us even without the passed-down chamber pot. Neither Barretts nor Randolphs dared to dispute the great man in their midst. My mother had to flee to Henrietta, to the other side of Harvard Square and then the oceans beyond, to escape my father. Elizabeth fled to Robert and to Italy to escape hers. Even in his final illness, Mr. Barrett returned all her letters unopened and refused to let his daughter cross the threshold of his door.

But perhaps my father was only trying to toughen me up for the world beyond my own threshold. Maybe dealing with the bully inside your door was how he prepared me for doing battle with the bully next door.

These days, my father isn't that bad. Kiki has mellowed him. Could it be the couples counseling she's talked him into? Who would have thought? But then who would have pictured him wearing a grass skirt and strumming the ukulele, as documented in the shocking photographic evidence from their Hawaiian honeymoon? On our Sunday telephone conversations between Cambridge and La Jolla, I can sense a bit of regret for old child-rearing ways now that he's seen the shock of the new. *That's very perceptive of you, Abigail,* he'll say to me when I make some prosaic observation like the reason Atticus is so slow tying his shoes is that kids all have Velcro now.

I may be perceptive, but my emotional intelligence as far as Ned and Lavinia were—and are—concerned plunged straight to the bottom of Stanford Binet's percentile pit.

Which offers a good reason to get through our mutual childhoods fast. I know you can go to the theater and see the abridged Shakespeare, all the comedies and tragedies acted out and boiled down into an hour including a ten-minute bathroom/Raisinets break.

Let's start with my corner of the world. Cambridge may be a city of 100,000, a city of diverse neighborhoods, a community—or several communities—proud of its multiculturalism. Our ethnic restaurants paste their high Zagat ratings and maps of Afghanistan, the Algarve, Ethiopia, Turkey on their windows and doors; our bookstores (not that I go into them) are Marxist, feminist, Buddhist, gay, architectural, revolutionary, culinary, foreign language; the kiosk in Harvard Square sells the *Sewanee Review* next to *Hustler* and *Penthouse, Daedalus, Seventeen, Hello!,* and Italian *Vogue*. Some Cantabrigians boycott the bridges to Boston, insisting that Cambridge alone can satisfy a person's every need.

You know Linnaeus's system of classification: kingdom, phylum, class, order, family, genus, species. Well, we were children of academics, a Cambridge subspecies but a kingdom unto ourselves. You wouldn't believe my childhood playmates; their parents and grandparents bore the titles of Nobel laureates, Bancroft, Pritzker, and Pulitzer Prize holders, MacArthur geniuses by the score. They advised governments, served as secretaries of state, headed the National Endowment for the Arts, donned the robes of Supreme Court justices. I guess I shouldn't name names without permission, and many of my old playmates, who fled Cambridge as soon as they came of age, would be a challenge to hunt down. They've joined twelve-step programs, are living in cabins in the woods, and are up to page 1200 of their memoirs, working on oil rigs in Alaska, construction sites in New Jersey. They're mostly people who realized Cambridge wasn't a kingdom any king could force you to be a subspecies of. Young adults who are now thrilled not to be known as the child of fill-in-the-blank. Who are no longer in a position to embarrass parents or maintain standards others have set up for them.

Some of course stayed and thrived. These merry few now hold the positions their parents held, reap the esteem their parents reaped. But it's the others who interest me. The falling/failing star kids of rising/risen star parents.

Unlike some of us, Lavinia never fit that category of the minister's daughter who ran wild, the professor's son who flunked out, the chef's offspring who burnt toast. She was everybody's pet. Let me rephrase this. She was the favorite of the grown-ups. The child our parents wished we could resemble more. *Why can't you be like Lavinia?* rang out throughout our West Cambridge neighborhood. *If only you had half her manners. Half her accomplishments.*

How can I explain this phenomenon? Here's an example. When we were kids, there was a toy store on Mass. Ave. called Irving's. The kind of store that no longer exists. It sold everything: penny candy, fancy candy, candy bars, puzzles, games, masks, Slinkies, not to mention educational toys and books—Lincoln Logs and *Make Way for Ducklings*—and the noneducational ones we all coveted—Conan the Barbarian comics and GI Joes and Barbie dolls. It also brought adults to its aisles stuffed with pots and pans, needles and thread, crepe paper and ribbon, paints and staple guns and screwdrivers. Irving and his wife, Doris, ran their store like a small municipality. White-haired and fake jovial, they barricaded themselves behind the front counter on stools, Buddha stomachs cushioning their laps and Santa Claus smiles stretched across their commerce-seeking faces. Our dimes and quarters bought Irving his big white Cadillac and their winters in Florida and the sapphires sparkling in Doris's ears.

When we came in with our parents, we were treated like precious little Shirley Temples and enchanting Lord Fauntleroys. *How Abigail has grown,* Irving would coo. *Pick yourself out a lollipop, sweetheart,* Doris would offer, and reach across the Matchstick cars to pat my pigtails and adjust my barrettes.

Once, however, my mother sent me in alone to return a plaster of Paris make-your-own-ballet-dancer kit. The plaster had solidified and cracked, its gray mass so dense there was no way you could follow the instructions and pour it into the ballet-dancer molds.

"You've used it wrong," Irving complained. "You've ruined it. Don't they teach you how to read directions at that fancy school of yours?"

"You broke it," Doris seconded. No smiles, no pats, no lollipops. "We have so much shoplifting from you spoiled brats, who can tell if you even paid for it."

I ran home in tears. My mother brought me back. "Oh, Mrs. Randolph," Irving oozed, "what an unreliable manufacturer. We'll order little Abigail another box immediately."

"How can you even suggest we'd accuse this adorable child of stealing or lying," Doris chimed in. "Obviously she has the overactive imagination of all creative types. She's one of our favorites." She reached for my braids. "Here, honeybunch," she said. "Pick out *two* lollipops."

What did I learn? Some people are nice to grown-ups and mean to kids.

That was Lavinia. Even as a kid.

Let me give you a couple of scenes from our childhood to illustrate this point.

Our families were neighbors. Our backyards abutted. We held duplicate keys to each other's houses. On summer nights our parents poured gin and tonics from the Potters' porch swing. In the winter, they filled brandy snifters in my father's library. We kids knew where the Potters kept the Ritz crackers and the Randolphs the Pepperidge Farm Goldfish. We knew the exact number and kind of toys in each other's rooms. We knew where to find the photographs of naked tribesmen in the books on Africa. We knew what encyclopedia volume hid *Lady Chatterley's Lover*. Though Ned, three years older, kept himself age appropriately aloof, Lavinia and I were born two weeks apart. All the stars aligned, all the fates conspired to make us best friends.

As I've already pointed out, the world of adults admired Lavinia's perfect manners, good grades, and charming personality. Far too clever to play Eddie Haskell—the ingratiating friend of Beaver's older brother Wally—a boy so transparently oily even grown-ups could see through his wiles, she was subtle enough to win over legions of natural skeptics and experts in early childhood development. She'd visit spinster aunts, slide drawings and thank-you notes through the mail slots of people who served her lemonade or offered a few branches pruned from their lilac trees. She was so persuasive that perfect strangers bought raffle tickets and Girl Scout cookies even though they'd tacked notes above their bells saying NO SOLICITING. She tithed her dollar allowance for the Save the Children Fund while the rest of us blew every cent at Irving's the morning we received it. She baked cookies for the sick, sipped tea in the kitchens of the boring. She practiced the piano for a full hour every afternoon no matter how temptingly the sun shone. She was appointed student representative to every parent-teacher committee from kindergarten on; she asked for extra work, read the optional selections on the reading list, her hand shot up as soon as anyone asked "Have I a volunteer?"

Where did I stand in relation to this saint who I might have scorned as a goody-goody if I hadn't been so clearly inferior? I was less concerned with the nameless others than with myself and my own small circle. I had trouble looking adults in the eye. My fish handshake needed work. My compositions were messy. My leadership qualities were not even incipient. But I was a good foil.

"You are my best friend," Lavinia declared over and over.

"And you are mine," I pledged. I slapped my hand against my heart.

"Let's mix our blood to prove it," she suggested.

She got a needle from her mother's sewing kit.

"Shouldn't we sterilize it?" I asked. I'd been looking at bugs in my father's entomology books.

"That's for babies. You go first."

I scrunched my eyes shut.

She pricked my finger. She squeezed it.

"Ouch," I yelled. Two bright red drops bubbled up on my thumb. My knees buckled. I grabbed the needle. "Your turn," I said.

She thrust out her hand. As soon as I reached for her wrist, she pulled it back. "You know," she said, "since I'm thinking about becoming a concert pianist, I'd better not take a risk of harming my fingertips."

One day much later, when we were in the middle grades of elementary school, our pediatrician appointments turned out to be scheduled back-to-back. We sensed inoculations were in order. Tetanus? Maybe diphtheria? Our mothers promised strawberry ice cream sodas afterward. They sat on the bench chatting. Two Wonder Woman dolls from Irving's were nestled inside their serviceable pocketbooks.

I went first. Okay, I confess, I cried. Not *that* loud. But it hurt. As soon as my sobs settled into sniffles, I got to choose a plaid Band-Aid and a Snoopy pin. "Who's your best friend?" Dr. Sherry asked. At the time I thought it was a casual question to distract me from my pricked arm and my acting-like-a-baby shame. Now I realize this question was another kind of probe: a diagnostic test of the is-my-patient-a-social-misfit? sort.

"Your best friend?" he repeated.

"Lavinia Potter," I replied. "Who else?"

My best friend Lavinia Potter's turn was next. I joined my mother on the bench. She put her arm around me.

"That hurt," I whined.

"I'll say. I heard you wail in there even though the door was shut."

When Lavinia went in, the door, stuck on a piece of swollen linoleum, stood slightly ajar. I couldn't see her. But I could hear her. Correction: or would have been able to. When Dr. Sherry gave her her shot, she didn't make a peep.

"What a brave girl," he marveled.

"How could I cry when the underprivileged children in Africa can't even get these shots to keep them dying from diphtheria?" she answered.

I waited.

"And who's your best friend?" I heard him ask.

She didn't pause. "Megan Parmenter," she said. *Emphatically*.

Well, I won't put you through our high school years, our college experiences (her Princeton summa, her Stanford Ph.D., her dates five nights a week and for Sunday brunch). I'll spare you my maid of honor role at her wedding at the Faculty Club. I know you'll think I'm petty when I tell you that the pink taffeta concoction I was forced to wear was something I'm sure she picked deliberately to be unflattering. Let's just say, in the whole history of our friendship, our roles never changed, she the queen bee, I the worker, the eager-to-please drudge. Why did I never question my role? Or, rather, when I did, why didn't I do anything about it?

I plead extenuating circumstances. Our parents' friendship; our physical proximity; Lavinia's dazzling charm when she cared to exercise it; my own weak self-image, which made me sufficiently content to touch the hem of her dress. Besides, being part of her circle—no matter how far from the center—brought prestige. Some of her gold rubbed off on me. Any friend of Lavinia's . . .

Or maybe I put up with it simply out of inertia. Or because old habits die hard. Or for the comfort of the familiar.

And then there was Ned. The sand in the oyster that, if I hung around long enough, I hoped would become a pearl. *My* pearl. As Lavinia's best friend, I could run through her house all hours of the day and night. I could sit next to him at the dinner table, in the breakfast nook. I could hear his music play from his bedroom across the hall from hers and copy down the names of his favorite groups. I could eavesdrop on his arguments over car privileges and curfews and agree his parents were being unfair. I could pick up the telephone and tell a honey-voiced cheerleader he wasn't available. I could pat his damp towels, the sweatpants tossed over the shower rail in the bathroom he and Lavinia shared. Pathetic, you might conclude. You don't know the half of it.

But Ned's out of the picture now. Except for the chamber pot. Which I, grateful for your patience, promise I'm getting to.

After the earthquake in India, after the memorial service in Appleton Chapel, after the funeral baked meats at the Faculty Club, after what was deemed a suitable period of mourning (because a lifetime of missing someone can't be quantified), after their landlord produced a new tenant and a list of repairs, it fell to Lavinia and me to clean out our mothers' apartment, divide our mothers' spoils. My father, already with Kiki in La Jolla and producing sons, had no interest in his former life. And Bickford Potter? I guess I forgot to tell you, but five years before, he'd had a massive fatal heart attack at the end of a lecture on Thoreau. It was the best lecture of his career, noted the memorial minute in the *Harvard University Gazette*.

Ned sent a letter endorsing his sister as his representative. She showed it to me. He was in New York, a forty-five-minute shuttle flight away, a four-hour Amtrak ride. A publishing deadline, he pled. Plumbing work in his apartment that he had to stay on-site for. He could as easily have been in China or Siberia. I didn't care. It was just as well. At the memorial service, he had sought me out even though I had managed to stick myself in the middle of my father's consoling colleagues, my mother's grieving friends. "Abby," he said. He grabbed my hand. His fingers curled around mine the way they always had. His eyes were soulful.

I tried not to look at them. I pulled my hand away.

"I'm so sorry," he said.

I nodded.

"For everything."

Though a lump the size of a zeppelin was ballooning in my throat, I wouldn't let myself cry. "Excuse me," I said. "Professor Morelli wants to have a word."

Lavinia and I met outside our mothers' apartment building on Remington Street. We each had keys. She was still living in the house in Concord though she was now divorced. She was working as a thinker for a think tank out near MIT. She wore a snappy suit, white silk blouse, medium-high heels. She carried a briefcase. I wore jeans and a sweatshirt that said GO AGGIES GO. It had been Clyde's; I'd salvaged it from the Goodwill bag. I'd stuffed my wallet and keys into the kangaroo pocket of Clyde's shirt. I looked at Lavinia. We were cleaning out a house, for God's sake.

We hugged each other. I smelled a perfume I couldn't recognize. Something new, I figured. Trendy. Expensive. Sold in a bottle of cutting-edge design.

"This will be tough," she said.

"I know."

"And sad."

I nodded.

"But we're in it together." She squeezed my arm. "I'm so glad I have you."

"Me, too," I managed to get out. "To have you, I mean."

We took the elevator to the fourth floor. Above the buttons someone had scrawled *A hates B*. Childish handwriting, but it seemed a sacrilege.

"The building's going to pot," Lavinia said. "And at the rent they paid." She adjusted a diamond stud. "These situations are stressful. Whole families have broken up over silly things like who gets Aunt Mabel's blender and Uncle Horace's baseball bat."

"But not us."

"Never us. We're both such good friends. We're both so reasonable."

And both distraught. The emptiness hit us the moment we opened the door. It wasn't that anything had been taken away; it wasn't that a single thing had been moved. No dust filmed the mahogany. No tarnish mottled the silver. No cobwebs laced the moldings, no Miss Havisham decay to underscore our emotional distress. Mrs. Leahy, the cleaning woman, had kept up her weekly ministrations all the time they were away, all the time after they'd died. And yet.

"Oh God," gasped Lavinia.

"I know," I said. We clasped hands, grateful for our deep enduring bond of sisterhood.

Which didn't last.

Lavinia dragged out a dining room chair. She set her briefcase down on the table. She opened it. She pulled out a sheaf of papers neatly clipped, a thick notebook, a manila folder, some sheets of waxy paper dotted with red stickers, the kind that mark Sold on works of art at gallery openings and fund-raising benefits.

"What's that?" I asked.

"I did a little research ahead of time."

"You did? What kind of research?"

She smiled. Her old Lavinia cat-got-the-mouse smile. "You know me. Always prepared."

I sat down next to her. My knees trembled. Adrenaline pumped. I recognized the old fright-or-flight response. I was damned if I'd let her see I was concerned.

But nothing got by Lavinia. "Don't be concerned," she said. "I did it for your benefit."

"Did what? For what benefit?"

"I made a list of our mothers' things. I called in an appraiser for the more valuable stuff."

"You what?" (I know, I know. Usually I'm more articulate.)

She fanned some pages out in front of me. There were photographs of the very furniture that now surrounded us. Valuations listed underneath. And in the margins, notes written in Lavinia's distinctive, unmistakable pinched hand.

"Without telling me?"

"As you know, Abby, I am a businesswoman. I'm used to taking charge. I'm organized, efficient. I have a job that demands those qualities. And you . . ." She turned toward me. Her eyes swept my for-cleaning-out-someone's-apartment jeans and sweatshirt. She wrinkled her nose as if she smelled something bad. "Well, you're the artistic one." With this she smiled her near–Eddie Haskell smile. "I know how you hate the details; I knew you would prefer to leave them to me."

"And you never thought to ask?"

"What was the need? When we are so close. When we know each other so well." She paused. But before I could begin to sputter out some answer, she jumped right in and cut me off. "Let's face it, you are a bit scattered. If it were up to you, we'd never get this done."

She had a point there, about my not wanting to get this done. But just this. Dismantling my mother's apartment. Removing all trace of her until these bare walls, these scrubbed floors could have belonged to just anybody. Who'd want to hurry to do that? Who'd want to rush to get that done?

"Let me remind you," she twisted in the knife, "you always have trouble finishing things."

"Had. Did," I said. But it was a puny response, its lack of conviction hardly lost on her.

"So I think we should dispose of this quickly, in as businesslike a manner and as unemotionally as we can. Not that we both don't feel sad, not that we both aren't devastated."

I felt all my limbs sink into a familiar slide of passive resistance. I would have been great on those marches of civil disobedience led by Gandhi and his followers. When the Raj police were about to hoist me onto prison-heading oxen carts, when the nationalist opposition was about to attack, I could make myself as limp and jointless as a slug.

"And good will come out of it, too. We'll have lovely things that belonged to our mothers. They did have fabulous taste, after all. And . . ."

"And . . . ?"

She hesitated. "I don't know quite how to put it. But you of all people will understand. Not that two women sharing households are that rare. Not that in this day and age alternative lifestyles aren't practically the norm. And believe me, I'm a regular donor to the AIDs Action Committee. I wrote the governor a scathing letter about his opposition to the Gay Marriage Act. Still, this is something we never really discussed, you and I. Understandably—given our community, Harvard, political correctness, our liberal values, our enlightened upbringing. Frankly, Abby, I feel—and I'm sure you do too—that it will come as quite a relief to erase all remnants of their unconventional lifestyle."

I pictured my mother and Henrietta in their Birkenstocks and denim wrap skirts, travel guides, maps, foreign currency sorted into their identical theftproof travel bags. I remembered their fine bone structure, their good manners, their gentleness, their gentlewomanliness. I rubbed my hand across the waxed mahogany dining table. A bowl of marble fruit sat in the center. The sideboard held candlesticks and a tea service. Cups in their saucers looked as if any minute they would be filled for arriving guests. In the kitchen hung their neat aprons; there were plants on the windowsills, and lavender sachets tucked into bedroom drawers. Everything spoke of quiet, order, comfort. Unconventional? "But they loved each other," I said.

"Love." Lavinia made the dismissive sound the French do when they push air through pursed lips.

"And they were so happy."

I expected her to tsk away happiness, too. Instead, she ignored me. "The situation was embarrassing. Not to mention my brother's stupid book . . ."

"Really? You were so supportive. You gave the book party for him."

"Which you refused to attend."

"For good reason, need I point out."

"One has to keep up appearances. Besides, he's my brother. You've got to be there for those you love. How would it look? And it *is* a novel. Not fact, but a work of fiction, after all."

I kept my mouth shut. I studied the photograph of the mirror that hung on the wall across from me. *Nineteenth century. Gold leaf. $1,200* was typed underneath its pasted Polaroid. Which one of us was going to end up with that? I could pretty much guess.

"Love. Happiness. Such fleeting abstractions broke up our family," she said.

"Hardly. They waited until we were grown. Until we were independent." I didn't mention that she had a husband at the time, the stiff and constipated Elliot, who had the bearing of a four-star general and the personality of a flea, and whose wedding ring I had handed over at the altar under the rose-and-lily-of-the-valley-festooned canopy. "They always put us first."

"Nonsense."

"What do you mean?"

"My father suffered terribly. Yours, well, he'd barely cut into those casseroles Emily had left behind in the freezer for him before he was hula-dancing with Kiki in some Maui resort. But *my* father. I blame Henrietta and Emily for his heart attack."

I pictured Bickford Potter, his Tweedledum shape, his glasses of port, his plates of pâté, his lust for sweetbreads and brains and tripe, *Awful offal,* Ned had called it. His hatred of exercise. He'd summon Henrietta from the kitchen to reach for a book off the shelf two feet away from him. I thought of his attacks of gout, his big toe grotesquely swollen on the piled pillows in the living room. I remembered the minor infarctions, the angioplasty, the midnight rushes to Mount Auburn Hospital well before Henrietta and Emily took their giant step.

"All water under the bridge," Lavinia announced. "Let's get down to business." She daubed dramatically at her eyes though I didn't see the gleam of a single tear brimming onto her shellacked cheek. She shuffled her papers. She put a stack in front of herself; a mere three pages in front of me. "I made a list of everything that belonged to my mother. Another list of everything that belonged to yours. The items we can't determine whose were whose, we'll discuss and divide." She waved a sheet of red stickers; it looked like those Candy Buttons we used to buy at Irving's when we were kids. "I thought I'd put these stickers on everything that's mine. Then everything that's yours will be stickerless."

"Shirts and skins," I pointed out. Though I sensed that our particular teams wouldn't be fairly matched in numbers or in strength.

"That's an interesting way to phrase it."

We'd received letters from our mothers' lawyers. They'd left us each separate small legacies—small because, guilt-ridden, they'd typically turned most of their own savings over to the husbands they'd abandoned. Knowing, the lawyer had explained, the husbands would in turn provide for their heirs. (Which Uncle Bick did, of course, for Ned and Lavinia when he died.) But all the household goods and personal belongings the lawyers were sure we would divide amicably in the spirit that our prematurely deceased mothers would have wished.

"So here's what I have figured is mine," Lavinia said amicably.

"Isn't the list a little lopsided?" I replied amicably.

"You may think so, but this list itemizes my mother's things."

"*Our* mothers' things. They bought everything jointly, shared everything."

"Not quite," Lavinia said. "I had many conversations with my mother before she died. She was very clear on what she wanted me to have."

"All news to me. How come I wasn't let in on any of this? Did she leave written instructions?"

"That's beside the point. I knew what she wanted. I was setting up a household. I had the big colonial in Concord to furnish."

"And what about me?" I asked, less amicably now.

"Your circumstances are different. You're renting that tiny apartment. No room for a dining table or sideboard. Any silver you'd leave there would be sure to be stolen. Let's face it, your neighborhood keeps turning up in the police blotter/crime watch column of the *Cambridge Chronicle*. Plus . . ." She paused.

"Plus?" Little Sir Echo, *c'est moi*.

"After my divorce, my rooms are emptier than ever. Elliot took loads."

"Excuse me, but you're *not* taking loads?"

She shook her head. "You have your little business. You're a collector. The kind of stuff our mothers amassed is not to your taste. You're more a flea-market, tag-sale, kitsch kind of gal."

"I beg your pardon?"

"Abby. You know I'm not materialistic. I never cared for 'things' the way you did. You were always a hoarder as a kid. Remember your collections of shells, and buttons, and colored pipe cleaners? I was better at sharing. Ask any of our parents' friends—you know how everyone always called me so generous. If it were up to me alone, I'd give you whatever you want."

"Oh, really?"

"Yes, really. But I have an obligation. It's my mother's dying wishes I need to honor." She sniffed. She squeezed out a crocodile tear. "I could never ever live with myself if I didn't take what she so patently wanted me to have."

And that, dear reader, is how I ended up with a few plates, the everyday silver, a small rug, some platters, a dieffenbachia plant, a photo of Henrietta and Emily on a camel, and the chamber pot.

6

I'm back in my booth. The place is deserted. Everyone's at Brimfield, dealers and buyers alike. I should have gone myself. Since my *Antiques Roadshow* appearance, stuff has been flying off my shelves. Now so many bald patches dot my four square feet that a transplant of *objets* is well overdue. How long can I trade on my fifteen minutes of fame? How long will the customers keep flocking in, hoping that a wobbly three-legged stool or a faded tapestry will be the next ticket to the *Antiques Roadshow*'s astonished O and a kid's college tuition or a grandparent's retirement RV? The way I figure it, I've got about one minute more to bask in the glow of Carol's makeup and my mother's ability to find the diamond in a haystack of cubic zirconias. In fact, I'm steeling myself for an eventual decline in traffic that I can't blame on Brimfield's week of mecca for the fanatic pilgrims of collectibles.

I suppose you assume it's residual feelings for Clyde that's keeping me from traipsing those farmers' fields in search of Stickley and Duncan Phyfe, Limoges and Imari, colonial samplers and oxidized fur coats. Just because I met Clyde at Brimfield doesn't mean that the sight of bed warmers and the smell of fried dough will provoke such a madeleine moment I'll have to take to my bed in my own Inman Square cork-lined room. I don't miss him. I don't mind hearing his name whispered among the dealers here in the constant breeze of gossip that circulates the stalls better than its stop-and-go ventilation system. I don't mind stories about the wedding to which everyone was invited except—understandably—me. (The *saumon en croûte* was a little dry, Gus loyally reported. The flowers, over the top. The bride far too gussied up for good taste, plus looking a little fat.) I am not affected when the fat turns out to be a pregnancy with twins. I don't even bother to do the arithmetic to prove that the seeds for those twins were sowed when their father was still planting a few seeds inside me under our mutually owned Amish quilt. I don't care that Clyde and his bride have opened a shop on the North Shore. I could not care less when I hear the shop is flourishing.

The reason I'm not going to Brimfield is much simpler. I have no extra money to spend. I've already used up too much replenishing my fast-depleting inventory. Wary of overconfidence, and because I come from save-for-a-rainy-day Yankee stock, I can't count on reruns to match the initial big bang of *Roadshow* luck. Plus, there's my Rindge and Latin part-time help. There's overhead. There are slices of pizza and movies at the Kendall Square Cinema. I've put the legacy from my mother into bonds, mad money saved only for an emergency. Meanwhile, I'm waiting to retake possession of my chamber pot. And trying not to focus on the implication for me that justice delayed is justice denied. If, like love, the course of true justice never runs smooth, this particular path of justice is stalled. Nevertheless, the legal fees accumulate at a whopping speed, outpacing both the tortoise and the hare. It's May. What's happened so far? you might ask.

Nothing, I'm forced to inform you. The chamber pot still sits in escrow in Mary Agnes's vault. I picture it, its plain utilitarian shape, its unmentionable-in-polite-company functionality. Confined to such hard cold steel quarters, flanked by grandma's tiaras and grandpa's blue-chip stock certificates, it's the wallflower. I feel a bond. I know what it's like to have your value so hidden few can appreciate it.

Meanwhile, lawyers write letters to each other. Their clients refuse to budge.

Are you surprised? Me? The wuss, the wimp, the pushover, the patsy, the mark. Aren't you astonished that I didn't say to Lavinia, Take it, it's yours.

Well, I didn't. Why?

Because it isn't hers. Because I'm developing a spine. Because Ned still absents himself and lets Lavinia speak for him. Because that makes me mad enough to refuse to allow former friends to take advantage of me. And because, deep down, it belonged to a poet who—with Robert—took enormous risks for love. A poet who scratched onto a humble vessel the title of her greatest testament to that love. And because my mother—with Henrietta—bought it in Florence, the city where she was happiest, then lugged it home. Because she would have wanted me to have it after she was gone.

"Right now it's Lavinia's word against yours," Mary Agnes had said to me. "Jim Snodgrass and I think the only solution is to sell it and divide the proceeds down the middle. Mind you, the offers are pouring in. Amazing the power of TV."

No less amazing than the stubborn streak I've just discovered, inherited no doubt from R. Griffin Randolph, Professor of Tenacity.

Maybe I would have been more flexible, under other circumstances. Maybe if I had been dealing with a real person, a person of understanding, sympathy, warmth. Maybe if Ned, for the sake of old times, old wounds, and overall fairness, had taken my side.

"Another solution," Mary Agnes went on, "might be for the two families to donate it to a university library. And get a huge tax credit. Not to mention the little plaque in the museum case saying *Gift of . . .*"

I thought of Lavinia's ostentatious philanthropy, her coercive childhood work on behalf of the Save the Children Fund, the two pages of volunteer activities touted in her CV, the duly reported charity benefits that she and Elliot held in their eighteenth-century Concord colonial. "Did you run this idea by Lavinia?" I asked.

"Yes."

"And . . . ?"

"Over her dead body, is what she said."

Now I shift my own body in my seat. For the last two hours I've been playing musical chairs; I'm starting to regret I sold the throne with the arms that ended in dragon's heads. All that reading I got done curled up in it. The Sheraton chair is too narrow, the Windsor too high, the bentwood too low. I feel like Goldilocks. I remember an architectural study that discovered no chair, even the most ergonomically designed, was ever comfortable for more than an hour. Today I could supply the proof to that theory since I haven't lasted more than thirty minutes in any one of them. Maybe I'm restless because I'm reading *Flush*. Let me confess that if I didn't have more than a literary interest, I might not make it through. *Flush*, no *To the Lighthouse*, is rather precious for my taste. I can't work up sufficient sympathy for his adventures with other mean dogs, nasty maids, and the bad guys who kidnap and torture him despite how easily some of his disasters could be metaphors for my own woes.

Yet what makes it all worth the tribulations of acting as a scab to cross my own private picket line into the Harvard Bookstore, of persisting in the book through three changes of chairs, are the following lines:

> *Flush was equally at a loss to account for Miss Barrett's emotions. There she would lie hour after hour passing her hand over a white page with a black stick . . . She had drawn "a very neat and characteristic portrait of Flush, humorously made rather like myself," and she had written underneath it that it "only fails of being an excellent substitute for mine through being more worthy than I can be counted."*

That the chamber pot shows up in a photograph of the Brownings' bedroom at Casa Guidi is more than great. Add to that a description, in Virginia Woolf's words, of Elizabeth Barrett Browning's attempts to sketch Flush—and, wow, even a semi-well-educated person such as myself can't begin to parse the thrill of it. All I can come up with is *priceless!*—an adjective pretty much devalued when you consider the MasterCard ad.

I picture the sweet drawing of the cocker spaniel with the word *Flush* written underneath it now sitting in Mary Agnes's vault. I miss my chamber pot. It's like a child sent to summer camp for the first time, a kid setting out for freshman year at a college on the West Coast, a quarantined pet. Not that an inanimate object requires Solomonic solutions. Still, Mary Agnes should understand that such feelings, such deep maternal yearnings, can only prove, beyond the shadow of a doubt, that this chamber pot belongs to me.

I shut the book. My bottom is sore from the nail heads, springs, and horsehair upholstery. Besides, it's almost lunchtime. Why not go home, make myself a sandwich, throw my laundry in the machine. I might pay some bills. I might call my lawyer and check on my case. It's a glorious day, not that you can actually see the sun in this windowless bunker of small and large treasures, of various degrees of junk, of twisting aisles of hulking dark mahogany.

I turn off my lights. I hang a CLOSED sign on a plaster bust of Marie Antoinette. Maybe I'll walk along the Charles. Business is so lousy it's not worth coming back this afternoon. Even Gus, who complains of the heat and what the muddy fields do to his bad knees, is at Brimfield; I miss not having someone to talk to just in case I wanted to talk to someone. I decide to bring *Kovels' Know Your Collectibles* to a bench at the Kennedy School park. So that, professionally speaking, I'm not wasting my time.

"Bye, Abby," says Frieda, who is filing her nails at the long desk opposite the entrance no one is entering. Over her head hangs an oxen yoke, which a certificate underneath guarantees as a true colonial artifact. "You've got the right idea. What with Brimfield and all, just sitting around here is a waste of a good salesperson's time."

Mail crams my box in the front hall. I unlock the metal grille with *A. Randolph* slotted into it. Who am I fooling? In contrast to the Daniel and the William and the Omar, the *A.* practically screams to any potential rapist there's a female living alone in 3B.

I dump the letters and magazines onto the communal table. *Antiques* magazine, *Maine Antiques Digest, Art & Antiques*. Bills. Ads. A letter from my lawyer . . . What now? I wonder. I set it aside.

At the bottom of the pile I spot a small yellow oblong box. A window is cut into the cardboard. Under its clear plastic lies a vial with a blue top. It looks like a smaller version of a bottle your doctor uses to collect a urine sample. But this is special. LOURDES WATER BOTTLE ENCLOSED! I read. PRECIOUS ITEM INSIDE! Don't you dare laugh, you who would dismiss this as junk mail without a second thought. Unlike me. Even as a nonbeliever, I still attach meaning to signs and miracles. After all, as Carol on *Antiques Roadshow* once pointed out, there are no atheists in foxholes. Who couldn't use a few healing sprinkles? Carefully I extract the Lourdes water bottle. Its precious liquid must be so pure I can hardly see it. I tear the box apart.

No wonder I can't make out the water; it's not there. If, however, I mail in twelve dollars and return the vial, my FREE, GENUINE Lourdes water will be poured into it and sent right back to me. What's more, if I up the ante to sixteen dollars, I can add prayers for—check one—financial difficulties, personal health, alcohol problems, world peace. What about love? I want to ask the scamming nuns. What about fairness? I want to ask the fraudulent priests. Where's the prayer for that? I throw the vial in the trash. Is nothing sacred? Isn't there anybody you can trust?

I pick up the letter from my lawyer. I open it. There's a small note stapled to a large Xerox. *From the desk of Mary Agnes . . .* festoons the top. Underneath, scrawled in red magic marker is: *A, FYI. Yrs., MA.*

She has sent me an article copied from the *New York Times*. The headline announces *T. Rex Bones, Uncovered with a Pick, Will Be Sold with a Hammer*. I sit down. I start to read. Here's the essence encapsulated and distilled:

A cowboy and his team in eastern Wyoming dug up hundreds of fossilized bones, which turned out to belong to a sixty-eight-million-year-old T. rex. The bones, about 20 percent of the whole animal, have been sent to an auction house where they are expected to fetch almost a million bucks. However, there's a dispute over their ownership. One of the cowboy's partners is divorcing and his wife claims the bones in the disposition of their assets. Other investors have come forth with their own claim to a piece of the dinosaur pie. As a result, there's no clear title. Lawyers warn of years of federal litigation and many boxes of documents filed in many different states. So far the court has ordered the bones to be sold at auction and the proceeds distributed among the various parties.

I read the article twice. What is Mary Agnes trying to tell me? That I should put the chamber pot up for auction before litigators are ringing my bell and boxes of legal documents are blocking my doorways and halls? I am starting to get mad. *My* Flush is no *Tyrannosaurus rex*. *My* chamber pot would never bring a million bucks.

And even if it did. What about sentimental value? What about honoring another's wishes? I swear I will never sell.

I look at Mary Agnes's note again. Maybe there's no hidden agenda. Maybe it is truly FYI from somebody who lived on your corridor, who lent you her hair dryer, who told an unwelcome suitor you weren't in. *Thought this might interest you. Thought you'd get a kick out of this. Look how small potatoes your dispute is compared to this.* Or *I promise that compared to this, yours will be resolved so much more easily.* Her attached Xerox bears no more significance than a clipped-out recipe or the engagement notice of someone you went to high school with. After all, Mary Agnes is not just my lawyer but also my friend.

I tuck the page into *Antiques* magazine. I gather up the rest of the mail. I lug it up my three flights. When I go into the living room, I see the light flickering on my answering machine. With a sudden any-news-is-bad-news instinct, I first pour myself a Diet Coke. I knock ice cubes out of the ice cube tray and into my glass. I go to refill the tray. I stop. I leave the tray in the sink. Perhaps because I'm sure that Lavinia, unlike me, would swish water back into those little compartments the second she emptied it.

I press Play.

"Hi, Abby, it's me," Clyde announces with typical arrogance. Never mind that I might have ten male callers leaving messages on my phone. Which, alas, I don't. But of course I'd know Clyde's voice anywhere; who could mistake those flattened midwestern syllables, that twang so close to a whine. His voice is staticky. I hear the whiz of traffic. He must be calling from the car he didn't have or the cell phone he couldn't afford back when we mixed our kitchen spatulas and our old depression glass.

"I need to see you," he says. "I'm in my car. Heading for the Square. Hope we can meet. Call me back on my cell." He rattles off some numbers. In the background, the radio spatters. A woman's voice starts to sing.

My hand hovers over the phone. Should I or shouldn't I? I dial.

I shouldn't have because the first thing he says is, "Hey, I heard about the chamber pot." I think of T. rex's disputed bones. I know that Clyde has no bone to pick with me, no leg to stand on in relation to the possession of my chamber pot. Unlike the bed warmer, our quilt, a few kitchen tools, there's no title here he could claim a portion of. Still, I clutch the receiver. My adrenaline is pumping both fright *and* flight. What is wrong with me?

"You looked real good. I liked what they did to your hair. You acted pretty surprised."

"Because I was."

"I'm happy for you. I really am. What with your mom's death and all. On top of that, the dissolution of our business. And, then, me leaving . . ." He pauses. I listen to a drawn-out cranking of gears, the sudden toot of a horn. "The Pike is your next left," I hear him yell.

"What do you want, Clyde? I'm busy. *Very,*" I stress.

"As I was saying. I'm glad for you. You deserve a break. I've got some things to tell you. Can we meet for coffee in the Square?"

"I figured you'd be at Brimfield. Like everyone else."

"It was my week to babysit the kids. Why weren't you there? Spending all that money from your chamber pot?"

I don't answer. What does he need to know of my internecine wars?

Obviously nothing, since he doesn't pursue it. "So where can we meet?" he presses on.

"What's the point?"

"I'll explain when I see you." *Who's sorry now* rises to a screech on the radio. I can just about make out *You had your way. Now you must pay.* "Look, don't worry. This has nothing to do with antiques. Or with money. I have no agenda here."

I get to the Pamplona early. It's warm enough that tables are set up in the little courtyard. I order gazpacho and a coffee ice cream parfait from one of the young, slim, white-shirted, black-trousered waiters who seem to have stayed the same since I was a kid coming here with my parents for flan and almond syrup poured over ice. That's the trouble with living in a college town. Every four years there's a fountain-of-new-youth turnover while you do nothing but unfashionably age.

A man at the next table is reading the *Harvard Law Review*. Two women under the tree toward the back talk animatedly in a Slavic-sounding language, Czech maybe, or Hungarian. Typical Cambridge scene.

Which is destroyed when Clyde pulls up in his sleek, atypical Cambridge BMW, no residential parking permit marring its atypically bumper-stickerless, atypically sparkling rearwindow glass. He parks right in front, wheels teetering on the curb, in the NO PARKING loading zone. He's not dressed in his usual Cambridge-cum-Midwest jeans and tattered denim shirt either. Country-club-like, he sports North Shore pressed khakis and a blue blazer, anchors shining on its brass buttons. At least he's not wearing pink pants printed with spouting whales.

"Abby!" he exclaims. His prematurely tanned face is suffused with glee. His hair sparkles with mousse. He leans in toward my cheek.

I smell too much cologne. I turn my head away.

He backs off. He holds up his hands in an I-surrender pose. "You're right. You're right. No way should I have approached your personal space without your explicit permission." He points to the chair opposite. "May I?" he asks.

Do I have a choice? I nod.

"Great to see you," he says. "It's been a while." The waiter slinks by. A small Spanish flag sticks out of his lapel. "Let's see. I'll have a cappuccino, *s'il vous plaît*." He points to my bowl. "And a cup of that tomato soup."

What did I ever see in him? I wonder. How could an antique bed warmer and the prospect of a warm body in bed—his body—have so blinded me? "Why did you want to meet me?" I ask.

He reaches into his breast pocket. He pulls out a folded paper. His wedding ring, a thick gold band embossed with entwined hearts and a Celtic cross, catches the light. Some sort of rope bracelet clasped with an ankh circles one wrist. "I'm on a journey," he says.

"To where?"

"Not that kind," he says. He makes the embarrassing eye contact of a crazy man ordered by invisible voices to stare at you. "Mine's a journey of self-evaluation. Of self-discovery. Of self-knowledge. Of meditation. Of contemplation. Of spirituality. Of redemption." He lowers his voice. "Of making amends."

"Oh, yeah?" I say. His eyes look so tired from gluing themselves onto mine that I add, more gently, "That's quite a list."

"You don't know the half of it." He unfolds his sheet of paper. He sets it on the table. He smooths it out. Some of the gazpacho drips onto it. "I've written down all the ways I've wronged you."

"Believe me, I know them. I don't need to hear them."

"But *I* need to recite them. It's part of the plan."

"What plan?"

He lifts his spoon across to my coffee ice cream parfait. "Do you mind?" He excavates the whole scoop. A melting mustache smears across his upper lip. "According to my spiritual director, I must get back in touch with those I have wronged and make amends before I reach the next level."

"Of beatification? Are you planning to become a saint?"

"It's not funny, Abby. I knew you wouldn't appreciate it." He stops himself. "Not that you haven't a God-given right to your personal opinion."

"That's a relief."

"Lately. Ever since the twins, I've been doing a lot of meditation. Been going on a lot of meditation retreats."

"Having twins must make you want to get away."

"Not how you mean it. You don't have to be so sarcastic. Not that—"

"Not that I don't have a right to be sarcastic," I fill in.

"In fact, the miracle of Edda and Rune's birth did just the opposite, propelled me into my personal journey of making amends. Remember, we are all our own people. We arrive at enlightenment as a matter of our own individual choice, at our own time."

I ignore the sermon. "So I gather you've been on the road?" I encourage.

"Not totally. Some of my wrongees, if you will, high school friends, family back home, I had to e-mail my amends. It was just too far, unfortunately. If it hadn't been for the twins, I would definitely have made the effort, though." He points to his car illegally hugging the curb. He smiles. "It would be a gas to press that pedal to the metal on the open highway." His face turns serious. "Naturally, the recommended way to right wrongs is face-to-face. Like us. Like now."

"I see."

"You sound skeptical. That's okay. Many people are at first. But when I'm done, you'll *really* see."

"I'm all ears."

"In that case, then, why don't I just get to the business at hand."

"Good idea." I order another coffee ice cream parfait. A girl needs her strength to face being amended to.

Clyde clears his throat. "In no particular order . . ."

"You mean you don't go from the least to the worst?"

"It's all relative. What I personally find the most egregious, to the other party may, in the catalogue of sins, be hardly worth mentioning." He looks at his watch.

"You have another wrongee scheduled after me?"

He nods. "In Cambridge. Near Porter Square. I just may be able to fit her in if I get through this fast . . ."

I don't tell him you can't hurry repentance. I don't exclaim, Another her in the city of my birth? Instead, I say, "Shoot."

Clyde looks me in the eye. He studies his list. He looks me in the eye again. His head is bobbing up and down like one of those spring-necked figures on the dashboards of pothole-seeking taxicabs. "In no particular order," he repeats. "Here goes:

"I should never have grabbed that bed warmer. You got there first. You had first dibs. I apologize.

"I should never have moved into your apartment without paying my half of the rent. I apologize.

"I should never have complained about your cooking when I wasn't willing to do it myself. Ditto your cleaning. Ditto your laundry and ironing. Ditto the way you made the bed. I apologize.

"I should never have slept in our bed with somebody else. I apologize.

"I should never have borrowed and not returned and then subsequently sold some of your smaller, not jointly owned antiques. I apologize.

"I should never have fallen asleep those two times—well, maybe more—in the middle of sex. I apologize.

"I should never have been more attracted to your family background, your family's house than I was to you. I apologize.

"I should never have bad-mouthed your antiques acumen to other members of our profession and in the place of our business. I apologize.

"I should never have hidden away invitations to parties for the two of us and gone myself. I apologize.

"I should never have picked up other women at those parties. I apologize.

"I should never have thrown into the trash letters addressed to you from other men who weren't your relatives. I apologize.

"I should never have told you something looked good on you when it didn't. I apologize.

"I should never have complained about your small breasts. I apologize.

"I should never have forgotten to give you certain telephone messages. I apologize.

"I should never have joked about your mother's lesbian relationship behind your back. I apologize.

"I should never have lied that I read all of *Ulysses*. I apologize.

"I should never have implied to others that you inherited your mother's sexual proclivities. I apologize.

"I should never have pretended at restaurants that I left my credit card at home. I apologize—"

I hold up my hand. "Stop!" I start to yell. "I've heard quite enough."

"But there's more."

"I get the gist."

He checks his watch again. "Well, maybe if I leave you the list, you can go over the rest. In fact, you can study the whole thing at your leisure. And realize how humbly and profusely and honestly I need to apologize."

I take the list. Its gazpacho drips make it look as if someone has bled all over it. Probably me. Except for the stains, it could be an official document, computer-generated. Laser-printed. And bulleted. "I'll save it for a rainy day. I'll save it for when I'm *really* depressed."

All irony is lost on him. He looks relieved. He jumps up from the table. Behind us a meter maid is slapping a ticket on his windshield. "Thank you. Thank you." He genuflects. "I feel so much better."

At least one of us does. I order my third ice cream parfait. Maybe I should have sent in for that Lourdes water after all.

Obviously he's reached the next level because he thanks me four more times. He pumps my hand. "You can see how much of a changed man I am!" he exclaims.

He smiles at the meter maid, grabs the ticket from behind the windshield wiper, then thanks her. He jumps into his car. Rolls down the window. Turns on the radio. Zooms away.

Who's sorry now. Whose heart is aching for breaking each vow.

He's a changed man, all right. But not so changed he hasn't left me with the bill.

7

I'm back in my apartment. I've drawn the shades. Unplugged the phone. Although it's a warm May afternoon, I'm in my bed piled with every coverlet I can find. The minute I got home, I gulped down three aspirin. I brewed a pot of herbal tea. Right now my wrist feels too weak to lift the translucent (early) Haviland cup from my night table to my parched and cracking lips.

If this domestic interior—woman with the vapors in darkened room—reminds you of Elizabeth Barrett Browning, I'm not surprised. She took to her bed because of bad lungs, a frail spine, and a domineering father. Okay, my lungs are healthy—knock wood—and my father's far enough away to give my healthy lungs some breathing room. Plus, as I've already told you, I'm building up my once-wobbly backbone with serious reinforcements of just-say-no grit. Still, doesn't my current prognosis sound glum?

I wouldn't want you to assume that EBB and I are in competition for the most impressive reason to stay in bed for the rest of our lives. Or that we're one-upping each other over who's got the hardest situation to deal with in a situation room full of them. Nevertheless, a frail poetess in a Florentine villa is bound to beat out a flea-market fiend in a third-floor Cambridge walk-up, particularly if you take the historical, more literary view. Just let me point out that EBB benefited from the mitigating circumstances of a great and lasting love. Don't I deserve a little affirmative action here? Wasn't what Clyde just did to me no less an affliction than the torment that forced Elizabeth to barricade herself inside her own four walls? Except for our nightwear—hers, I imagine, a gossamer silk gown edged in Alençon lace; mine, a T-shirt advocating OUT OF IRAQ—we could be twins.

For a long time I was sure she was a fellow Sagittarian. You only have to read her sonnets, or see her through Flush's eyes, or take in a revival of *The Barretts of Wimpole Street* to recognize those Sagittarian adjectives: Loyal. Generous. Original thinker. Optimistic even though hopes are dashed. When I found out she was born in March, I was hardly fazed. I didn't need a Carol from *Antiques Roadshow* to tell me what I already knew—however different our signs, they were fated to be complementary ones. Anyway, just because we're not twins of the Edda and Rune sort doesn't mean we're not twins in suffering.

I roll over onto my stomach. I bury my face in my pillow. My brow burns as feverish as that of any delicate English poetess confined to the shades-drawn mausoleum of a boudoir. I am never going to leave this room. I will call friends to bring round bowls of nourishing bouillon; I will fill in with takeout menus and bicycle deliverers. I will stack newspapers and magazines up to the stained and flaking ceiling until my subscriptions expire.

Outside my darkened window, traffic hums. The skateboards of kids just released from school spin and clank. Women call to each other in Portuguese. A dog—cocker spaniel?—barks. Squirrels scrabble under the eaves. Life goes on. Inman Square, Cambridge, New England, America, the world, the universe, is oblivious to the agony of Abigail Elizabeth Randolph. *Clyde?* my father once asked. *How could you take up with a boy with a name like that? Sounds like a criminal.*

Little did he know. I groan. I moan. I touch my forehead. I'm not kidding, I'm really sick. I will concede, however, that three coffee ice cream parfaits might account for a portion of the nausea now keeping me pinned to my mattress and swearing off nourishment. I clutch my stomach. Just in case, I've slid a wastebasket underneath my bed the way Elizabeth once kept her chamber pot. At least she couldn't blame a lover—or ex-lover—for making her ill. Don't you agree that Clyde's twelve-step program of righting wrongs face-to-face is far worse than the behind-my-back wrongs he needed to right?

Under my pillow lies Clyde the Criminal's list. Compulsively I've been reading it. Masochistically I've been scrolling though the litany of apologies. From top to bottom. From bottom to top. And what stands out, like the one suppurating sore in a pockmarked brow, like the most decayed apple in a crate of rotten Granny Smiths, worse than infidelity, worse than theft, is this:

I should never have thrown into the trash letters addressed to you from other men who weren't your relatives. I apologize.

And this:

I should never have forgotten to give you certain telephone messages. I apologize.

I groan again even though it's pretty sad to hear the cry of my lone mewling voice in the wilderness. I have never felt so cut off from everyone. What if Ned had telephoned me? What if Ned had written me?

Because so much time has passed, maybe Ned figured a new appeal to my senses might start to melt my steely heart and bend my stiffened backbone. Not that anything could weaken my resolve. Though I will never be deterred from my hatred of him for what he did to me, I'm still curious about any flimsy excuse he's managed to concoct. Let's face it, you want to receive the invitation even when you're compelled to send your regrets.

But more likely, it's not the old wound at all, but the new, rawer sore now resting in Mary Agnes's vault. What if he'd committed to paper or my answering machine his personal and heartfelt opinion—not filtered through the legalese channels of Snodgrass, Drinkwater, et al.—on the subject of the chamber pot? I'm on your side. It's yours. You have first claim. Possession is nine-tenths of the law. Your mother picked it out. Lavinia gave it up. You deserve it.

And if so, how would Ned then have interpreted my lack of response?

Damn Clyde!

My first impulse when I staggered into my apartment was to ring Clyde on his cell phone in the middle of righting another wrong. What letters? What messages? I wanted to ask. Any return address, any *Abby please telephone Ned* marring that clean slate of yours? I hesitated. It was too late now for damage control. And besides, I knew how selective his memory could be. Maybe I'd just tell him off. *Asshole! Asshole!* I'd scream so loud his next apologee couldn't help hearing. But before I finished dialing, I imagined his zealot's joy at knitting my anger into another layer of his hair shirt. You're right. You're right, he'd shake, rattle, and roll. Go ahead, call me every name in the book!

Now sweat drips from my brow and stings my face. My meeting with Clyde has driven me nuts. The fact is, Clyde was long gone before any chamber-pot issues surfaced. But not, I remind myself (igniting more anger flames), before possible state-of-the-union, state-of-the-relationship, abject *I'm sorry* calls and messages from Ned. I get up. I stagger to the bathroom. I run cold water. I squeeze into my palms a hefty dollop of CVS apricot liquid cleanser, highly recommended by the *Allure* survey I tore from the dentist's waiting room. I wash my face.

I stop. I gasp. My skin feels burned, chafed, sandblasted, scoured. As if I've rubbed gravel all over it. I check the mirror. Big welts are rising on my cheeks; one eye is swelling shut; my jaw looks like it has been hacked by a rusty razor. Oh, God! What do I do? Call 911? Am I having an allergic reaction to my life? Has too much of Clyde and too little of Ned sent me into anaphylactic shock? I wait for my throat to close up, my body to crash to the floor. But nothing happens. Whatever it is seems confined to my stinging skin. Calm down, Abby, I tell myself. Calm down. I take deep breaths. If Clyde were here he could lead me in meditation, suggest a suitable mantra, help me reach the next level.

Which is what?

They'll be sorry, I crow, imagining my dramatic end, the tears at my funeral, the died-young-before-reaching-her-full-potential eulogies. I'd hate to miss the ceremony.

As soon as I realize that death is not imminent, I search for clues to my distress. It doesn't take long. I have mistaken the orange bottle of toothpaste, with its teeth-whitening touch of citrus, for the apricot bottle of apricot scrub. In a few minutes, my complexion will be cavity-free and whiter than white. This doesn't cheer me. I goop half a jar of aloe onto my assaulted, inflamed epidermis. I feel assaulted, inflamed. But not from the toothpaste. Not completely. I smell like orange Kool-Aid.

On the way back to bed, I pass my desk. I open the bottom drawer. There, under school reports and family documents and old postcards and canceled checks is the hard-to-miss blue envelope with its interlaced hearts, lipstick kisses, and border of *x*'s and *o*'s. I tried to throw it away. I really did. But at least give me credit for burying it in this drawer, for not looking at it for a whole year and a month. And for taping it shut.

I take it into bed with me. I arrange my pillows. I turn on the lamp. I rip the tape off with a fingernail file. I pull out the photograph.

It's a picture of Ned and me and Professor Chauncey Coolidge Thayer in front of St. Barnaby's Chapel in Kerry, New Hampshire. The leaded windows sparkle with the sun. The spire rises amid red and yellow autumn leaves. Professor Thayer stands between us. He has his arms around each of our shoulders. We are all smiling. I remember who took the picture. A fourth former wearing a maroon blazer with a gold school crest on his pocket and a beanie on his head. He had chapel duty, he explained. He called us "sir" and "ma'am." He didn't bark out the usual Say cheese. But we all grinned cheese anyway. I was bursting with joy. It was the day, the hour, the minute, the second I realized my longtime childish crush on Ned had turned into full-blown love.

And it was the day, the hour, the minute, the second that, miracle of miracles, Ned told me he felt the same.

Let me backtrack a bit here. As I've described to you, our houses abutted, our families were friends; at least four out of seven of the group, at various stages, were more than friends. To us kids, the Potter household was the place to hang out. Henrietta was always ready to stick another lamb chop in the broiler for an extra mouth. There were sleeping bags for overnight visitors rolled into a corner of the third floor. I, however, got a season's pass to the second maple four-poster in Lavinia's room wallpapered with urns and the columned temples of ancient Greece.

My father was more like Mr. Barrett; he barely tolerated my friends. Though he talked about undue influence, a lack of seriousness, the truth was he couldn't stand any disturbance to his routine. In his own curmudgeonly way, he did accept the presence of Lavinia and Ned and other faculty brats whose parents held long-tenured and lauded positions in Harvard's more prestigious departments. It was a tenure system for kids. A college of intellectual snobbery my father was chancellor of.

Uncle Bick was a dictator, too, but a benevolent one. Unlike my father, he enjoyed the muffled chorus of our voices, not to mention the pitter-patter of our not-so-little feet. If you were walking by his study, he'd invite you in for a drink. A drink, however, for which you'd have to fetch the bottle, find the glasses, chip the ice from the old-fashioned Frigidaire. He gave me my first port when I was ten, clinking my goblet with an untranslatable toast. He'd ask about our studies, our interests, what we wanted to be when we grew up, in the kindly but distracted way of an absentminded professor. We knew to avoid the topics of baseball, TV programs, pop songs, movie stars. Instead, we discussed math projects, music lessons, the Shakespeare for Children our mothers had dragged us to.

Ah, yes. Ah, yes, he'd say, brushing crumbs from his lunch-stained shirt. When I was little, I was convinced he was Santa Claus.

The Potter welcome was not so effusive as to fit the protesting-too-much category that set off any kid's antennae for the dishonest and the uncool. It just existed like dust motes in the sun and geraniums on the windowsill. That, and my designated best friend Lavinia, kept me running through their door. But, looking back, I think what drew me the most was an only child's—and a girl's—curiosity about Ned. What were these creatures called boys? What were their manners, habits, habitats? How did they talk and walk and do innumerable things to a ball? Why did they pinch and tickle and tease their sister, then ignore her? Why were their voices so loud? Their feet so big? Their smells so distinct? Why were their rooms stuffed with old rocks, broken bicycle parts, notebooks of Little League box scores? And how about their bodies? What was it like to have all those messy things hanging off you while we girls were so nicely and neatly tucked up inside? Even at an early age, I was savvy enough to know that my father didn't qualify. Had my father ever been a boy? Though he started many sentences—usually ones that would end in criticism of contemporary life—with *When I was a boy,* I never believed he hadn't been born full-grown with a beard and a watch chain clutching *The Decline and Fall of the Roman Empire.*

While I spent more time studying Ned than I did on my homework assignments, Ned hardly seemed to notice me. I was simply Lavinia's friend, the girl next door, Abby underfoot, no more remarkable than the table in the corner that had been there since he was born.

Except for one occasion. On the most thrilling day of my childhood, he taught me how to ride a two-wheeler. In retrospect I'm sure this gesture of generosity had less to do with me than with my bike. Ned was obsessed with bikes the way some of us preadolescent girls were with horses. He was always out in the backyard tinkering with his brakes, polishing the fenders, shining the handlebars, hanging streamers, tilting the seat, sticking cards on the spokes of his wheels.

I was ten, inching along the sidewalk on my embarrassing training wheels, when Ned spun by on his own shiny red Schwinn like Prince Charming atop his Arabian steed. He was doing wheelies; a box of new baseball cards peeked out of an Irving's bag. He actually noticed me; he actually stopped. "Why don't we take off those baby things and I'll teach you really how to ride, Abby," he offered.

In seconds he'd whipped out his tool kit; with two deft twirls of a screwdriver, the training wheels were lying in the pachysandra. He gave me a couple of go-team-go! instructions; he adjusted the height of my seat. He stepped a few feet in front of me; he held out his arms. "Now ride to me!" he commanded.

How could I not? So I did. Over and over. As he backed farther and farther away. "You can do it!" he cheered. "One more time."

One more time too many. Maybe I was cocky. Maybe I was showing off, but I hit a rock and went flying. I scraped my knee. I looked at the bloody mess of gravel and blood and mauled skin. I tried not to cry.

"All bikers have falls," Ned soothed. "Let me clean up that cut." He went into his house, came back toting the Potter family first-aid kit. With the same kind of care I'd watched him lavish on his Schwinn—maybe in that instance he saw me as an extension of his bicycle—Ned examined the gash, picked the pebbles out of my knee, daubed at the scrape, and applied the Band-Aid in a precise horizontal that covered every bit of damaged flesh. I inspected the lovely back of his neck. I studied his silky hair. I felt his breath on my knee. I'd never been this close. "Are you going to be a doctor when you grow up?" I'd asked.

"Dunno. Dad expects I'll end up a Harvard professor. You'll probably have a scar."

I have a scar. And when I touch it, I can remember Ned, how he taught me to ride, how he made me get back up on that seat, the way he picked, one by one, the pebbles out of my wound, and especially the sweet back of his head as he bent over me.

You'd hardly be surprised that from that day on, I held him in even greater awe. When he'd talk to me—*How's it going, Abby?* he'd ask. Or *What are you girls up to today?* Or simply *Hey* as he passed in the hall—I was so thrilled I barely noticed he never bothered to wait for the answer poised flightless as a dodo bird on the tip of my preteen tongue. "Ned spoke to me," I'd report to my mother in the incredulous tones of the pauper invited into the palace of the prince.

"Well, of course he did," she'd say with a laugh. "You are a charming, intelligent human being." She was working on the build-your-daughter's-self-esteem resolve of a woman who was perhaps starting to doubt her own reliance on a man.

Although I worried that she might disapprove of my crush, for lesbian, feminist, political reasons, she was actually pleased. I once overheard her and Henrietta in our kitchen, heads bent together conspiratorially, Emily drying, Henrietta rinsing, their dialogue going something like this:

"What if Ned and Abigail . . . ?"

"Could we even dare hope?"

"She has such a crush on him."

"No wonder. He *is* your son."

"They suit each other. He'll come to see that eventually."

"It would be so perfect."

"So perfect that we have to be careful not to let them sense that's what we want for them."

"The kiss of death."

"I quite agree."

"They need to discover this for themselves."

"They have so much in common. Someday they'll realize it."

What did we have in common? I wondered. A neighborhood, a city, a childhood, genus, species, kingdom trapped under the bell jar of academia? Years later, I managed to figure it out. In our own separate ways, in our own separate families, neither of us was quite up to snuff. My father would call my academic slump, failure. Ned's would call his a march to a different drummer. But tomayto or tomahto, neither of us was the golden apple of anybody's eye.

Like me, Ned was a dropout. He decided he wanted to be a writer. "What decent writer could even begin to pen a single sentence on a single page without a thorough grounding in literature?" the Professors Randolph and Potter would snort, each in his own way.

"Let them find themselves," chimed the Greek chorus of our mothers in perfect harmony.

I was working part-time in an antiques/junk shop in Central Square. I hoped to learn the business. Mainly I drank coffee and folded the vintage T-shirts bannered with the names of rock bands that had broken up. At night, I waitressed in a Greek restaurant where the waiters all wanted me to marry their sons.

Ned was writing in the old third-floor sleeping-bag room. He'd found a three-days-a-week job driving around a famous retired law professor who had a bad hip.

We were both living in our parents' houses for lack of funds. We were both depressed. At loose ends. Those of our friends nearby seemed set on a straight trajectory smack-dab into the professions; the others had slung backpacks over their shoulders to travel as far away from home as possible. If only we had stayed in school, our fathers complained. "Where's Abigail?" "Where's Ned?" a colleague might ask. "Harvard." "Princeton," they could reply with a certain puff of pride.

Now what did a father say? Chauffeuring? Waitressing? Passing off plastic bracelets as Bakelite?

The mothers both said, of course, writing. Studying antiques. Having life experiences. On-the-job training for finding themselves.

But if we weren't finding ourselves, we were finding each other. How could I not help bumping into Ned? How could Ned avoid me? Two outcasts with odd hours living next door burdened with the disappointments of fathers and even more deflated by the perky hopes of our mothers. "How's it going?" Ned would inquire, he leaving for his job, me coming home from mine.

"Don't ask."

And we'd nod in understanding, our eyes mirrors of each other's misery.

"Maybe we could have a coffee sometime?" he suggested one rainy morning as we fished our damp *Boston Globe*s from the sidewalk hedge.

"Maybe," I answered. I made my voice noncommittal, not from flirting, coyness, or adherence to *The Rules,* but simply from depression and the long drumming unrequitedness of my feeling for Ned so settled into my bones that to imagine anything else was impossible.

"You're both at loose ends," my mother advised. "Why not spend time together?"

"That's all I need," I said. Is that what I need? I wondered.

"A cup of coffee doesn't mean a wedding, Abigail."

"Mother!" I screeched, like a thirteen-year-old.

We had the cup of coffee. And another. Pizza. A movie. Bookstore reading. Long talks on the Potters' porch swing. Bike rides along the Charles. A gradual accumulation of spending time together like steady increments of an inoculation so you don't notice that you've gotten over your allergy. Soon I was washing my hair every day, shaving my legs, and standing at the kiosk in Harvard Square thumbing through *Vogue* while next to me my Cambridge sisters were buying up the *London Review of Books* and *Scientific American.* When Anastasio Aloupis, the maître d' at the restaurant, brought his son Damien—a hunk with a Greek-god build and a newly minted M.B.A.—in to meet me, I declined sharing a baklava and a retsina in the corner booth. *I'm seeing someone,* I told Damien, and knocked three times on the Formica countertop. Don't get your hopes up, I'd warn myself. It's proximity. Convenience. The girl-next-door syndrome. Just wait till he sells a story, gets his own apartment, meets somebody else, just wait till he's out of here.

"I can't believe this. My kid sister's bratty friend whom I've known forever. You grew up," he marveled.

"That happens. Not that you ever noticed me thrusting my training bra and Maybellined eyelashes in your face."

"I was a slow developer."

"You've caught up."

He took my hand. "Just like they say, search the world over and find what you're looking for right in your own backyard."

I wanted to ask, Have you? But I was too afraid to ruin the spell.

Though, later, the spell wasn't so much ruined as obliterated. An atomic bomb that laid waste a whole relationship. Considering how it all turned out, what's the point of giving you much more of Abby and Ned, the early days. I think you can pretty much fill in the blanks with your own experience of young love. Needless to say, our colluding mothers found excuses to be away from home when our fathers were in their offices, pleading errands (camouflage, I now imagine, for their own trysts) and giving us the run of the many bedrooms nestled in Cambridge Victorians. As far as the sex, I plead Yankee reticence. Besides, if you take into account what's going on—or rather not going on—in the present, past fabulous sex is irrelevant. Just know that while the things you wait for so often turn out to be disappointing, this wasn't. Not in the least.

So in the interest of moving the narrative along, let's skip to Ned and me and Chauncey Coolidge Thayer, professor emeritus at Harvard Law School. "What does he teach?" I asked Ned.

"Estates and Future Interests."

"Which is . . . ?"

"Estates, you can figure out. Future Interests involves the right to own property after a death or expiration of a specific term of years."

"Ah," I said, not realizing at the time that I should be tapping the resource in the seat in front of me.

Three days a week, Ned drove Professor Thayer to visit the chapels of New England prep schools. The old man was fascinated by spires and altars, pulpits and lecterns, church bells, stained-glass windows, spandrels and buttresses. He loved to examine prayer books and pipe organs and choir lofts, memorial plaques and the initials schoolboys had carved into the backs of pews. He studied the plantings around the chapels and the views from their towers. He and Ned had covered most of Massachusetts and were setting out for the greener prep school pastures of New Hampshire and Vermont.

"Come with us," Ned suggested one morning. We were sharing a sleeping bag in the third-floor attic, having rejected torture-rack horsehair mattresses and the prison-narrow twin-bedded ones. The Professors Potter and Randolph and the Mizzes Potter and Randolph were in Washington for intellectual festivities at the Library of Congress and the Mary Cassatt exhibit at the National Museum for Women in the Arts. "Professor Thayer wants to meet you."

"You've told him about me?"

"Of course." He took my hand in his hand. He wrapped his fingers around my fingers. "Look," he said. He lifted our joined hands. "How perfectly your hand fits. Like a bird in its nest. Like a nut in its shell."

"A nut?" I exclaimed. I studied our clasped hands. Was there anything more beautiful?

I snuggled close. His breath was warm. Velvety. "What did you say about me to Professor Thayer?" I asked.

He squeezed my fingers. "That you're this pesky girl who grew up next door and follows me around. That I can't get rid of you."

"Ned," I said. I laughed. I gave him a playful punch. I shook my head. And wondered if that's how he really thought of me.

It was the kind of October day that a writer I once read somewhere described as crisp as a Macintosh. Professor Thayer and his wife were waiting in front of their Memorial Drive apartment building as we drove up. He was a gnomelike man leaning on two canes, dressed in academic tweeds, vest, and striped silk tie. His eyes, two bright black coals in a wizened, ancient face, twinkled with a surprising (for Harvard) lack of self-importance. His wife, taller, thinner, and wiry, had a white pageboy set off by a headband, and a face of finely etched skin over beautiful bones. She was wearing an embroidered Guatemalan skirt topped by a Mexican serape. Pinned to it was a brooch I recognized as a copy of an Egyptian artifact from the Fogg Museum store. White Reeboks gleamed on her feet. A bag printed ATHENAEUM LIBRARY was strung across her chest. One hand clutched Professor Thayer; the other, an ancient three-speed Raleigh with a bright blue snazzy new helmet hanging over the handlebars. "There you are, Chauncey," she said, passing her husband to Ned like a grocery bag handed over to a customer. "And you must be Abby." She held out her hand, dry and papery as parchment with a grasp a politician would envy. "Ned, you must bring her for tea after your little trip." She strapped on her helmet. "I'm just off to the store to get us some nibbles. Tea is a euphemism, my dear, for sherry, of course. Now you have a good outing, Chauncey, and don't bore the young 'uns with your naves and apses."

"You know very well, Virginia, that naves and apses apply only to cathedrals," Professor Thayer sputtered.

"Indeed I do, dear, after sixty years of wedded bliss." She steered the bike out onto Mem Drive, clambered onto the seat, and pedaled off, an octogenarian Lance Armstrong in support hose.

Following much *After you, Alphonse, No, Gaston, after you* discussion and my insistence that I didn't get carsick, wouldn't feel like a second-class citizen, didn't have to sit next to my "beau," I scrambled into the backseat while Ned managed to settle Professor Thayer, his trick knees, his two canes, and his iffy hip in the front.

On the way to New Hampshire, up 93, onto the turnpike, they talked. I listened. It was the kind of conversation I was used to at my own table, in the Potters' dining room, at the dinners and breakfasts and lunches of my parents' friends. Wide-ranging, intellectual, grammatically precise discussions of books, politics, the Napoleonic Code, the Supreme Court, the latest theatrical desecration of the classics at the American Repertory Theatre, the declining quality of best-seller lists. The kind of conversation I could let wash over me like a lullaby, its familiar lilts and rhythms so soothing you hardly noticed them. *Jeez!* a public high school friend from the town soccer league once exclaimed after a family dinner my mother forced me to invite her to. (My mother insisted I mix with other zip codes to get a sense of the world outside my privileged one.) *Jeez*, she repeated. *In my house, you talk about Wal-Mart, Madonna, gas prices, baseball scores, Oprah. That is, if you talk at all, considering the TV's always on.*

No, what I paid attention to was Ned. His kindness, his gentleness to Professor Thayer. His deference, his courtesy, his hearty appreciation for stories of the good old days and even heartier reappreciation when the old man repeated himself. Unlike me, he didn't just let the sound of Professor Thayer's voice perfume the air; instead, like the most attentive student taking notes from the front row of the lecture hall, he asked questions. He mulled answers. That he was interested in Professor

Thayer, that he cared, intensified my own interest in Ned, made me care for him. To the exclusion of Professor Thayer, I'm forced to admit. For me, that day, there was only one person in the car. From my backseat perch, it was easy to study him. I noticed the way he leaned over to tug at Professor Thayer's seat belt to make sure it wasn't too tight; the way he asked him if he wanted to stop, to stretch his legs, to use the gas station facilities. The way he drove steadily, surely, avoiding potholes and sudden swerves. Every so often, through the rearview mirror he'd smile at me, then turn his attention back to how the law school students had changed since Professor Thayer first started teaching there.

We were in our twenties then, and though the hippie adage *Don't trust anyone over thirty* had both originated and died in our parents' generation, not many of our peers, me included, would have taken such delight three times a week in the company of an octogenarian. I craned my neck toward the rearview mirror. Traffic had knotted up, pinning Ned's lovely hazel eyes to the road. A thatch of brown hair fell boyishly over his brow.

Two weeks before, I'd been to the wedding of my friend Marnie, who'd married the boy she'd played in the sandbox with at the Cambridge Nursery School. They'd been a couple throughout kindergarten, grammar school, high school, and college. "Imagine," one or another of us had exclaimed admiring the photographs of the two of them set out in the foyer of the church, photographs that could have stood in for those growth charts of boys and girls at every stage of their development. "Guess there'll be no surprises with Jono. Marnie must know him as well as any person can know anyone," said Marnie's maid of honor in her toast to the newlyweds.

Can you find your soul mate as a kid? Can you keep him in your sights until you're out in the world with your own credit card and sauté pan? I scrutinized the sweet back of Ned's neck and listened to Professor Thayer expound on the disclaimer provision of the gift tax law.

Soon enough we pulled up to St. Barnaby's Chapel. People talk of Chartres, how when you drive from Paris to the Loire Valley, the cathedral starts to emerge in pieces, a spire, an arch, a rose window, a tower, a block of medieval stone, until the whole glorious creation rises up from the Plain of Beauce and takes your breath away. A spiritual experience, such people report.

The term *spiritual,* let me warn you, is not in my vocabulary (despite my anomalous fling with astrology). I come from a family of atheists. We are proudly secular. Our church affiliations are these: weddings, funerals, memorial services in Appleton Chapel, and poetry readings in the Unitarian Church. Old clothes get bundled into boxes and left off at the Quaker Meetinghouse in Longfellow Park, destined for the most oppressed population depending on what conflict was currently oppressing what part of the third world.

And yet when I first saw St. Barnaby's Chapel, I had this startling and intense ecstatic response that, for lack of a better word, I can only call spiritual. This chapel couldn't have been less like Chartres. A small New England building of white clapboard, plain leaded-glass windows, some framed with black shutters, cresting the rise of a gently sloping hill, its spire peeking up through a grove of trees fluttering with red, yellow, and orange autumn leaves.

We all rushed to the open double doors. *Rushed* used euphemistically since Professor Thayer's hips, two canes, our firm hands on his elbows cranked our pilgrims' progress into slow gear.

The chapel was empty. I sat on a pew, the wood underneath scooped by centuries of bottoms. I took in the elegant, eloquent simplicity of line, of space, of air. Outside the leaves rustled; faraway young voices rose from playing fields. Inside there was a hush broken only by Ned and Professor Thayer's quiet murmuring and the *tap-tap-tap* of the old man's cane. I felt the kind of contentment I had as a child when a warm bath, a story, an ice cream cone, a bunch of us kids playing tag at dusk, the smells of supper wafting through the screen doors was enough evidence to prove all's right with the world.

Ned was helping Professor Thayer up onto the pulpit. Professor Thayer started to examine a stack of prayer books on the table behind the lectern. I looked at Ned. He stood still as a statue. A shaft of light angled in from a high clerestory window and turned him golden. There in that plain New Hampshire church, the sun shining through old bubbled glass, he was lit like a Renaissance saint. I love him, I thought. This is the man I love.

Ned walked down from the pulpit. He sat beside me in the pew. He took my hand. His fingers circled mine. "Abby," he whispered. "The most extraordinary thing. I was just standing there and this light came from the window behind you and illuminated you in such a way . . ." He stopped.

He kissed me. The kind of kiss not suitable for a chapel, not suitable for a room where a student might any second run in through the open door, not suitable in the presence of an elderly professor now examining the window that had just anointed your one true love. Not suitable for a public place. Not suitable, but he kissed me anyway. *How do I love thee? Let me count the ways.*

The words came out in a rush. "We'll get married. Here. In this chapel. When I've finished my novel. When you've got your business up and running. When we've laid a little groundwork to build a life together as husband and wife. Isn't it amazing? You've been here all along, right in my own backyard." *The lark's on the wing; / The snail's on the thorn: / God's in his heaven— / All's right with the world.*

Then we went outside. Where the fourth former in blazer and beanie took our beaming, in-love, ecstatic, revelatory photograph.

We would have preferred not to stay for tea. We would have preferred to go back to the Potters' third floor and seal our declarations of love in the time-honored way. But an invitation accepted is an invitation that can't be declined. Like so much of everything, we were beginning to discover, we agreed on that.

Mrs. Thayer had set out sherry on a silver tray in the library. The apartment was a big rambling one, much like our houses, with river views and books piled everywhere. Paintings of stern ancestors in dour suits and wasp-waisted ball gowns covered those spaces between bookshelves. Stacks of legal journals filled a brass coal shuttle. My in-the-process-of-being-educated eye focused on the antiques. Sheraton sideboard, Chippendale chairs, Queen Anne footstools, tapestries with moth holes and ragged edges, lacquered Chinese tables. Scattered throughout, like guests who'd wandered into the wrong party in the wrong century, were some bent plywood tables, bright plastic stools, and pale oak chairs. I remember my mother once telling me how shocked she was when she visited one of England's stately homes—Chatsworth? Blenheim?—to see a Donald Duck telephone, a vinyl butterfly chair, a 1950s pole lamp of wrought iron and chrome. The Thayers' anachronistic pieces I recognized from the old Design Research on the corner of Brattle and Story streets. The Thayers must have filled gaps when the antiques they'd inherited started to spread too thin.

Now Mrs. Thayer spilled out the contents of her Athenaeum Library bag. "Here are the nibbles," she said, sifting them into a series of blue-and-white Chinese export bowls. "Unfortunately the bounty is limited to what I could bring home on my bicycle. There was the loveliest wedge of Limburger, but I decided it just might tip the balance."

"Not to mention the smell, my dear," added Professor Thayer with a pinch to his nose.

She passed around the bowls. Smoked almonds, olives, sunflower seeds, wasabi peas, Goldfish crackers—the ones with smiles. She smiled. "So I trust you had a good trip to St. Barnaby's."

Professor Thayer popped a Goldfish into his mouth. "Most gratifying. Quite a nice 1789 Book of Common Prayer. An original bell tower, too. The pulpit looked new, though. You can always tell by—"

"Enough, dear. I'm sure the young people had more than their ration of the ecclesiastical for the day." She fanned out four white linen cocktail napkins monogrammed *VGT*. "I had wanted to arrange some entertainment for them. I called Amelia and Geoffrey to see if they could come upstairs for a game of Latin anagrams."

"What a splendid idea," the professor said.

Ned and I looked at each other, panic mapping our faces, the panic fueled by that old nightmare of students everywhere: you're in a room taking an exam and realize you've studied the wrong lesson, read the wrong book.

Mrs. Thayer didn't seem to notice. "Unfortunately they have a grandchild—or is it a great-grandchild?—visiting them," she went on.

"Who could certainly join us, dear."

"Of course I suggested that very thing to Amelia. 'We have other young people coming,' I explained." She paused. "Chauncey, you will be shocked to hear her reply."

"I'll try to withstand it, my dear. Do tell."

"That the grandchild. Or great-grandchild. I don't know the sex either. But the fact is that he or she never studied Latin. Not even a term."

"What a disgrace. An entirely sorry state of affairs. Latin is the basis of all knowledge."

"Amelia explained that she or he is learning Spanish, or was it Portuguese? Very useful in our multicultural society, she added. All well and good, I told her, but a person needs a foundation in the classics. One can't build on anything without due respect for the roots of the past." She turned to Ned. "Don't you think so?" she asked.

He nodded. "The roots of the past are very important."

Professor Thayer poured the sherry into the thimble-sized stemmed glasses. His hands trembled. Some liquid spilled over onto the tray.

I saw Ned start to lean forward to help him, then think the better of it. We are of the same mind, I concluded, my first instinct to reach out to help, my second not to let Professor Thayer know I noticed any infirmity.

Our same mind was underscored even more by our shared relief—and debt to the grand or great, the him or her—not to have to risk certain humiliation in a game of Latin anagrams.

Was our relief so apparent? Perhaps so, because Mrs. Thayer then nodded at us. "I'm sure the two of you studied Latin," she declared.

"Four years," confessed Ned. *"Omnia Gallia in tres partes divisa est."*

"Two," I added. *"Amo, amas, amat."* I paused. I gathered steam. *"Agricolae poetae sunt,"* I recited. I couldn't help myself.

She clapped. "See, I knew you were both properly educated."

"What a pity we can't play. It's not quite the same with just four," her husband said.

"What a pity," Ned echoed.

"Next time," Professor Thayer consoled. He poured more sherry into an already-overflowing glass. This welcome diversion cascaded onto the tray, over the table's edge, onto Professor's Thayer's tweed knee, and onto the Heriz carpet at his feet.

I brought the tray into the kitchen. Mrs. Thayer pulled out a roll of paper towels. "Oh, men." She sighed. A word of exasperation stated with such affection it made us both smile.

A soup tureen of pale blue china sat in the middle of the kitchen table. Painted on it were pairs of cupids dancing, jumping, cavorting over fields of wildflowers. Birds and butterflies filled a brilliant sky. Picturesque ruins crumbled artistically next to waterfalls. "How beautiful!" I exclaimed.

"Isn't it? Chauncey and I got it on our honeymoon. In Italy." She stopped. Her eyes filmed with far-off memories. "To this day, more than sixty years, every time I serve a lobster bisque, I'm reminded of those magical weeks." She ran her fingers over the tureen's cover, rested them on its handle, a knobbed red apple attached to a sleek purple plum. She patted a cupid. "Chauncey is so fond of Ned."

"Driving Professor Thayer is the best job he's ever had. Ned adores him."

"And Ned seems so fond of you."

"You think so?"

"I can always tell."

Back in the library, Professor Thayer was asleep in his chair. His chin bobbed on his chest. The sound of gentle snores mixed with the clang of dishes and glasses being cleared.

"It's time for us to go," Ned said. "Stay there, Mrs. Thayer. We'll let ourselves out."

At the door, we turned to wave.

Mrs. Thayer didn't see us. She was sitting next to her husband. Her hand was on his knee. She leaned toward him. She whispered something. Then planted a kiss on a cheek that, I was certain, seemed as smooth to her as that of a young man, her young man, her bridegroom, in Italy more than sixty years ago.

8

I'm still in bed when the buzzer rings. I stick my head under the pillow. "Go away," I yell. "I am retreating from the world." Not that anyone can hear me. The buzzer keeps screeching like those car alarms that bring old ladies into the street wearing fuzzy slippers and waving rolling pins. Is it stuck? Now that I shall never leave my apartment, now that I shall never leave my bed, am I to be tormented by a jammed and insistent buzzer that will turn me into one more crazy hermit in a city full of them? Who could it be? I wonder. And the second I think this, I pounce on you-know-who. And dismiss that thought.

Mailman? UPS? Someone soliciting for Common Cause despite the NO SOLICITATION signs stuck all over the downstairs hall? These rarely deter the kids putting themselves through college by selling magazine subscriptions to *Auto Digest*, though never *Art & Antiques*. Or the earnest souls collecting for disease of the month, terrorizing you into handing over five dollars lest tumors map your body and rot your skin. I touch my still-stinging face—rot has afflicted me already. Maybe it's Clyde, who left behind in his ticketed car another doctoral thesis's worth of apologies.

I shall never answer my door, I decide. The minute I take this stance, the buzzing stops. What a sense of power I feel, the power of semipositive thinking. Too bad I can't vanquish thoughts the way I can vanquish annoying visitors.

But I've spoken too soon, for now there's pounding at my door. Ceaseless, unrelenting pounding. Followed by the voice. "Abby, open up. I know you're in there. I've already been at Objects of Desire. I know you've gone home. Open up. I am going to keep knocking until you let me in."

It's Lavinia.

"Go away," I call again. But my heart's not in it. I recognize a hopeless case when I see it, and Lavinia's stubbornness and persistence are as immutable as the Berlin Wall—more, if you consider they tore the wall down.

I force myself out of bed. My legs are weak; maybe my calf muscles have already started to atrophy. I pull on sweatpants over my plain white 100 percent cotton serviceable underpants. I've tucked away my Victoria's Secret silk bikinis along with my hopes in the back of my bureau drawer. I have seen my bleak future. No sex. Bodily fluids as dry as my shriveled, shrinking skin.

I open the door.

"My God, what's happened to your face?" Lavinia shouts.

"Hello to you, too."

"Stress," she diagnoses.

"Actually some allergic reaction to a face cream," I say. I do not admit rubbing toothpaste all over my delicate brow.

"No wonder you're hiding out." She walks inside. Flings a jacket I have hung over the back of a chair onto the floor, pushes away a pair of jeans, and sits down. "Just so you know, some lady who lives in the building, on her way back from the market, let me in. You should have a rule. It's hideously unsafe."

"If we had a rule, you wouldn't be here now," I reasonably point out.

She brushes this off. "I need to talk to you."

"Is conversation between us permitted?" I ask. "Considering our lawyers." Since my *Bleak House* legal problems, I've been watching even more *Law & Order*.

"We're friends."

Were, I start to amend, then slam my mouth shut.

"Besides, we're not jurors blabbing to the press." She looks around my living room.

I view my own four walls through her two eyes.

She doesn't say, What a dump, but I can read it on her face.

I touch my own face. "I've been feeling so under the weather I haven't got around to cleaning this up."

"With all this stuff, I can't imagine you'd have room for anything more."

Does she mean room to fit a chamber pot? Does she mean room for our mothers' antiques, ninety-nine point ninety-nine percent of which she arranged to have crated and moved to her Concord house? "I'm sorting it out. Some of the stuff is going to my booth," I lie.

She studies my sofa, draped with my none-too-clean, all-too-practical underwear. "I'm getting married again," she announces.

I do a double take. She has stated this in the same way she'd say she was going to the store to pick up a jar of pickles. "Oh," I remark, neutral as Switzerland. I feel a sadness for what, in a normal friendship, would have been the scenario to follow such news: the jumping up and down. The flinging of arms. The examining of the ring. The pulling out of photographs. The who, what, and where asked and answered with mounting excitement verging on gushiness.

"Yes. And I want to start this marriage with a clean slate."

"Which has what to do with me?"

"Everything. The chamber pot, for example." She smooths her skirt. She points to my OUT OF IRAQ T. "Aren't you a little too old to be wearing that?"

"I feel strongly about the war."

"You're not a college student anymore."

"Does that make me less of an involved citizen?" I stare at her. At her neat red suit and diamond studs and red-leather-trimmed pocketbook. "Omigod!" I exclaim. "Is your husband-to-be a *Republican*?"

To her credit, she has the good grace to blush. "Political affiliations are private," she snorts. "Besides, my forthcoming marriage is not the purpose of this visit."

"Explain to me again what the purpose is."

"To resolve the issue of this chamber pot."

"I assume your heavy-hitting Snodgrass X, Y, and Z law firm was in charge of this particular assault." I pat my T-shirt. "These weapons of mass destruction on a civilian population unable to defend itself."

"Stop it, Abby. You're becoming tiresome." She sighs her long-suffering Lavinia sigh. "My lawyers, in fact, would not wish me to be here talking to you."

"You mean consorting with the enemy?"

She ignores this. "They feel my case is the superior one. That my mother wanted me to have the chamber pot, herein stated same, and as such it rightly belongs to me. But even given the probable positive outcome of my case, I am, as you know, not a selfish person."

"Always thinking of others. Generous to a fault. Awash in the milk of human kindness."

All irony is lost on her, maybe because she keeps talking like a lawyer. "And, as a result, to avoid litigation insofar as I can focus on my upcoming marriage, this *happy* event—*very happy event*—I've decided to go against counsel's advice and offer to sell the chamber pot and split the proceeds with you." She looks at me with a self-congratulatory tilt of the chin.

Am I supposed to melt at her feet into a puddle of gratitude?

She waves her fingers in the direction of my underwear-upholstered sofa, my clutter of bric-a-brac and flea-market finds, my pizza boxes and Chinese food cartons waiting to be put out in the trash, my mottled lumpy face in desperate need of an ace dermatologist, my T-shirt and sweatpants begging for a fashion makeover. "It seems to me you could certainly use the money," she adds, noblesse oblige winning out over *Let them eat cake*.

My spine, put through its character-building paces, gratifyingly stiffens. "The chamber pot was meant for me. It was my mother's. I'll never part with it." I pause. "Besides, you didn't want it until I took it onto *Antiques Roadshow*. It was *my* mother's," I repeat. "You rejected it. I kept it. Too bad."

"Well, then let me point something else out. How would you like your mother's—and my mother's—life together broadcast all over the Boston tabloids?"

"Believe me, no newspaper would be interested in the domestic arrangements of two mousy academic wives."

"You wanna bet? When there's a chamber pot that once belonged to Elizabeth Barrett Browning involved? When you stick yourself and it up on one of PBS's most popular programs, broadcast on channels across the fifty-two states? With reruns shown more than twice a week, dare I calculate. Almost every time I turn on the TV—which isn't often, as I prefer to use my few free moments to read—there you are with your eyes popping out and your mouth agape. 'You're kidding,' you scream." She shakes her head. "Don't be naïve, Abby. You asked for it. Boy, the media can't wait to shove the knife into us Brattle Street Harvard types. The whole story of our lives will be right out there for every Tom, Dick, and Harry to read. Your grocer. Your dentist."

"Not to mention your new fiancé." I was going to say Republican fiancé but I didn't have the hard evidence. I paused. "Lavinia, it isn't as though our story hasn't been told before. It isn't as though your brother didn't publish his book."

"Which was a *novel*. Not a piece of mass-market yellow journalism."

"You were upset at the time."

"I got over it." She waits. "Unlike you."

I don't defend myself.

But she defends Ned. "The book didn't get the recognition it deserved. It sold zilch copies. Due not to Ned but to the bad marketing of his publisher. I'd rather keep our story in the family than let the newspapers make hay of our private affairs."

"Nothing changes my mind. You didn't want it. Finder's keepers."

She gets up in a huff. "I would have hoped you'd be reasonable. But why would I have thought that, as you've never been reasonable in your whole life."

"Not reasonable like you," I say sweetly. "Not so unselfish as you, either."

She turns toward the door. Some of the upholstery in the chair must have ripped as feathers and bits of cotton batten dot the seat of her red skirt. I smile.

"I don't know why you're smiling, Abigail. You've made a stupid mistake." She sticks out her jaw like a toddler incubating a tantrum. "I'll see you in court."

I keep smiling. "I bet you've always wanted to say those words."

She puts her hand on the doorknob. "Next will come the depositions." She opens the door. She turns to me. "I assume Ned will be subpoenaed to testify."

Ned. Ned. I've delayed this part long enough. I'm not surprised you're getting restless. I pour myself a glass of wine even though, as Uncle Bick would have said, the sun hasn't passed over the yardarm yet. I get back into bed, where I promptly dribble wine on the pillowcase to join the Rorschach blots of pepperoni pizza and Buddha's Delight. I take another, more careful sip.

Here goes. I'll try to make it fast in the way that, as with a Band-Aid, the quicker you pull the less it hurts. When I left off telling you Ned's story, it was at the highest point of my life: St. Barnaby's Chapel, Professor Thayer, glorious light, declarations of love. If I've learned anything in my thirty-three years, it's that highs are often followed by lows. And the lows last longer.

But the highs made it through the three more years it took Ned to finish his novel, the waiting period between the proposal and the day the actual event would occur. *We'll get married. Here. In this chapel. When I've finished my novel,* was what he said. If all happy families are alike, so are all happy lovers. Our world blazed in Technicolor. Food never tasted so good; music never had so much charm to soothe a savage breast; our words were sonnets that spilled out. In bed we read to each other the poetry that as students we had scorned.

I opened my heart to Ned. My most private thoughts, any secret I ever buried, I revealed to him. My deepest feelings about my friends, my insecurities about my place in the world, my guilt about my privileged Cambridge life and my failure to live up to it, my bewilderment over my mother's lifestyle choices and my teenage confusions, my grievances against my father and my hopeless sense of having disappointed him. I came to understand that my lovemaking with Ned was a physical manifestation of this opening up, a dramatization, a choreography, a profound, creative expression, the stuff of an epic or a symphony. Sex with Tom, Dick, and Harry (and three was pretty much the extent of it) was thrilling and fun, but it was never like this, never like sex with the person you trotted after as a child and beheld, when you grew up, in a dazzling shaft of light. He wrote. I worked. We made plans for our future together.

"Can I read the work in progress?" I'd asked Ned.

"I'm superstitious. Wait till I'm done."

Months passed. More months passed.

"How is it going?" I'd inquire. "Almost near the end?"

"In a while," he'd say.

Then, "I'm getting there."

Then, "Soon. I'm starting to reach the home stretch."

It was a beautiful day when he finished. Afterward I remembered that. I wondered if things always went bad on glorious days. I thought of September 11. Not a cloud in the sky, just a hint of the crispness of fall, a day in which you're sure all's right with the world.

Back then, when Ned finished, my mood was as sunny as the day. It was the middle of the afternoon, a summer afternoon, the two words Henry James called the most beautiful in the English language. A Sunday. I was on the Potters' porch swing. The house was up for sale. Our mothers were in India. My father was in Hawaii fertilizing Kiki's eggs. Uncle Bick had died the year before, and I'd moved in with Ned. Next door, in my old house, I could hear the cries of the young children of the new owners protesting being put down for their naps. Ned came out onto the porch carrying a typewriter paper box, a bottle of champagne, and two of Henrietta's best Baccarat flutes. "I finished," he said.

It was a solemn moment. A hush in the cathedral. We were silent. I wondered what it must be like to complete something so big. We opened the champagne with no talk of whether the sun had passed over the yardarm. Ned poured. We each had a single glass that we raised in a toast. "To finishing," he said.

"To your novel," I said.

He passed the box to me. *The Cambridge Ladies Who Live in Furnished Souls* was typed in bold across the top. "Cummings," he said. "Though I'm sure you know."

I nodded. I lifted the title page. *This book is dedicated to Abigail Elizabeth Randolph, soul mate and light of my life,* I read.

"Ned." I started to sob.

"Don't cry yet," he ordered. He held up a traffic-cop hand. "If you're going to start it now," he said, "I'll have to leave the house." He kissed me. He unlocked his bicycle from the porch rail. He put on his helmet and set off for Concord. To Lavinia's.

I settled back into the porch swing. I turned to Chapter One. I was high on joy. On hope for the future. On the realization that all the waiting was over. On dreams of St. Barnaby's Chapel. On my life with Ned. On love for my fellow man. On love for one fellow man in particular. *This is the most perfect moment of my life,* I thought. My heart swelled.

By page thirty my heart had shrunk into a tiny, hard, cold nub. Joy had turned to misery. Love to shock.

Every little secret I had ever told Ned, every fear and embarrassment and doubt bellowed out there from the page. My troubles with my father; my worries about my mother; my own childhood crush on him, all wrapped up into a scathing critique of our Cambridge lives, our Cambridge friends, generic Cambridge ladies, and our own Cambridge mothers in particular. If you flipped through at random, here's what you'd see: There I was dropping out of school. There was my first failed love affair. There was the scene where I stole two Snickers from Irving's, illuminated by my abject confession and my father-edited note of apology. All building up to the crescendo of the moment when, in my pink-striped bedroom described down to my periodic table quilt, my mother told me about Henrietta, mother-daughter dialogue recreated almost verbatim from the conversation I'd revealed to Ned.

Was the book any good? How could I tell? Why would I care? Who could see the forest for my barbed-wire, knife-edged, stiletto-branched trees? I was pierced, beaten, pounded, flattened, kicked so low I could have dropped to China through one of those holes we used to dig as children in the Potters' backyard. This is the lowest day of my life, I knew.

What should I do? My first instinct was to flee to Lavinia, who was still my best friend. For obvious reasons, I couldn't go there. I packed a bag. I poured out the rest of the champagne into the hydrangea bush. I left a note, weighted by a stone, on top of the manuscript box. *Please don't try to contact me*, I wrote. Then crossed out the *Please*. I made a few phone calls and accepted the first offer of a living room couch. In two days I'd sublet the Inman Square apartment from a techie who'd decided to make a trek to Nepal. On day three I moved in. And, yes, just as you'd assume, I took to my bed. I threw out Ned's letters without opening them. I monitored all calls. I refused to talk to Lavinia, who left unctuous and then increasingly angry messages on my answering machine. I didn't go to my door except for the pizza delivery man and the plumber the superintendent sent to test the pipes.

Finally, they stopped. The letters. The calls. Finally, I got out of bed.

It took a year and a half for Ned's book to be published. During that time our mothers had died in the earthquake in India. And I'd met Clyde. Typical rebound scenario, you'd diagnose. I'd have to agree. But for a while Clyde helped me, if not to forget, then to avoid the obsessional hand-wringing and chest-smacking that took over every second of my life since I opened Ned's manuscript.

The Cambridge Ladies Who Live in Furnished Souls bombed.

There were three local readings. Not well attended, reported my spies, except for a handful of brave *It's fiction* family members, including Lavinia putting on a public face, and a couple of loyal friends scattered among the usual suspects showing up for the free coffee and shoppers stopping by to take a load off their feet.

The reviews were lousy. The few there were.

"Amateur writing," wrote the critic in the *Boston Globe*. "Warmed-over Cambridge quiche. Nothing you haven't heard, and heard better told, before." He called the protagonists' lives "boring and dreary," their problems, "tiny tempests in Wedgwood teapots." "What reader could ever care about such people who lack vision and will?" he asked. "If this is all they can do with their Harvard educations, then they deserve each other."

I should have been glad Ned's exploitative book got panned. I should have cherished the starless ratings on Amazon. The mean words. The speed at which his novel got moved from bookstores' center tables and into the spine-out Siberia of back shelves. It was what the book deserved. Just desserts. The sweet smell of revenge. Bad deeds that *did* get punished.

But I was sad for him. A residual feeling like the scar that marks the long-ago childhood bout of chicken pox.

I avoided bookstores. I avoided his books. I avoided Ned, who must have avoided me, too. But I couldn't avoid Lavinia. She came into my booth.

"What are you doing here?" I asked. It was yet another quiet day; no one rummaging through my brass doorknobs, the ersatz Currier & Ives, the china gravy boats and coin silver demitasse spoons, no one to impress Lavinia with my industry, my business acumen.

"It's a public place," she said. She was all dressed up in her ladylike color-coordinated clothes. I—well, you can imagine what I was wearing—carpenter's pants, a Greek sailor's shirt, my usual scruffy glad rags (accessorized by a vintage scarf, I might add). She picked up a saucer painted with silhouettes of George and Martha Washington. She put it down.

"This is ridiculous," she said.

"These saucers are very popular."

"You know what I mean." She banged her fist on a cherry wood table. A piece of veneer fell off. "Though I can't understand why, you seem to have broken my brother's heart. He's moved to New York."

"The center of publishing. All the better for his literary career."

"Look, Abby, I got over it. Why can't you?"

I stopped. My body went limp. I felt knocked sideways by despair. My whole sad life came washing over me, my whole sad life documented in Ned's tell-all book. "I can't, Lavinia. It was *my* life Ned stole. I just can't."

"That changes everything," she said. With not even a good-bye, with not even a wave, she turned on her two-inch stacked heel and walked away.

9

Mary Agnes Finch calls me. "The deposition's been set for six weeks from today," she reports. "I'll mail you the official notice. I must say that the logistics have been a nightmare, for such a little case—"

"A little case!" I exclaim.

"Well, not to you, of course, but in the larger scheme of things, in the legal world . . ." Her voice trails off. Between the lines I read I'm a pain in the ass, I'm being unreasonable. But what about Lavinia? I want to shout. What about Ned? It's not my fault, I'm tempted to cry, a child unjustly accused of hogging the shovel and pail while others are trying to grab them away from her. I need to be grateful to Mary Agnes.

I know she wouldn't have taken this on if we hadn't gone to school together. "I can't thank you enough. I really am so—"

She cuts me off. "If we hadn't gone to school together, Abby, I might not have agreed to pursue this. I usually accept cases with much higher stakes."

"I understand that a chamber pot isn't a multimillion-dollar estate," I admit. "Still . . ."

"Of course, to *you,* it's high stakes."

"Yes. Plus there's always the principle of the thing."

"Naturally."

But I can recognize a lukewarm response when I hear it. I change the subject. "You mentioned the logistical nightmares?"

"Yes, agreeing on a date, agreeing on a time, agreeing on a place. Getting everyone together—the other lawyers, parties to the dispute, the stenographer. Jim Snodgrass and I are in accord about forgoing the expense of videotape. For convenience, we've decided to depose you all at once. I've set aside a conference room in my office. Ned will take the shuttle back and forth. We're hoping to get through everything in two days."

"Two days?" What was I thinking? A morning of discomfort followed by the lollypop of a Filene's Basement trip?

"Often depositions take *weeks.*"

I collapse onto the nearest chair. Something sticks into my butt. When I slide it out, I see it's *Flush: A Biography*. I hold it against my heart. Could there be a more profound signal to walk on through the storm? Which at least won't show up on videotape. Small consolation.

No consolation at all when I hear what Mary Agnes says next. "You realize that you'll all be deposed not only at the same time but also in the same room, that you'll all sit in on each other's testimony."

"What?" My throat closes up. I start to sputter. I can barely get the words out. "I assumed we'd be deliberately segregated, that our schedule would be set up for avoidance." I must be thinking of Feydeau farces, the slamming doors timed so precisely that actors keep missing each other by the tip of a toe or the knob of an elbow. "In *Law & Order,*" I instruct, "witnesses are always brought to separate interrogation rooms. The Sam Waterston character takes great pains to hide one witness from the opposing one."

Do I hear Mary Agnes snort at the source of my legal expertise? "That's for a criminal case. Depositions are preliminary." She pauses. "Abby, are you sure you want to go through with this?"

I stroke the cover of *Flush*. If I weren't so sane, I'd swear the cocker spaniel is winking at me. My chamber pot has been in Mary Agnes's vault for so long I've forgotten what it looks like. My mother has been dead for so long I can hardly re-create the contours of her face, the sweet comfort of her smile. What I do know, however, is that she'd want me, who barely finishes anything, to finish this. "Never surer of anything more in my life," I swear.

"Well, then," she says, "I'll send you a copy of the notice of deposition. I'll also give you a little booklet I had made up for clients who are about to be deposed."

"It will be like college again. The studying," I add.

"In a way. We'll meet beforehand for a little coaching." She laughs. "A Kaplan cram course. A Princeton Review prep."

"Uh-oh."

"Come on, Abby. You, a Harvard student."

I'm about to answer, Faculty brat, but let it go. After all, Mary Agnes Finch, from blue-collar South Boston, doesn't need to be reminded that Harvard is not always a meritocracy.

Mary Agnes continues. "You do understand now that though the three of you will be in the same room, will be hearing each other's testimony, it won't be like a trial. You won't have the chance to reply."

"I understand."

"And let me just warn you that the questions can get quite personal."

I sit up. "What do you mean?"

"No holds barred. Your background, your family relationships, your sexual history, secrets, feelings, problems you may not necessarily want to talk about. All grist for the deposition mill."

"You're kidding," I say. This time my voice contains horror, not the delight that followed the valuation of my chamber pot. Will I have to talk about my feelings for Ned in front of Ned? The highs of our life together. The lows of our life apart. How he betrayed me, the embarrassing things there were to betray.

"It won't be easy."

She's thrown down the gauntlet. Does she think I'm not up to it? "I'm up to it," I state with a bravado I don't feel.

"I heard from Jim Snodgrass that Lavinia went to see you. That she offered to sell the pot, to split the proceeds fifty-fifty."

"So?"

"You might want to reconsider. She might be persuaded to extend the offer again."

I shake my head. "Never."

"Even without taking into account legal fees and expenditures of time, this kind of compromise will save a lot of emotional distress."

I picture *The Cambridge Ladies Who Live in Furnished Souls*. All my distress is catalogued there—347 pages' worth in ten-point Galliard, on ivory stock, filed in the Library of Congress, sporting an ISBN, for sale to any comer for $24.95, Ned's photograph on the back flap. And inside, my heart exposed, my guts eviscerated and spilling out. "Over my dead body," I say, "to quote an ex-friend of mine."

Since I've got a whole six weeks until the deposition, I decide to get to work on my brilliant career. I boot up my computer. I look up flea markets and country auctions in the Greater New England area. It's time to add more to my stock. I've been so focused on Lavinia in the present, Ned in the past, my legal woes, I haven't kept you up to date on my professional activities.

Well, at least something's turning out better than I would have thought. As a realist, I expected the increase in business from my *Antiques Roadshow* appearance to be short-term. The flavor-of-the-month effect. The on-to-the-next-brilliant-discoverer fickleness. And true enough, after every spike, there'd be the kind of significant drop to make me start worrying about my rent. But thanks to endless reruns, my fifteen minutes of fame has turned out to be the gift that keeps on giving. People are still walking into my booth saying *I saw you on TV* months after the event, months after the chamber pot found its (temporary, I hope) resting spot in Mary Agnes Finch's repository.

I stop typing. My fingers freeze. My hands hover, trembling, over the keys like the hands of a séance-conducting medium. *Tag Sale: Country furniture, china, washstands, farm implements, chamber pots, Route 193, Kerry, New Hampshire,* I read. I read it again. *Kerry, New Hampshire,* the site of St. Barnaby's, the site of my only marriage proposal (if you discount Johnny Aherne's in third grade), the sad reminder of things past. I move my eyes to *chamber pots,* the object both of my improved circumstance and of my current misery. Lightning can't strike twice, I comfort myself—neither with the good a chamber pot can bring nor with the bad. If Elizabeth Barrett Browning had only known in the nineteenth century what complications her plain, humble, utilitarian chamber pot would work in the twenty-first, she'd have written an ode on the subject. I highlight the tag sale, click on bold, and bracket the date with two stars.

I force myself back to the next flea market on the list. I am struggling not to obsess about the deposition, about seeing Ned. When I was a teenager, up to my erupted skin in adolescent angst, my mother suggested I bring all my worries to her between four and four-thirty every afternoon. We would worry together, then and only then. The rest of our hours would be productive and glorious. For a while this ploy worked, if you agree that *productive* and *glorious* are adjectives subject to interpretation and full of flexibility. But now that I'm grown, the tsunami of worries washes over me twenty-four hours out of a twenty-four-hour day. If my mother were here, I'd call her up the way you call up your sponsor in AA. *I feel a worry coming on,* I'd confess, *I can't stop myself*. And she'd rush right over and hold my hand until the craving passed.

How I wish my mother were here. How I miss her. When I picture her and Henrietta in front of the Taj Mahal, one lover's monument to his beloved, I am cheered. The fact of her happiness at that moment cushions my loss. Underneath the hum of the computer, the tap of the keys, the click of the cursor, the stop and go of my heart, the up and down of my despair-o-meter, I can almost hear her voice. *Keep busy, dear,* she says to me. *Time and work are the great healers. Work makes the time pass.*

I reach for my date book, which is sadly underutilized. I can just imagine Lavinia's dance card, her daily planner cluttered with lunches, dinners, appointments, benefits, second wedding, lawyers' meetings, torment-your-friend meetings, all jotted down in her cramped, clear, anal hand. I mark my own calendar: flea markets, tag sales, teeth cleaning a month from now, lunch date with a friend who is bringing her two children down from Maine to follow in the footsteps of Paul Revere. La-di-da! You won't be surprised to see that my Friday and Saturday nights are blank. At thirty-three, I find those empty spaces are harder to fill than at twenty. Especially if you no longer have a Clyde on your arm for a movie at the Brattle Theatre, a hamburger at Bartley's, a drink at the Casablanca bar. Searching for Mr. Right—or even Mr. Just Okay—while getting over one man and legally entwined with the other is worse than cooking fudge when you've got twenty pounds to lose. I pencil in *Tag Sale, Kerry, New Hampshire,* under Saturday. *Viewing,* as it says in the ad, *from ten till all the merchandise is gone.*

Just then the phone rings. I pick it up. "Abigail Randolph?" a man's voice asks.

"Who wants her?"

"The *Boston Globe*."

"I already subscribe."

I'm about to hang up when the voice cuts in. A laugh followed by, "Wait. I'm a reporter."

It's a word that should come with a warning: *Reporter: Danger Ahead.* A word that should trigger my flight response, but, well, what can I say? He is a man, his voice sounds deeply masculine, I am staring at a crossword puzzle's worth of fill-in-the-blank squares for all weekend nights. "Yes?" I answer, careful to keep any eagerness or encouragement out of my tone.

"Todd Tucker. I'm doing a piece on the follow-up to *Antiques Roadshow*. What happens to people and their objects once they've been featured on the program."

Well, if that isn't a signal to slam down the phone and flee in the opposite direction, then my name isn't Abigail Elizabeth Randolph. Maybe it isn't, maybe I'm adopted, because I don't do any of those things. I plead loneliness. I plead stupidity.

And also a susceptibility to flattery, as you can gather by what comes next. "I saw you on TV with your chamber pot," he admits. "You were terrific. Believe me, I've been watching the program for an age trying to find just the right person to interview. Can I take you to lunch?"

But then the sensible single-woman-in-the-city kicks in, the new me whose distrust has been honed by Clyde's leaving, Ned's betrayal, Lavinia's threats. Boy, can a chamber pot in a lawyer's vault and a looming deposition change a person's people-are-really-good-at-heart philosophy. I wouldn't put it past Lavinia to have hired a private detective posing as a reporter. How many times have I seen *that* ploy on the television programs I used to feel ashamed to watch but can now claim as essential research? "Actually," I say, "can I call you back? I need to dig up my date book and check my schedule."

He gives me the number of his direct line. "I'll be here for another hour or so."

"It won't take that long." I search the yellow pages for the *Boston Globe*. "Do you have a Todd Tucker on your staff?" I ask the "This is Phyllis" woman who answers the phone.

"City and Region section," she supplies. "Shall I put you through?"

He picks up on the first ring.

Yes, reader, I say yes. You can't admonish me any more than I admonish myself. What is my excuse? Mankind is weak and a woman in need of a man, a woman with legal problems and a single carton of yogurt and a frozen chicken à la king for one in her refrigerator, is weaker still.

We arrange to meet at the East Coast Grill at noon. Brownie points on the thoughtfulness front, he's chosen a place in my neighborhood. "No need for the red carnation in the lapel," he jokes. "I've already seen you on my Sony portable."

If I'd already seen *him*, I wouldn't have been so tempted to leave a note with the hostess explaining that Abigail Randolph had been taken away for an emergency appendectomy. The minute he walks through the door, all second thoughts fly right out that door. He's tall and big with a Kennedy thatch of hair and a Cary Grant cleft in his chin sexy enough to make a girl regret any resolution to swear off men. What would you expect with a name like Todd Tucker? A movie star name if ever there was one. Tab Hunter. Troy Donahue. Nick Nolte. Jude Law. Brad Pitt. "Abby," he says. He heads straight for my table even though there are a few nymphish waifs picking at salads and reading Kierkegaard.

We split a rack of ribs. "Let's splurge for boutique beer," he suggests. "I'm on an expense account."

He tells me he got his B.A. from Wisconsin, majored in English, specialized in nineteenth-century British poets. "I went through a real Elizabeth and Robert phase," he confides.

"You're kidding."

"'Fraid not. Am I the only living nonacademic male under seventy to dig the Brownings?"

"Probably."

"The reason why I'm convinced your story is meant for me." He laughs. "Even though I decided to quit my own poetry. I figured I had to make a living."

My fork stops in midair. "You're a poet?" I exclaim.

"Barely." He shrugs his (very broad) shoulders with disarming modesty. He waves a dismissive (well-modeled) hand. "Well, I placed a couple of my verses in a few literary journals. The kind that pay you in two copies."

"I'll have to look them up."

"The quarterlies are so obscure they're impossible to find. In fact they're probably defunct. I'll show them to you"—he pauses—"when I know you better."

He's a poet. He's going to know me better. He's going to show me his poems. He's handsome. Stop it, Abigail, I tell myself, you're not thirteen.

"So I decided to forgo poetic suffering and went to the J-school at Columbia," he continues.

"Any misgivings?"

"Sometimes. When I pick up Elizabeth or Robert. Or Wallace or E.E. You know, that alone-in-bed-in-the-middle-of-the-night thing." He pauses. "Not that you . . ."

I stare at him. I am starting to rue the ribs. I'm afraid the grease has smeared my lipstick way beyond acceptable boundaries; strings of pork are no doubt sticking between my teeth. I've lost my appetite.

"I like a girl who eats," Todd says. He means it as a compliment though I'm sure the women nearby with their salads, dressing on the side, their bottled water, slice of lemon on a saucer next to it, wouldn't take it that way. I don't tell him about my empty refrigerator, how I hardly leave my apartment, how I'm living on pizza slices and dregs from my fast-diminishing supply of Chardonnay. Let him think I'm a healthy girl with a healthy appetite, a healthy social life, and a healthy lack of stress. A girl with a special regard for iambic pentameter. I study the cleft in his chin. What would it be like to slide a finger right into that cranny? How would it feel? Maybe like a little cocktail frank snug in its little cocktail bun. Maybe like a perfectly contained haiku? Is that a healthy thought? I wonder. I grab a paper napkin. I wipe my mouth. For a reporter about to conduct an interview, he's barely posed a question yet.

He clears his throat. Here it comes. "Are you married?" he asks.

Not what I expect. Is that a professional or personal query? I'm tempted to answer. Why do you want to know? I want to ask. "Uh-uh." I shake my head.

He leans closer. "I was married for about two minutes," he confides. "When I was young. One of those first-love things that are pretty much destined to peter out."

"I know what you mean," I second. "Not the marriage but the first-love bit."

"A rite of passage. Hard on the heart but good for poetry." He sighs. "We'll have to exchange war stories someday."

Before I grow too hopeful, I remind myself where I am and why and what for. Maybe the you're-terrific, what-a-good-eater, I-adore-poetry-too, I-have-also-loved-and-lost, we'll-discuss-this-at-a-later-date is simply journalistic foreplay. Besides, as I know all too well from past experience, writers spell trouble. "Are these"—I cast around for the right words—"these *personal questions* part of the interview?"

"Strictly off the record. And totally unprofessional." He checks his watch. "I suppose"—he draws the syllables out—"I'd better start gathering some of the information I need. Let's order another round of beer and get to work." He signals for the waiter.

"Is this so tough we need a lot of drinking to cushion the blow?"

He smiles. "Painless, I promise." He takes out a small notebook, folds the cover over like a steno pad, and pulls a pen from his shirt pocket.

"At least you don't have a tape recorder."

"Never use them. In my experience, it sets up a wall between the reporter and the subject." His eyes hold mine. They're mocha, soft as a cocker spaniel's.

Despite my best intentions, I drink another beer. I try to warn myself that flirting—can I still recognize flirting?—is part of a reporter's bag of tricks, There's probably a whole course at the J-school on how to butter up a subject to get her to reveal her innermost secrets against her will. I should view his questions in the same category as deposing a witness. There ought to be a manual to prepare you for an interview like Mary Agnes's workbook for witnesses. I need to be wary. But it's hard to think legal, professional, *Law & Order* when you're gnawing at ribs and swilling beer with a guy with a cleft in his chin.

He starts slowly, my education, where I grew up, how I became interested in antiques.

I relax. "My mother was a flea-market hound," I explain. "A collector. She took me to auctions when I was a kid. I still have the doll I bid on and won when I was seven."

"Maybe we can get a photograph of that doll. Of you holding it."

I tuck my hair behind my ears. "A photograph?"

"Of course. A picture's worth a . . . you know. Readers crave them. Can you describe the doll?"

I take another swig. I settle back. This is easy, I decide. I don't have to reveal the truth about Henrietta, my father, my like-everyone-else's dysfunctional family, dysfunctional in its own way. I can talk about a doll's gingham dress. Its button blue eyes. I can arrange the facts of my life into a recipe of my choosing to make the prettiest, most decorative cake I myself select.

Todd jots down a hieroglyphic or two. He nods. He smiles. He laughs. He slaps his knee. "Go on," he says.

I go on. Would you think me vain if I told you others have pronounced me an amusing conversationalist? Would you find it unseemly if I confess that he seems fascinated with everything that comes out of my mouth? Granted it's his job, but nevertheless, his spellbound absorption provokes some on-the-spot polishing of my recently tarnished storytelling skills. I spin sentences. He throws back his head and howls at them.

He asks about my booth, how I arranged it, my pricing system, my sales. "Describe *Antiques Roadshow* and all the steps leading up to it," he coaches. Has anybody cared that much about the details of my life? At least since my mother died? Since my split with Ned? Don't worry. Just because I've been living on the margins so long, a few temporary and strictly business moments at the center of attention will hardly turn my head. Still, it's funny how being treated not even as an object of desire, but simply as an object of interest, can build one's self-esteem. I feel warmth rise from my toes to my brow; I could have scrubbed my whole body with orange citrus toothpaste the way my skin tingles.

I tell Todd about lugging my chamber pot on the T, about the snaking lines, about other people's treasures so easily and tactfully dismissed, about my progress through the five stations of the *Roadshow* cross until I'm in front of TV cameras and seated next to the expert on chamber pots. I tell him about Carol, about her carpenter's apron full of jars and potions, about her way with an astrological chart.

He leans closer. "What did she say about you? About your sign?"

I duck my chin. "I couldn't possibly."

"Come on," he encourages.

I don't need much encouragement. Even though I've been raised not to be boastful, how could it be boastful, I rationalize, to repeat the words of an astrologer? Words applicable to everyone born from mid-November to mid-December. "She said—not that she *knows*—I'm an original thinker. Optimistic even when my hopes are dashed." Charmed and plied with booze as I am, I still have the sense not to report the rest of Carol's analysis: that when I meet the right man, hidden passions will surge and, well, world, watch out. "Not that anyone can ever believe any of that garbage," I add.

"I believe it about you," he says. "You've got original thinker written all over you." He folds his napkin. He stirs sugar into his coffee. "As far as dashed hopes, from what I can see there aren't too many." He taps his pen. "So how did you feel when you first heard what the chamber pot was worth?"

"You'd probably need a poet to do *that* justice," I say. If the Eskimos have one thousand words for snow, how hard could it be for me to come up with something more sophisticated than the *cool* or *awesome* that first leaps to my tongue. How can I try to describe the pure ecstasy of that moment, before the joy got tainted with all that followed? If *Antiques Roadshow* wasn't quite up there with St. Barnaby's Chapel, it was still right up there. "Well," I begin. "The surprise itself, of its being worth something, of the Barrett connection and the dog . . ." I hesitate.

"Keep going. You're doing fine."

"Well, I count it as one of the most delicious moments of my life."

"I can understand that. What's so absolutely awesome," he adds, "so cool, is not just the Browning stuff. But Flush. The irony of the word itself associated with the chamber pot."

"Bathroom humor."

"Yes. I'm afraid I'm stuck with a toddler's delight in scatology. But besides that, I especially like the literary connotation."

"Is there anything you don't know?" I ask.

He reddens becomingly. "Rocket science."

I laugh. "I mean, you're familiar with the book *Flush*?" I stop. "But of course you would be, having studied Browning and all."

"Anybody who's familiar with nineteenth-century English lit would have come across Elizabeth's poem."

"Not *anybody*," I say. Not me, I don't divulge.

He gives a self-effacing shrug. "I must admit I'm partial to cocker spaniels. When my marriage broke up, I got Wordsworth, who, I now realize, is the spitting image of the picture of Flush on the Woolf paperback. When you see him, I'm sure you'll agree."

So there'll be a next time. That is, if I can believe him. That is, if he's not another Clyde.

That is, if he's not another Ned.

He rubs his chin. "I read *Flush* for the interview. My homework. So I have you to thank for this discovery. Until this assignment, I never knew about Woolf's biography. A charming story particularly for what it tells about Browning and Casa Guidi. I think the scenes showing Flush's jealousy of Robert are spot-on. The kidnapping—dognapping, I guess—is hilarious."

I smile.

He smiles. "Sometimes—this time at any rate—I'm very happy I became a journalist." He shakes his head. "Let's face it, there are these pockets of pleasure—though often few and far between—when you can just about agree with Browning that 'God's in his heaven— / All's right with the world.' "

Do I agree? I thought so with Ned, perhaps, once in a while, with Clyde. And look what happened. Why haven't I learned my lesson? Bad luck comes in threes, my inner lawyer warns. Three on a match. Three strikes and you're out. Try as I might, I can't sway my jury of one. I need a Mary Agnes Finch to make the case.

Maybe it's the beer. Maybe it's the remarkable eyes, maybe it's the poetry, maybe it's simply the novelty of male attention even if it comes from someone doing his job. No matter. Just let me state right now, right here, at this table in the comer of the East Coast Grill, in Inman Square, in Cambridge, Massachusetts, in zip code oh-two-one-three-nine, all's right with my world.

As soon as I have this thought, I want to issue a retraction. Not only because the minute you declare you're content, the ax starts to fall, but also because I must have communicated an uncharacteristic, positive, optimistic, moment-in-time worldview to Todd. Granting him the tools to dig a little deeper. "So what else happened," he asks, "in the aftermath? How has your life changed?"

My face must register something less than joy since he immediately holds up his hand. "I've taken enough of your time," he apologizes. "I'm sure your schedule is packed."

If he only knew. Even so, I can act the part. I bustle. I smooth my skirt. I heft my pocketbook. I look at my watch. "Since you bring it up . . ." I moan, as if my harassed secretary were just now prioritizing my packed schedule like a triage team in the emergency room.

He waves for the check. "Why don't we stop here. My deadline is flexible. We'll have plenty of opportunity to explore these issues more." He slides his notebook into his pocket. He walks around to my side of the table. He pulls out my chair. For a second he holds my elbow. His fingers tighten in what I'm almost sure is a definite, though slight, squeeze. When he lets go, I feel an inexplicable sense of loss. "Let me be your shadow," he suggests. "If it's all right, if you consent, I'd love to come along to a flea market or tag sale with you, to follow you around, to watch you work."

"I'm not sure . . ." I pause. "It's not very exciting. For a nondealer, that is. Traipsing through muddy fields. Sifting through junk."

"Compared to listening to the minutes of a city council meeting? Compared to asking a lottery winner what kind of car he'll buy?" He shakes his head. "My goal would be to pick up pointers for my readers. To convey to them a sense of how a professional eye operates."

"I'll be pretty preoccupied," I warn. "It's one thing to have lunch like this, quite another to be actually on the job out in the field."

He grins. "I can promise good publicity."

"In that case . . ." I concede, businesswoman to the core.

"I swear you'll hardly know I'm there." My shadow claps his hands, a problem-solved, that's-settled gesture. "So, are there any treasure-hunting opportunities coming up?"

"As a matter of fact . . ." I dig into my pocketbook. I make a big fuss of pulling out my calendar, of riffling through it, as if I can barely turn the pages, so heavy are they with obligations both personal and professional. "Umm, let's see," I consider. "Well, what do you know! There's a tag sale this Saturday morning in Kerry, New Hampshire." I stop. "Which might be too far away."

"Not at all. It sounds like a blast. We can make a day of it." He tucks a wad of bills under the saucer for the tip. "I'll pick you up."

Are things moving too fast? "That's very nice of you but not necessary. I usually lease a car from Rent-A-Wreck. A wagon, since I often have a load to cart home."

"I can offer a roof rack and a ton of bungee cords. How early should we leave?"

"Seven?"

He winces. "On a Saturday morning? The things I do for my job."

"It's important to get there early. Before the best stuff is sold. Tell your readers that."

"Will do." He opens the restaurant door. He lets the Kierkegaard-reading waif slip through, then holds it wide for me. "And as a reward, Saturday night I'll take you to dinner."

"Really?" I pause. "As part of your job?" I ask. I'm not the only one anxious to get the facts straight.

He takes a step back. He sweeps his arm across his waist. He bows. "For the pleasure of your company."

IO

I get up at six. Enough time to take a shower and shave my legs. I've come a long way since my middle school days and those off-the-feminist-wagon college moments devoted to the un-Cambridge-like ritual of showering, depilating, tweezing, moisturizing, deep-cleansing, blow-drying, manicuring, and flossing for a date. Was I deluding myself that those seventh grade boys hadn't seen me in gym shorts with gum stuck to my hair? And as for Ned—and my desperate Ned-related attempts at self-beautification—what glamour-puss makeover could mask the kid underneath, the kid underfoot, muddied and scraped after a fall from her bike? What cosmetic transformation could hide the preteen, her teeth in braces, Clearasil dotting her adolescent zits? Thank

God the era has ended when the arrival of *Seventeen* marked the highlight of my month.

Don't worry. I haven't pulled out my Victoria's Secret underwear from the back of my drawer. I have no plans to bury the three-to-a-pack white cotton granny skivvies. I'm under no illusion that my role as passenger in a car driven by a reporter nosing out a story equals being with a man. A Saturday night dinner hardly counts as a date if the meal is payment for allowing him to shadow me. Can he expense it? I wonder. Will the *Globe* pick up the check?

No matter. I pull on my just-pressed jeans. I find a clean T-shirt that doesn't broadcast a far-left-of-center cause. I wouldn't want to discourage a New Hampshire dealer from giving me a good price. Since I look a little pale at this hour of the morning, I bronze my cheeks. I wish I'd paid more attention to how Carol had mapped my face and less to how she'd read my sign. As a concession to a close-quarters three-hour drive, I check my cache of perfume. I eliminate anything containing musk. I reject all scents advertised by a sultry model with implants and collagen-puffed lips. I settle for light and lemony. I wouldn't want Todd to feel trapped in his car with one of those Pine-Sol'd green trees cabdrivers dangle from their rearview mirrors.

He rings my bell at the dot of seven. "You look nice," he says as I slink down my tenement treads with the grace of Isabella Stewart Gardner descending her Italianate marble stairs.

I don't tell him how nice he looks. The charm of that just-woke-up-and-rolled-out-of-bed dishabille. Hair askew, unironed jeans, wrinkled denim shirt he might have slept in, buttons buttoned wrong to expose a whorl of chest hair that I can't help gawking at.

"Far too nice," he adds, "to be digging around in some New Hampshire farmer's barn."

I pat my Levi's. "These old things" bursts out of my mouth, surprising me. Where did I steal that line? What movie actress in Balenciaga mouthed those words?

"I'm not talking about your clothes."

"Oh, come on," I groan.

His car—an egg-yolk-yellow VW Beetle with roof rack and a backseat the size of a chamber pot—is parked outside my building, hazard lights flashing. He opens the door for me. He tilts his head toward my ear. "And by the way," he whispers, "the perfume is dynamite."

Inside, between our seats, tucked into a plastic double mug holder, sit two steaming Dunkin' Donuts Styrofoam coffee cups. On a tray beside them lie packets of sugar and Sweet'n Low, along with sealed thimbles of half-and-half.

"You've thought of everything."

He shifts gears. He pulls out onto Cambridge Street. "It's a long drive," he says.

A glut of traffic is leaving town all at once. I'm grateful. Between that and the coffee and the many ROAD NARROWS, CONSTRUCTION AHEAD, FORM SINGLE LANE signs, our conversation is safely desultory. "I'm not great in the morning," Todd admits. He speeds up to keep a signaling car from cutting in. "I really come awake at night."

I look at him. Does dinner count as night? Should I be nervous about a whole day and evening with someone I hardly know? In a car? In a farmer's field? In a restaurant? An apt setting for Colonel Mustard at a tag sale with a farm implement. And you know the outcome of *that* scenario.

What have I done? I've climbed into a car with a stranger. One of the first *don'ts* you learn as a child. We're setting off to cross the state line. Those hazard lights were blinking for a reason. Why didn't I do a background search, a criminal records check on the Internet? Even though I did call the *Globe,* did I bother to verify? Did I ask to see his reporter's badge the way any sensible victim of crime, any knowledgeable criminal, any intelligent witness demands to inspect a *Law & Order* cop's ID?

I've worked myself into a state when I realize we are indeed on the road to New Hampshire, the doors aren't locked, and Todd's got a folder marked *The Boston Globe* on the backseat of the car. "Do you mind reaching into the glove compartment for my sunglasses?" he asks.

It's not the voice of a serial killer, I reassure myself. Not even the voice of a serial apology compiler. I open the glove compartment. There on the top, next to his glasses, is a photo of a dog. I bring it out.

Todd slides on the glasses. Instant movie star. He should be gliding along Hollywood Boulevard rather than rolling past New Hampshire discount liquor stores. He nods at the photograph. "That's Wordsworth," he informs. The cocker spaniel is reddish gold with beseeching eyes. Except for his tartan collar, he could be the clone of Flush. "My pride and joy." He sighs.

He passes two trucks on the right and cuts in front.

The driver honks.

"Your mother, too," Todd shouts. Then, nodding to me, appends, "Pardon my French."

I think of my family's every-ten-years turnover of stately Volvo wagons. "The safest car, studies show," my father would claim, driving at his funeral-procession pace. He once got stopped by a trooper for going *below* the highway minimum. "I'm a Harvard professor," he announced, to my mortification and my mother's tsking disapproval.

The trooper shoved the citation through the window's one-inch-open slit. "Buddy, I don't care if you're Einstein."

"Einstein couldn't drive worth a damn," my father lectured him.

I'm sure by now my father owns a sports car that he races at terrifying speeds, though never with his children. No doubt Kiki will mention this in her next Christmas letter: *Professor R. Griffin Randolph treated his midlife crisis to a bright red sports car. The boys and I give it a wide berth. It's Daddy's toy, I explain. And truth to tell, he looks so adorable in it and is having such a good time I can't begrudge my darling this particular mistress (initials MG!). Enclosed is a photograph . . .*

Now Todd weaves across three lanes, his hand on the horn. "There's nothing like a dog to spice up your life," Todd goes on. "I can totally understand Elizabeth's devotion to Flush. Do you know there's a dating service called Date My Pet dot-com?"

"To fix up dogs?"

He laughs. "For pet owners to meet people who share their love of cocker spaniels, for instance." He flips down the sun visor. He flicks his hair out of his face. "But mostly it's to make sure the person you date is approved of by your pet."

"Have you tried Date My Pet dot-com?"

"No way. Personally, I'd never use a dating service."

"I didn't mean to imply . . ." I stammer.

"Not that I wouldn't, if I ever felt that was the only method of meeting someone suitable. So far the old-fashioned technique works just fine." He switches his eyes from the road to wink at me. "I just brought this up to point out, in a rather convoluted manner, that Wordsworth would quite approve of you."

I shake my head. I know this type. A man who flirts with women the way others salivate at a side of fries. Still, I turn my face to the window so he won't glimpse my silly pleasure at this remark. When I look out, I see a green roadside sign. ST. BARNABY'S CHAPEL, EXIT 8, I read. All pleasure disappears. My chin drops. My shoulders sink.

Todd swerves to avoid a fallen-off hubcap straddling two lanes. I bump my head against the glass. Which seems to knock some sense into me. My despair passes. Besides, the St. Barnaby's sign, like my sadness, I remind myself, is now half a mile behind me. A dot in the dust. A symbol of a fading memory. *Put it behind you* is the mantra of the twenty-first century, meaning scandal, war, misdeeds, bad choices, lost love.

"We'll be there soon," Todd says now. "I'm sure you're relieved that I haven't continued our interview in the car. It seemed unfair. Captive prisoner and all. Plus I couldn't exactly take down your answers in my trusty notebook."

"I'm glad for a break."

"Enjoy it now. I'll have a million questions once we get to Kerry, once I see you in action." He pauses. He reaches for the radio dial. "Would you like to listen to the radio?"

"Sure."

But when he switches it on, I don't hear the familiar tones of Renée Montaigne, Scott Simon, Bob Edwards, or Terry Gross on NPR. No *The Connection,* no *BBC World Service,* no *Fresh Air,* no Boston Symphony, no cutting-edge jazz, no left-of-the-dial alternative rock. It's an FM Lite station, oozing the kind of music that bombards you in supermarkets, elevators, beauty salons, and dentists' offices. Everywhere but Harvard Square, that is.

For the rest of the ride, Todd Tucker's clear tenor rings out—word-perfect, pitch-perfect—tripping lightly through the lyrics of "The Shadow of Your Smile," "Sentimental Journey," "Misty," "When You Walk Through a Storm."

And "Memories."

A number of vans, pickup trucks, SUVs, and cars toting roof racks and pulling trailers are already parked in haphazard zigzags on the farmer's field when we get there at exactly five of ten. The minute I step out of the car onto the patches of mud, tufts of grass, dried bristles of hay, I tremble with the frisson of excitement I always feel right before the chase. My hunter-gatherer instinct is on full alert. I am cavewoman with club, calculator, and magnifying glass. At flea markets, auctions, tag sales, all things are possible (even romance, cf Clyde). Buried treasure lurks under the junk. Somewhere one particular item will speak to me and change my life. It has already happened of course. But that time it was my mother's sharp eye (perhaps a bit of Henrietta's, too) that deserved full credit for the chamber pot. This time I'll flaunt my own discernment, my own professional expertise to Todd Tucker, to the readers of the *Boston Globe,* to my colleagues in the antiques field, to my father who insisted I couldn't set foot in the world without a Ph.D., to my lawyer, to my legal adversaries. And to one adversary in particular. Let the world know that the treasure-tapping gene has been passed down in my DNA. Not that, to be fair, one could ever overlook the element of luck.

"Are you feeling lucky, Abby?" Todd asks. He's got on a tattered straw hat a scarecrow might sport. His notebook and pen stick out of his shirt pocket. I notice his pen has leaked. A black amoeba-shaped blob marks his heart. I think of *The Wizard of Oz*. The missing heart. Yet it wasn't the heart the Scarecrow lacked, I correct, but a brain. There's nothing wrong with Todd's brain, however. Proved by a man who's both a poet and a reporter, yin and yang, a man who loves the Brownings, who knows *Flush,* whose dog is called Wordsworth, a man who reads E. E. Cummings in bed. "You've got that dog-on-the-scent look," he declares.

I laugh. Since what matters is context, I'm more than happy to be compared to a dog. "And you . . ." I begin.

He snaps up a stick of hay. He jabs it into the side of his mouth. He chews on it.

"And you," I repeat. "*Agricolae poetae sunt.*"

For a second I hear Ned's voice: *Omnia Gallia in tres partes divisa est.* I picture his face in the Thayers' living room. He's smiling. He's balancing a glass of sherry on his knee. He's holding a bowl of toasted almonds. I listen to my own voice quote *Amo, amas, amat.* I love. You love. He loves. So long ago. Another place. Another me. Once upon a time when those words meant everything.

"Come again?" Todd asks.

"It's Latin."

"Which is all Greek to me."

"It means farmers are poets." I stop. "You never studied Latin?"

He shakes his head. Clumps of straw fall off his hat. "But now I will." He bangs his hand over his ink-stained heart. "I swear on it."

Picnic tables heaped with glass, china, yellowing linens, headless, armless dolls, rusted nails, broken clocks—a community's discards—ring the barn. Furniture, orphaned and forlorn, dots the grass: chairs missing a leg or a seat, chairs whose ripped and unraveled caning hangs in shreds like the torn hem of a skirt. Over there lies a toppled washstand minus its basin. Here, a chest of drawers, knobs Scotch-taped to its bowed front. A row of small porcelain sinks bolted together might have arrived intact from a grammar school. In fact, two old-fashioned school desks with holes for inkwells and entwined initials carved into its scarred oak, stand ready for girls in smocked pinafores and boys in short pants to open their composition books. I spot a box of toasters, entrails spilling out. Another, of ancient radios. A man is carrying away a sled and a rusted rake. "I'm not sure about this," Todd ventures.

"First appearances don't count," I lecture. "It takes a practiced eye to appreciate the beauty that lies beneath an unlovely surface." I'm back to Ned again, my childhood idol. I look at Todd. "And sometimes it's vice versa. What's beautiful turns out to be worthless." I hold up a pedagogical finger. "Lesson number one. Write it down. First impressions are irrelevant." I pause. "In antiques, if not in life," I amend.

"That I'll remember. No need to take notes." He grabs a child's tricycle marked $5. It has streamers attached to the handlebars and a shiny silver bell. "This isn't bad," he says.

"Do you have a kid in mind?"

He puts the bike down. "Not really." He takes a few steps back. He twists around. "Over there." He points. "Chamber pots."

We walk across the patch of dried mud to where five chamber pots have been laid out on a frayed quilt. "Aren't you proud of me?" Todd asks. "I can now identify the real thing—not as the washbowls or planters I would once have taken them for."

"If I had a gold star, I'd paste it on your forehead right here and now."

He chuckles. "You needn't go to extremes." He picks up one of the pots by its rim. He holds it away from his body. As if it's something nasty. As if it's about to bite.

"It won't bite," says a plump woman sitting on a stool and waving a tattered *Reader's Digest* back and forth in front of her red face. She balances a pad of receipts on her lap. A fanny pack clipped with an elastic extension ties around her waist. This holds change, which rattles as she flaps her arm. Dollar bills stick up from the half-closed zipper like a clot of snared cloth.

Todd sets the pot back on the quilt. He pulls out his notebook. "Can you tell me the history of this particular object?" he asks.

"Sat under the bed before indoor plumbing. Could've been used by some founding father for all we know." She laughs. "George Washington pissed here." She slaps her *Reader's Digest* against her massive thigh. "Folks use 'em for planters these days. I've even seen them set out at church suppers filled with molded salads or franks and beans."

She must notice Todd shudder because she stops in mid-fan. "They've been cleaned out, dear," she soothes. "Scrubbed and sterilized. Not to worry. I'll sell you the one you just had in your hands for twenty-five bucks."

"Thank you. I'll think about it." He turns to me. "Anything, Abby, that catches your eye?"

I study the chamber pots. Porcelain. Tin. Ironstone. Flowered. Plain. Inside a pale blue-sprigged vessel, curlicued script limns a proverbial *Please keep me clean so I won't tell what I have seen.* For a minute I linger over that one. I picture it in my booth. A classic example of the genre. After all, as the high-profile chamber-pot lady, don't I need it for a talisman? But when I turn it over, I see a large chip. I point at it. "This decreases the value," I enlighten Todd. "Signs of age, crazing, fading, discoloring, are good. But actual chips and cracks lower the worth."

"Ten dollars," says the woman on the stool to a lady who has come up behind me.

Arpège wafts around her blond pageboy. She's wearing a pantsuit with double rows of brass buttons and inappropriate little heels that dig into the dirt. Thanks to my vast experience of the species, right away I nail her as a decorator, the kind whose silver sang its siren song to Clyde. She pulls ten dollars out of a black quilted purse swinging from a double gold chain.

"I'll take it," she says. "Isn't it sweet? It's perfect for my client's new laundry facility. I can just picture it filled with tulips. Or fat pink peonies."

"Wait one minute," orders Todd. He places his hands on his hips. He stomps his feet apart. He looks like one of those G.I. Joes lined up on a shelf at Irving's, the toy soldiers all the boys in the neighborhood craved and all their peace-marching parents forbade. *Here's a little plastic Buddha,* a mother might coax. *Or how about this darling action figure of Martin Luther King Jr.?*

Todd turns to the woman, who is already cradling the chamber pot, now swathed in old newspapers. "We were here first," he warns.

I touch his elbow. "It's okay," I whisper. "We don't want any of these. Elizabeth's is one in a million. What are the odds of getting lucky a second time?" I nudge him forward. "Let's see what's inside the barn."

He relents. "I'm just trying to make sure you get what you want, Abby," he says. "I'd hate you to miss out on anything because you're too polite to stand up for yourself."

"Believe me, I don't feel I'm missing out on anything." I stop. "When it's something I really want, I'm perfectly capable of going after it," I stress. What I don't tell him—because I'm leaving the realm of antiques here—is that I don't always know what I really want. I don't always know what I *should* want either. Or what's worth fighting for.

But in the realm of antiques, inside the barn, I hit pay dirt. Within ten minutes, I have filled a New Hampshire discount liquor store box—kindly provided to customers—with a creamware platter, coin silver spoons, candy molds, crocheted place mats, a corncob doll, old postcards of New England factories, a gravy boat, and three corkscrews, their handles made from twisted olive wood.

Todd himself has picked up a cribbage set, a distinguished service medal from the Korean War, a penknife initialed *T*, a silver loving cup awarded to the winner of a country club croquet tournament, and a copy of Longfellow's *Evangeline*. Heady with success, Todd goes to the corner of the barn to interview a specialist in mechanical banks.

I rummage through a table marked—lowercase—ODDS AND ENDS. I check out a carton of small farm implements. $15 FOR THE LOT is scribbled across its dangling tag. I turn over a weeder, a small shovel, a horseshoe (good luck!), a branding iron, a wrench, three bolts, a copper whistle, and a mysterious gadget in blackened metal shaped like a coffee grinder. I pick it up. *Nebraska* in raised letters runs down one side. Numbers stamp the bottom, then, scratched underneath, I read: *WC-EL*. I turn the crank; a spiked disk on the top moves. While farm implements are hardly my area of expertise, I'm intrigued. Their rustic quality. The reasonable price. The good omen of a horseshoe.

Though the objects aren't beautiful, I decide to take my own first-appearances-don't-matter advice. Besides, there's a bit of American history in the box. Maybe the man who deals in old tools and farm implements and blacksmith memorabilia at Objects of Desire might be persuaded to fork over fifty dollars for such an assortment. I bought a print from him of a spreading chestnut tree for my father and Kiki's wedding present. *One of a kind*, he promised. Gus said I overpaid. *Wildly* overpaid. Kiki didn't get the Longfellow reference. In her thank-you note, she admitted she was partial to palms but hoped to branch out (ha-ha!) and see a lot of spreading chestnuts when she came East. If she could tear my father away from his backyard swimming pool.

I turn the coffee grinder wheel again. Perhaps I can recoup a little of that spreading chestnut money. The day after I bought the print, an identical one was hanging back on the same wall. Identical down to its distressed, wormholed frame and spotted mat. I run a finger along the raised *Nebraska*.

"That's a corn sheller," a man's voice edifies.

I look up. He's standing across the table straightening out a row of hammers. A large man with a gray beard and hair caught into a ponytail. He's wearing a plaid shirt and denim overalls. He's the spitting image of a farmer. But you never know, considering these days of Ivy Leaguers in camouflage pants and Army/Navy-store dog tags, couch potatoes in running gear, holders of academic chairs in Hawaiian shirts. "Herbert Morgan. This here's my barn."

"Then you're a dealer?"

He shakes his head. "Insurance. Retired. The wife inherited the property. We lend it out. This is the last year, though. Bought ourselves an RV and are heading down to Florida." He stops to pump the hand of a six-foot-five man he calls Tiny. "Though I learned plenty of lessons from all these swindlers and junk pickers over the years."

This prompts laughs from Tiny and a cluster of his equally untiny friends. Who move away in a single file, each slapping Herbert on the back like the losing team in a football match.

I hold up the utensil. "What is a corn sheller?" I ask.

"Take a guess, kid."

I shake my head.

"Give it a stab. You don't need a college degree."

I blush. I'm tempted to boast of three and a half semesters at Harvard, but I stem the urge. "I don't mean what *is* it," I defend myself. "I mean how does it work?"

He takes it out of my hands. His hands are huge, the skin red and coarse, farmer's hands even if they're used for filling out actuarial reports. He turns the wheel. "See, you put the cob in this here gizmo, the kernels fall to the bottom—you'd stick a container under here to catch them—and then"—he points to another opening—"the cob comes out sideways through this hole."

"Pretty ingenious," I marvel.

He nods. "These New Hampshire folks knew a thing or two."

"But this one says 'Nebraska.' "

"I'll be . . ." He examines it. "Funny," he says. "Wonder how it got all the way up here?"

I point to the letters. *WC-EL.* "Do you know what they stand for?"

"Can't say that I do. They don't look like they've been etched into the metal by any machine. Got to be homemade. Somebody scratched them on." He winks. "Maybe a couple of lovebirds, is what I'd guess."

I spin the disk. "It hard to believe someone would give a loved one a gift of this."

"For you and me maybe. But for a couple of farmers this might be more appreciated than your average say-it-with-flowers boo-kay."

"Perhaps," I concede, still skeptical. *Lovebirds. Nebraska. WC. EL. Lovebirds. Nebraska. WC. EL.* These reel through my head like the revolving disk now in my hand. Somewhere in my not-fully-educated brain, a lightbulb starts to pop. The wattage increasing with every spin of the disk, with every repetition of *WC-EL.* Could it possibly? I wonder. Is there a chance? I ask myself. My excitement is mounting so fast it takes every bit of my will not to let it show. The evidence is irrefutable. All the pieces add up. "Well, maybe I'll buy this lot." I sigh, assuming my most casual, can't-be-bothered voice. "The horseshoe's the big selling point."

"A pretty girl like you must have plenty of luck."

"Who couldn't use more?"

He nods. His ponytail flaps. "That's the truth." He sifts through the box. He studies the wrench. He clangs a couple of bolts. "You won't be sorry. Take a gander at the ton of good stuff in here."

All I want to do is grab the box, throw money at Mr. Morgan, and hightail it out of there. But I'm a professional. I speak slowly. As if I have all the time in the world. As if I'm doing Mr. Morgan a favor by clearing out his barn, by hauling away some of his trash. As if my philanthropy alone will get his actuarial hide all the more quickly into his RV and onto the beaches of Florida. I swallow hard. "Will you take ten?"

His face suffuses into a theatrical mask of disbelief. His eyebrows arch. His mouth drops open. "Come on, the wrench itself is worth more than such a piddling amount."

I point. I scowl. "This old thing."

"It's got real age."

"That's rust."

"*Patina*. Patina is what the professionals call it."

"Look, Mr. Morgan . . ."

"Herbert."

"Look, Herbert." My tongue trips dulcetly over the syllables of his name. "Just between you and me, this is an impulse buy." I sigh. I shake my head. "This kind of junk isn't anything I personally collect." I pretend to walk away, though my hands clench the box, glue themselves to its corners. You'd need more than a rusted, aged wrench to ply each finger from its inch of claimed cardboard, its squatters-rights stake.

"Ten bucks won't put the gas in my RV."

I shrug. "Then forget it."

He throws up his hands. "Just because I like you. And I'm feeling softhearted today, let's split the difference."

But Abigail Elizabeth Randolph takes no prisoners. "Eleven-fifty," I order.

Herbert Morgan pulls at his ear. "Split the difference and I won't charge you tax."

I flash a gotcha! grin. "This is New Hampshire. Live Free or Die. No tax!" I click my tongue. "Besides, I have a dealer's number."

"Okay. Okay. You drive a hard bargain. Twelve. It's my final price."

I hand over the twelve with the kind of reluctance that implies I've given away the money that would buy me my last supper here on earth. "I'll probably regret this," I gripe.

Mr. Morgan—Herbert—shoves a green garbage bag at me. I stick my box inside. "What's done is done. Put those regrets behind you," he advises.

"Good luck in Florida. Slather on the sunscreen," I call over my shoulder as I rush outside the barn.

Across the field, I can just make out Todd, his straw hat askew, at the end of a long line of people waiting for the Porta Potti. Just as well, I decide. I'm not going to tell him of my suspicions, my second strike of lightning, until I have the curatorial proof. Then and only then will I award him the gift of a spectacular, she's-done-it-again ending for his feature article on Abigail Elizabeth Randolph, ace detective, treasure hunter extraordinaire.

I find an unpopulated tree. I plop down with not the slightest concern about the immaculateness of my clothes. I look around. I hug my bundle, a miser guarding his gold. No one's watching me. A few yards away, a whole family has laid out a picnic. The mother is nursing a baby; her shirt discreetly curtains the infant's face. Fat dimpled legs kick the air. The father is squirting squiggles of mustard on a row of hot dogs for two older boys. Just behind them, in a patch of sun, three gray-haired ladies chat on folding chairs. They wear floppy hats and clutch straw pocketbooks appliquéd with hot pink flowers. No muggers, thieves, or plunderers seem to be haunting this farmer's field in Kerry, New Hampshire.

I lean back against the trunk. It's an ordinary maple, though for storytelling purposes and to close yet another circle in my amazingly circular world, I wish I could christen it a spreading chestnut. I pull up a dandelion puff. I blow on it. It vanishes. *I want my work to resonate,* Ned used to tell me after a morning of struggling with what he called nonresonating paragraphs. Right now, my own work, my own life, is resonating so much I'm vibrating like a tuning fork.

Funny how bits of your past show up in future surprising places.

How what you once interpreted as self-indulgence or irrelevance or avoidance or rebellion turns out to hold an entirely different meaning years later. I think of that sophomore course I took on the Writers of the Plains. *Your choice of study seems arbitrary at best*, my father would complain. *Not to mention the lack of focus on a career.*

If only I could tell you that this urban Inman Square dweller had a passion for agrarian themes, vanished America, pioneer life. But—full disclosure—Writers of the Plains met at eleven in the morning Tuesdays and Thursdays—promising long weekends and indolent hours of extra beauty sleep. And it was a gut, according to the *Harvard Confidential Guide*, which noted the limited reading, few papers, and an absent-minded professor about to become emeritus.

Now I pull out the corn sheller. The horseshoe is wrapped around the handle of its crank. I detach this example of the smithy's art. I lay it on the grass next to a tangle of unruly dandelions. I turn the corn sheller upside down. I look at the initials. I examine the *Nebraska*.

And I know. Thanks to my sleep-craving, it's-a-gut-seeking academic choices, I am so certain I'd bet my chamber pot on it. Eureka! I want to scream. Because what I am holding in my hand is a tool Willa Cather herself clasped in her own presumably callused farmer's hand. Yes, Willa Cather, journalist, essayist, short story writer, poet, critic, novelist, winner of the Pulitzer Prize.

I set out my case. The corn sheller is from Nebraska. Willa Cather grew up on a farm there. Her longtime companion was EL, Edith Lewis. Cather was also a great friend of Sarah Orne Jewett. From New Hampshire, where Cather is buried. This explains the location of a corn sheller from Nebraska in a farmer's field in New Hampshire. Evidence piled upon evidence. Irrefutable evidence, even Mary Agnes Finch would agree. I have come across another literary artifact. *Agricolae poetae sunt.*

There's more. Connections that might not carry much weight in the marketplace but have personal meaning for me. Willa Cather and Edith Lewis were lovers. Like my mother and Henrietta. Wheels within wheels. Signs and more signs. I tap the horseshoe now on the grass next to my hip. I am grateful to my mother for taking me to flea markets; I am grateful to my education for bringing me to the literature of the plains. I am grateful to my character flaws that made possible the study of Willa Cather. I am grateful to my mother's lesbian relationship for leading me to an appreciation of alternative lifestyles and, as a result, perhaps a subconscious interest in Cather herself. I am grateful to the chamber pot, which opened the door. To Clyde who shut it. To Todd whose interest brought me here. To Ned . . .

Ned. I stop. What about Ned? His name has popped up in this trio of men as automatic as a breath. But he doesn't enter into this particular equation. He's history. I've put him behind me. I clutch my corn sheller to my heart. I run my hands over its blackened, well-used surfaces. I crank its wheel; I watch its little disk spin. Has there ever been an object more beautiful? And valuable? If I could tape it inside my bra, I would. If I could helicopter it to Mary Agnes's vault, I would. If I could hire an armed Brinks van, I would. I look around again. I plant a kiss on the initials *WC-EL.* I put it back inside the box surrounded by its less worthy companions. I add the horseshoe. I knot the bag. I bend my knees, and tuck it under them.

"Abby?"

I look up. Todd is walking toward me carrying a tray. Fried dough, lemonade, hot dogs, onion rings, a pink cloud of cotton candy. Junk food for junk hunters. I smile. I wave. I am ravenous.

It's after six when we finally leave the field. Todd has interviewed more dealers. He's bought three more knives and an old BB gun. "Boys' toys," he excuses with such unabashed glee as to make the peaceloving, guys-can-cook and girls-can-hammer enlightened males I've grown up with seem to be missing a key chromosome. In the eight hours we've been here, I've delivered enough of a treatise on collecting, searching, digging, bargaining, verifying to qualify for a doctorate. Todd has gone through two notebooks on my words alone. It's amazing how eloquent you can be when your every syllable is recorded, if not for posterity, then for a daily newspaper with a daunting circulation and an online version that people the world over could conceivably download. Whenever I sag, whenever I catch myself in an infelicitous phrase or dumb observation, I stop. "You're not going to put that in?" I caution.

"Not if you don't want me to," he assures. "But remember, it's all good publicity for your booth."

If only my father could see me now, a woman overcoming her shyness and personal privacy for the sake of her booth. A woman with an eye on the prize who will not be derailed by misgivings, depositions, and the betrayal of an old and now-guttering flame. Even more, a woman who will never, in turn, betray that flame, however deserving of the spilled beans he himself has already spilled. Would I ever divulge a confidence? Would I ever reveal the secrets of those close to me? No! My father needs to take a long, hard look at his rod-of-steel backboned daughter. I am a woman in charge. A woman who can control her own spin.

Not to mention a woman who'd never let a reporter down. For Todd Tucker's sake, I've trudged from table to table putting on a good show, but with none of the fire in my belly for any other gewgaw or rusted artifact carefully laid out on an ironed cloth or varnished board. The corn sheller—favorite, pet, best-in-show—commands all my loyalty.

Todd locks our purchases in the VW's trunk. We collapse into the front seats. He tosses his hat into the back. He runs his arm across his brow. "Phew." He sighs. "I'm in awe of you. How do you keep up this pace?"

Has anyone ever been in awe of me? I allow myself a humble shrug. "This isn't something I do every day," I remind him. "Most of the time I'm sitting in my booth, twiddling my thumbs, waiting for a sale."

"Thank goodness. Otherwise you'd qualify as some kind of god. *Goddess,*" he corrects. "Not that you don't have goddesslike attributes."

Name them, I want to demand. List my attributes so that in some deep dark despairing night of the soul I might scroll through them like a self-help tape and feel buoyed. Instead, I shake my head. I shut my lips.

Gestures that have no effect on Todd. Can he read my mind? He holds his right hand up. He snaps his fingers out, one at a time. His mouth flies open. "Let's see. A great eye. A good appetite. Business acumen. Persistence. Endurance," he reels off. Then he hoists his left hand. He taps his thumb. "Plus a love of poetry."

Is that all? a lesser person might ask. A person more susceptible to flattery. The kind of person who'll fish for a compliment. "I suppose we should be getting back," I say instead.

He drops his head on the steering wheel. "I owe you dinner. But considering what we've just consumed . . ."

"I, for one, will never eat again." I groan.

"Eating again should be delayed as long as possible."

I pat my stomach, now roiling with fried dough and lemonade and FDA-unapproved additives. I loosen my belt. "The later the better."

"Agreed. But the prospect of three hours on the highway . . ." He shudders. "Let's get a drink first."

"Drink and drive?" I ask. Prissy words I regret the minute they're out of my mouth.

He grins. "I haven't lost an interviewee yet. One drink. Lots of coffee. I know an inn nearby with a big front porch."

The porch *is* big. The inn is painted a blazing yellow with green shutters and petunias spilling out from window boxes. We sink into the kind of Casablanca wicker chairs that once might have supported Sydney Greenstreet's white-suited, Panama-hatted corpulence.

"I'll have a mart," demands Todd to the fresh-faced student-slash-waitress in khaki shorts and lime-green polo shirt.

"Pardon?"

"A martini," he spells out. "Grey Goose. With an olive. *And* a twist."

"I'm not sure . . ." The waitress drops her pencil.

Todd picks it up. "Never mind. Your standard martini, please." He pauses. He points at me. "You, Abby?"

"Pinot Grigio," I answer. I look at the girl. "House white wine," I amend.

When the waitress comes back with our drinks, she sets them down on cardboard coasters printed with a Lake Winnipesaukee sunrise. Todd takes a sip. "Cheap gin. A country martini. A *New Hampshire* martini. Though it has its charms."

I drink my wine. "In the right setting, almost anything does."

He flashes me a boyish, aw-shucks grin. A bad-boy grin. His mother must have had a hard time resisting him, I imagine. Chocolate chip cookies between meals and unconditional use of the family car.

"What a great day. I must admit when I first proposed shadowing you at a flea market, I looked at it like some kind of hardship duty. Muddy fields. Boring junk. Boy, was I wrong."

"It grows on you."

"Especially when you have a knowledgeable, savvy guide." He drains his glass. He fishes out his olive. He places the pit carefully in the middle of Lake Winnipesaukee's rising sun. It looks like a belly button. "Thanks to you, Abby, I may have caught the bug. I may become a collecting fiend. It's great how contagious another person's enthusiasm can be. *Yours* in particular."

I feel a wave of dizziness. It's the wine, I'm sure, and not the words going to my head.

"Can we do this again? Can I come with you to your next tag sale?" He stops. He brightens. "Maybe there'll be an auction. I've never been to one."

"Haven't you got enough for your story?" I ask.

"This would not be for my *story*."

I remind myself to check the flea market/tag sale/auction schedule the minute I get home. Now is the season. There are probably two a day. I could plan another excursion next weekend. Or even tomorrow if Todd were so inclined.

He orders another drink. "How about you?" he asks.

"Oh, I might as well," I allow. "It *has* been a great day." If bad luck comes in threes, why not good? I have a lot to celebrate—one, my corn sheller; two, the present company, who extols my virtues and has yet to discover my faults; three, who knows? I settle back in the wicker chair on the New Hampshire front porch, the world beyond its banisters suddenly rife with possibility.

"Hungry?" my present company asks.

"Not in the least." By mutual junk-food-stuffed consent, the bowl of peanuts on our table stays untouched.

He yawns. He stretches. "I've got an idea."

I lean forward.

"Let's get us a couple of rooms here for the night."

I look at my watch. "It's just eight. If we leave now, we can make it home by eleven; at the latest, half past."

"I'm afraid my limbs don't have the strength to hold the wheel, to press the gas." He yawns again. His chest expands to show more adorable whorls of hair. "Unless you want to . . ."

I shake my head. "I don't feel comfortable driving someone else's car." Which is news to me, who has operated automobiles of friends, relatives, neighbors, and mere acquaintances over the almost twenty years since I first got my driver's license. And who holds the best safety record of any client of Rent-A-Wreck. "And perhaps," I say delicately, "we've both had too much to drink."

Considering his exhaustion, he jumps up with surprising pep. "Wait here. I'll make the arrangements."

In five minutes he's back, dangling a key. "There's a bit of a hitch." He peers up at me from under Princess Diana–style, bashful half-closed lids. "The desk clerk says there's only one room left."

My eyes must widen in alarm because he rushes to add, "I can sleep in the car."

I picture his little yellow VW Bug. He'd have to sleep curled up, pretzeled arms and legs. Let's face it—even *summer* nights in New Hampshire can get really cold.

"Unless . . . ?" he offers.

"Well . . ." I begin.

"I'll be a perfect gentleman," he promises. He salutes. "Scout's honor. I can stretch out on the floor."

As we head upstairs, we pass the reception desk. A middle-aged couple has just arrived, two suitcases in tow. "We don't have reservations," they apologize.

"No matter," the desk clerk consoles. He checks the computer. "We can offer you a choice of queen, king, or two twins. It's a slow night."

Slow night for *some* people, you might snort. And expect me to call him on his lie. You're a few steps ahead of me here. To you, it's patently obvious there's only one right response. You assume any sensible, ethical person will take appropriate action when she catches someone in a fib: rent a car. Call for a taxi. Get a bus schedule. Go to the front desk and demand her own room. Kick that good-for-nothing Todd Tucker out of her life. He's not for you, you'll tell me. You hardly know him, you'll insist. A road-rage driver, a reporter, a dissembler, a heavy drinker (my two glasses of wine don't count—good manners made me keep up), a flatterer. Look, you'll point out, the column of negatives towers over the shallow pluses of good looks, charm, attentive interest, dog ownership, a burgeoning attraction to flea markets. It's a no-brainer. Get rid of him.

Okay, you've made your point. Now I ask you: What would a *man* do? Would a *man* not bed a woman because she lied about a room? Would a *man* need an emotional connection to have sex?

Can I blame two glasses of wine for leading me to the Old Man of the Mountain Room? For collaborating with what you seem to see as the enemy? Can I blame my secret Willa Cather triumph demanding celebration? Can I offer the excuse of more wine? (He ordered a bottle sent up along with turkey club sandwiches.) One bed? Cole Porter's "Just One of Those Things" on the radio? The kissing couple in a poster of Chagall's *Birthday* hanging on the wall across from us? Low self-esteem? High sexual desire?

Just one of those things.

So we do it. And may I inform you that Todd Tucker is to foreplay what Chippendale is to the mahogany claw-and-ball foot. He proceeds systematically. He takes off my clothes. Shirt. Jeans. Utilitarian underpants. Each item he folds into a tidy isosceles triangle like the American flag given to the widows of veterans. He's a veteran. A veteran of sexual combat, a soldier on the Masters and Johnson front line. He removes my necklace. Detaches the hoops from my ears. Slides off my bracelet. Unbuckles my watch. "Friction," he explains. He lowers a strap.

If he's not just-one-of-those-things spontaneous, he's done his homework. Could there be a better practitioner of premeditated seduction? His scripted moves are so precise he can throw away the script. Ah, the choreography. *Fly me to the moon,* he hums while his hands fly all over my body, alighting here, then there. "This?" he asks. "Or that?" he invites, like an ophthalmologist trying to test the best lens to correct your stigmatism. "Like this? Or do you prefer that?"

Let me count the ways.

And you know what? Though my body pings like a Stradivarius in a virtuoso's hands, though my body is having one hell of a time, my brain seems focused somewhere else. On corn shellers and Imari vases and piecework tablecloths. On grocery lists and to-do lists and to-read lists. I turn my head toward the night table. The Old Man of the Mountain calendar is taking on the profile of Ned.

Later. A lot later, we empty the bottle of wine and spoon postcoitally on our trampled aftermath-of-a-war bed. He whispers in my ear. "So tell me," he says, punctuated by the darting in and out of a tongue.

"Tell you what?"

He sucks on my earlobe. "What happened afterward? With your chamber pot? I sense some tragedy there. Something very dark."

"Nothing."

His tongue moves down to my breast.

"Nothing."

And keeps moving.

I blame the wine again. I blame a body missing a man's—any man's—touch. I blame the thumbscrews of pillow talk.

He slides between my thighs.

I name names. My mother. Henrietta. Lavinia. Ned. I hate myself.

He turns me over. "Did you love him?" he asks.

But my head has detached from my body. I don't answer him. I *can't* answer him. "This!" I groan. "That!" I demand.

After, he gets out of bed, stumbles around in the dark.

"What are you looking for?" I ask.

"My shirt. Oh, here it is." He tiptoes into the bathroom. He shuts the door. I hear the lock click. I hear the toilet seat slam down.

He's in there for a long time. I listen for the splash of the shower. The filling of the bath. Silence. Why does he need his shirt? I wonder. I picture the reporter's notebook tucked into his breast pocket. His leaky pen. The black blob that marks his heart. Is he in there taking notes?

I pull up the covers. I slide my hip away from the wet spots on the sheet under me. Big deal, I tell myself. So what? We had sex. It's amazing how body parts can carry on even if hearts don't beat as one. Is it such a big deal that for a woman, this woman anyway, sex doesn't scale mountains without an element of love? It still feels good. Why should I start entertaining thoughts of guilt?

When he comes back, he licks the nape of my neck. "One last question," he says.

"No more. Let's get some sleep."

"What's the title of Ned's novel?"

"Over my dead body."

"I'm a reporter. I can find anything out."

"I made your work too easy. I've already told you quite enough."

"Just one click on the Internet . . ."

All my muscles tense. "You're not going to read it? For your article or anything?"

"If you don't want me to, I won't. Cross my heart." He crosses his heart. The mattress shifts. "I'm an ethical guy."

His tongue finds my ear again.

Can I sink any lower? *"The Cambridge Ladies Who Live in Furnished Souls."*

"No way!" he exclaims. He laughs. His shoulders rise and fall. The bed shakes. "What a clunker. No wonder it bombed."

I hoist myself up on one elbow. "It's the title of a poem by E. E. Cummings," I sneer. "One of your favorites. One of the poets you turn to for that—let me quote—'alone-in-the-middle-of-the-night thing.' One of the poets you read in bed."

II

I wrap the farm implements in tissue paper. I use three extra layers for the corn sheller. I tuck all the tools into an old discarded briefcase of my father's, expandable and with a lock and key. I add some old socks for extra padding. I turn the key in the lock. Just above the brass plate are the initials *RGR,* half worn away from years of a rain, sleet, snow, and gloom-of-night trudge to Harvard Yard, bulky Emily-knit gloves rubbing against the monogram. I find a bungee cord in the closet. I wind that twice around the case, then attach the metal hooks under the briefcase handle.

I'm taking no chances. Still, when I look at my bundle, I have to pause. Has anything more clearly shouted *Valuables inside!*? I remember reading once about the diamond merchants of Amsterdam. How they walk around with diamonds loose in their pockets, rattling like spare change, or swinging in a cheap plastic bag from the Dutch equivalent of the five-and-ten. Who would ever suspect such humble carriers to contain such important gems?

Nevertheless, I can't steal a page from a diamond merchant's book. I'm too new at this game. And too scared. I read the Crime Watch page in the *Cambridge Chronicle*. I know about the gangs of kids in my neighborhood filching hubcaps and car radios. The drug addict who snatched a Gold Star mother's pocketbook. The mugger who lifted a Rolex off the wrist of a tourist from Bangor, Maine. Just my luck that when my personal thief opened the briefcase, he'd dismiss the contents as junk and toss them away. Thus dooming my treasure, one of a kind, historically priceless, never to grace a pawnshop's window or appear on eBay or even to end up lovingly catalogued in the collection of a hardened criminal.

I clutch the briefcase with both hands in front of me and walk the two blocks to my place of business. I hug the buildings. I stay away from the curb. How easy for a motorist to reach through an open window and grab my bag. I feel a bit like that marine, the one who follows the president everywhere. You can see him on the news, in photographs, fingers fused to the nondescript valise that holds the phone for ordering a nuclear attack.

An elderly man blocks my path. He wobbles on spindly legs and an unreliable aluminum cane. His hand trembles with the effort of reaching out to me. "Need help with that, young lady?" he asks. "You're hunched over something awful. It must weigh a ton."

"No thanks. It's not as heavy as it looks," I say. I swing it to demonstrate its eternal lightness of being. Despite their heavy padding, the farm implements clang and clink.

The old man chuckles. "What did you do? Rob Fort Knox?"

In my booth, I set down my bag. Without ballast, my spirits soar. Dealers are hanging around the front desk drinking coffee and trading tales of woe. "So this woman comes up to me holding some god-awful painting of a cat," I hear one person say. "'What can you tell me about this work of art?' she demands. 'Lady,' I answer, 'that's not mine. That belongs to the guy in the next booth. I'm the one selling the big furniture nobody wants to buy.'" A gale of laughter greets this remark. What's so funny? I wonder. I know all too well how it feels to pass whole days without a sale. To have something nobody wants.

Though not anymore. Not with the chamber pot. Not with the treasure now hidden underneath a pair of needlepoint pillows. I knock on the flimsy wall between me and Les Antiquaires de Versailles. "Gus?" I call.

He appears right away, like the genie at the rub of a lamp. Some lonely nights, against my better judgment, tamping down the suspicions I was used, I wish I could summon Todd that fast. Isn't there a chance—however faint—that he manipulated me into bed because he wanted *me*, not my spilled beans? "I'm no one-night-stand kind of guy," he said when he dropped me off.

"I talked too much. The wine . . . I might have told you things I didn't intend . . ."

He put his hands on my shoulders. He looked me in the eye. "I don't remember a word you said."

Give him a chance, I tell myself now. Maybe I can learn to like him more. The bird-in-hand approach. Who's perfect anyway? How can I resent his E. E. Cummings claims when I myself have lied about reading all of Proust? Was I that taken with Ned—or even with Clyde, that liar extraordinaire—from the start?

I'm afraid I'd have to say yes.

Never mind. Todd's working on a deadline, he's informed me.

"Night and day. Damn shame." So he is temporarily unavailable for the repeat R & R he assures me he's pining for. Funny how his unavailability commands the attention that just one in a thousand and one nights of an ongoing assignation would never have drawn. I think of the advice from a fifties dating manual my mother used to scorn: Make yourself scarce, play hard to get, leave them wanting more, let them realize how precious you are. It's the same with antiques: The one in a million is the one everybody wants, the object of greatest desire. Who even notices the dime-a-dozen quotidian bits and pieces we surround ourselves with? Who even notices the girl next door who once surrounded you?

"At your service, Abby." Gus salutes. "What's up?" His mustache is curled and waxed to even more of a fare-thee-well. A watch chain stretches across his brocade vest. All he needs is a white-powdered wig to peg him as a dandy in an eighteenth-century French court. Just the impression I'm sure he wants to convey. He twirls his mustache. He fingers the old acorn-shaped fob etched with somebody else's coat of arms.

"How's business?" I ask, wanting to spin out the suspense and milk my climactic scene of all its dramatic possibilities.

"Sold almost a dozen cherubs in the last few days. Not to mention a couple of matched pairs of those china dogs. Dogs and cats, Abby. Haven't I always told you that?" He pats his brocaded stomach. "And angels, of course." He pauses. "So where've you been lately? I haven't seen you around here for an age. Are you neglecting your job?"

"I've been on the job. Tag sales and the like. Up in New Hampshire."

He leans closer. He scrutinizes my face. "Alone?"

Do I look different? Does *Had Sex Recently* flame from my face like a tabloid headline? Maybe it takes the cultural intuition of a Frenchman—a French Canadian—to ferret out the kind of change a night in bed with a kama sutra expert might promote. "Of course alone." I make myself meet his eye.

He winks. "If you say so."

I switch into my diversionary business mode. "I need your advice,"

I plead. I lean over the edge of my chair. I pull out the briefcase. I unwind the bungee cord, taking care that it doesn't snap and bruise a face apparently already bruised with remnants of lust. I unlock the clasp. I click open the flap.

Gus is all business, too. He lowers himself to the floor. His knees crack and creak. "Ahh, *ma petite chouchoute,* what have we here?"

I check the aisle to make sure no one is walking by. I lower my voice. "You're not going to believe this," I whisper.

"Try me."

I take out the farm implements. One by one I unwrap them. I arrange them on the kilim that covers part of the floor. I'm a doctor laying out her instruments for surgery. Scalpel. Tongs. Retractor. I save the triple-wrapped corn sheller for last. "Voilà!" I exclaim. I hoist it above my head like the Statue of Liberty's torch.

Gus doesn't seem to notice. Instead he picks up the branding iron. He is turning it over and over in his hand. He holds it close to the lamp. He tilts the shade. He sticks it next to the bulb. He studies it.

"Never mind that," I order. "Take a peek at this."

He looks up. "Oh, a corn sheller," he remarks in the same blasé tone he might have used to say, Oh, a frying pan.

"You know what it is?"

"Of course. They're very common."

I am not deterred. "Not this one," I stress. I award him my cat-that-swallowed-the-canary smile. "This is something else again."

"How so?" he asks.

"Because . . ." I say. I stick the utensil two inches in front of his pince-nez—"it was made in Nebraska. It has the initials *WC-EL* scratched right here." I point. "Willa Cather—*WC*—was the lover of Edith Lewis—*EL*. She was born in Nebraska. She was buried in New Hampshire. *Quod erat demonstrandum.*" I stop. I wait. "Ta-da! This corn sheller belonged to Willa Cather!"

Do I expect him to burst into the "Hallelujah!" chorus? To jump?

To throw his hands about and praise the Lord? Maybe a little, because my heart sinks when he says, "So, you're planning on another coup along the lines of your chamber pot?"

I stiffen. "Why not?"

"I have my doubts."

"Just because it's another writer? Another literary artifact? Making the whole thing too neat a package, too convenient to be believable? The lightning-doesn't-strike-twice-in-the-same-place phenomenon?"

"Not that. I'm not much up on farm implements, though I did read a book on them once—there are quite a few avid collectors in Canada—but . . ." He hesitates.

"But?"

"If I can remember right, there was a company called something like Witchell that produced a slew of them."

"Which still doesn't mean . . ."

"No, it doesn't, but you need to prepare yourself for disappointment." He smiles so broadly I can see the gold fillings glint in his teeth.

"Why are you smiling? Considering I'm about to be disappointed. Considering you're about to tell me my literary corn sheller is merely run-of-the-mill. Run-of-the-cornmeal-mill."

He keeps smiling. "I'm not telling you anything. We'll ask Milligan."

I think of the multiple spreading chestnut trees. "That crook?"

"It *is* his area of expertise."

I shake my head. I lean back against the chair.

I must look as deflated as I feel because Gus reaches over and taps my shoulder. Is all that gold he's exposing between his grinning lips *real*? "However . . ."

"However what?"

He holds up the branding iron. "This particular item." He twirls it like a baton. Back and forth. Up and down. Figure eights. Fishtails. Arm rolls. I remind myself to ask him about a previous life in a marching band. "I think you've got something way, way, *très, très,* valuable here."

"What?" I exclaim. "That?" I point. My mouth puckers in distaste.

"Let's take this over to Milligan." He makes come-hither wiggles with his eyebrows. "Just you wait."

If you added a bowler and a cane, Fred Milligan could be Charlie Chaplin in *The Tramp*. Which doesn't inspire confidence. He's a small man sporting baggy black pants, a crown of unruly curls, a little coal lozenge of a mustache, and pulled-down, sad-clown eyes. His booth is a mess. Buckets and pails crowd the floor, stacks of magazines teeter in the corners, prints of cows and farmhouses and fields and, yes, the spreading chestnut tree overlap on the walls like shingles on a roof. A wagon wheel minus most of its spokes leans against a barrel with broken, splinter-threatening staves. In contrast, a three-shelved glass case, lit from within, displays a cache of rusted tools laid out in precise, equally spaced rows. A bottle of Windex alongside a roll of paper towels garnishes the top of the case. A lingering ammonia smell and the sparkling glass testify to a loving, ongoing, however selective, maintenance.

Fred Milligan skips the preliminaries. "What you got there, Gus?" He points to the rewrapped, tissue-papered branding iron.

"Abby here"—Gus nudges my elbow—"and I want your professional opinion." He pulls off the tissue paper. The crumpled pieces fall to the floor.

Fred Milligan doesn't notice. His eyes stay on the branding iron. He doesn't say a word. He breathes in and out with a smoker's telltale rasp. And then his face and body do this amazing Chaplinesque thing. He sinks to the chair like a rag doll, all the stuffing out of him. His eyes and mouth drop even lower into even sadder expressions. His head flops. If, in a game of charades, his selection ordered him to act out disappointment and boredom and couldn't-care-less, he'd win first prize. "So?" he asks, in the robotic, without-affect voice of a telephone operator.

Gus puts the branding iron in Fred's lap. "Quite the poker face," he adds.

Fred flinches as if Gus has handed him raw sewage. "So, where did you get this?" he asks. Under what rock did you turn up this piece of crap? is what his tone implies.

"At a tag sale in New Hampshire."

He doesn't respond.

"I figured it might be worth something," I blow my own horn, and neglect to mention how I passed over the branding iron in favor of a joint—and less significant—occupant of the same New Hampshire liquor store box.

Gus keeps my secret like a loyal coconspirator.

Fred yawns.

"Is it anything valuable?" I persist.

He yawns again. Unlike Gus, he does not flaunt expensive dental work, but instead chipped teeth dotted with blackened silver overlays. "I'll tell you what," he says, syllables flat and uninflected. "I'll give you a thousand bucks to take this rusted bit of iron off your hands."

I hold my breath. "Hmm," I ponder. Gus squeezes my arm.

"Just as I thought," Gus exults. He slaps me a high five. "You old rascal," he says to Fred. "There's no way Abby's going to sell it to you. Even if you offer ten times your piddling peanut sum." He pauses. He twirls his mustache. "So you might as well tell us if what we've got is what I think it is."

Fred Milligan is a changed man. He sits up. His eyes and mouth, defying gravity, twist up into crescent moons. His whole expression switches to jaunty. Alert. A sheepish grin plasters his lower jaw. "Well, it was worth a try." He guffaws. He smacks his knee. "If you weren't sticking your big Canuck nose in, Gus, I'd have my kids' down payment on their first house right here in my hot little hands."

Gus reaches for the iron. He wrests it from Fred's vise of a grip. "You don't have kids, Fred."

"With that, I could get me a few." He laughs. "And a couple of wives to go with them."

"What is it?" I ask.

"And you an antiques dealer. You mean you bought it without knowing what it is?"

Once again Gus comes to my rescue. "The girl's got an eye," he boasts. Proud parental glee shines from his face. What he doesn't confide—an omission for which I'm grateful enough to buy a few cupid sconces myself—is that my eye was on the wrong prize, a corn sheller made by the Witchell manufacturing company, a corn sheller rattled off an assembly line along with a zillion of its clones.

"One of a kind," Fred says now. He pulls out a couple of rickety old chairs. "Take a load off," he says, "and I'll explain."

He clears his throat. Smooths his hair. Straightens his shoulders. I recognize the all-too-familiar professorial grinding of the gears. And when he starts to speak, his tone is professorial, too. I lean forward, half expecting to hear, Dim the lights, here's the first slide.

"Here's the story," he starts. He takes his time, though Gus is emitting impatient, get-on-with-it sighs.

"Get on with it," Gus groans.

"Well, back in the old days, your 1700s, our li'l ole colonies were rich in natural resources. As I'm sure you know." He raises his eyebrows.

"Yes," we chime.

"And some of these resources were considered the exclusive property of the king. The English king." He stops.

"Yes," we prompt.

"So, at any rate . . ."

"So at any rate," I coach.

"What is this, some kind of choral reading?" Gus snorts. "Get on with it, Fred."

He picks up the pace. "At any rate, there were huge forests of white pine in New England. The best kind of wood for shipbuilding. For masts. So the king, being a king, made a law that any tree a foot from the ground and two feet in diameter belonged to his navy. And to drive this rule home, to make sure there were no mistakes, they decided they needed some kind of X-marks-the-spot doohickey." He stops. He clears his throat again. It sounds like he's gargling. He shoots his thumb at the iron Gus is now clutching close to his chest.

By this point Gus and I are both nodding and exhaling in perfect unison, such mirror images of each other we could be synchronistic swimmers butterfly-stroking and somersaulting for Team USA. "So . . . ?" we push.

"So this is it. The King's Arrow. Take a look."

We all screech our chairs together in a neat little circle and examine the branding iron's base. The three crude lines—which I previously dismissed as, well, three crude lines—now flaunt their intrinsic arrowness. How could I not have spotted this? I wonder. I blame the distraction of Todd Tucker. I blame my immersion in the literature of the plains. Underneath in raised metal blocks is *GR III*. Letters and numerals I would have rejected, in another less enlightened moment, as grade three, third choice, third place, undesirable.

"Georgeus Rexus the third," Fred says, gloating. "Or however you say that bugger's name in Latin. Mad King George, the tea party dude." Do his eyes mist up? He brushes away something glistening on his cheek. "Never seen another one myself. Scarcer than hen's teeth."

Gus runs his finger over *GR III*. He cradles the King's Arrow like a newborn. He's almost rocking it. "I had a hunch about this," he says. "Didn't I, Abby?"

I nod. "Full credit where credit is due. And I'm awfully glad you did," I add.

"You're one lucky dame, Abby," Fred crows.

If my first instinct is to answer luck had nothing to do with it, I can't bring myself to lie. "I know," I admit, a gracious concession if I say so myself. "Now what do I do?"

"Put it in a vault. A safe. Until you have a plan."

I think of my chamber pot in Mary Agnes's vault. Not that I would ever send the King's Arrow off to join its fellow antique. Who knows what contamination from legal disputes it might suffer just by sharing the same space. Add to that the possibilities of a mix-up with one client's trust indentures, another client's emerald lavaliere.

"I bet I can probably find someplace to keep it in this building here," Fred volunteers.

"I'll take it to the bank," I decide. "A safety deposit box. It should just about fit." I pause. "Then what?" I ask. "What do I do next?"

Fred stands up. He performs a Charlie Chaplin dance. His shoelaces are undone, though his shoes, still-bright Reeboks dotted with holes, aren't anything I could imagine Charlie Chaplin putting in a pot and serving for lunch. "Take it on to *Antiques Roadshow*. It sure worked for you before with that potty your English poet lowered her delicate butt onto."

I think of *Antiques Roadshow*, the disaster in its wake, the repercussions still ahead of me. "Gus?" I implore.

"No way!"

"Please?"

"Absolutely not."

"Come on, do it for the little lady," Fred joins in.

"Stay out of it, Milligan. The little lady, my ass. You were going to take this little lady for a ride."

"Just business," Fred excuses.

"It would mean so much to me," I beg.

His mouth shuts. He fiddles with his watch fob.

"You'd be so great on TV," I add. "Plus think of all the cherubs you'll sell."

I've got him. He twirls his mustache. He passes me the King's Arrow as if he's passing me an Olympic torch. "For you, Abby," he promises. "The next time the program comes to our area."

12

By the time I make it home from the bank, I'm exhausted. My new treasure's safe passage to the Cambridge Trust involved even more of a CIA operative mind-set than the paranoid scuttling elicited by my misplaced faith in a corn sheller tied to Willa Cather's Nebraska roots and lesbian love affair. There's a lesson in all of this, I tell myself. A lesson I'm sure has been stated eloquently by poets and philosophers and hit lyricists. I'll have to flip through Bartlett's to find the exact quote. But here's the gist: Don't be so blinded by the wrong thing you can't see the right just in front of your nose.

Not that such a lesson holds any meaning for me, in the romance department at least. As soon as I think this, I hear Clyde's voice: *It's not funny, Abby. I knew you wouldn't appreciate it. Not that you haven't a God-given right to your personal opinion.* Words my mother would call giving with one hand and taking away with the other. I consider Clyde's method of righting wrongs. His apologies for previous complaints about my small breasts, lousy housekeeping, lack of enough sexual enchantment to keep him awake during intercourse, Are these *so sorrys* supposed to make me feel better? What did he expect? That I'd see how opposites attract and manage, like Jack Sprat and the missus, to work together to lick that plate clean? Hardly. It's more the seesaw effect. A lightening of his conscience that drops me into the slough of despond. I click off the postadolescent wrong men who have blinded me: Ned, a couple of insignificant others, and Clyde.

Soon I'll be adding Todd. I'm starting to realize I made a big mistake. I should have ditched him right away, especially because I have the sinking feeling he's already ditched me. How did that best seller phrase it—*He's Just Not That into You.* Well, he was into me, Old-Man-of-the-Mountain-Room, king-size bed into me. Once he achieved what he wanted, however, he disappeared. Exactly what our mothers always warned us about. Though my case turned out to be a twist on the same old story—it wasn't my body he was after; it was selected sordid scenes from a life he seduced out of me. For a while I refused to see this. Doesn't everyone deserve the benefit of the doubt? I asked myself. And let me reassure you that the fact that he was the only game in town was completely irrelevant.

Oh, God, what have *I* done? What is *he* going to do?

I've left messages on his voice machine at the *Globe*. I've e-mailed him so many times carpal tunnel is setting in. For any hope of damage control, I need to speak to him. Of course, having lived with a writer, I understand the obsessiveness of the species, how the world can fall away, how time and place can dissolve. But would a *reporter* hide in that cave of creativity, suffer that darkness of the soul? A journalist?

A member of the fourth estate who receives a regular paycheck along with a cubicle, a desk, and press privileges?

Only a louse.

But maybe—and don't think I'm being too vain here—since the subject of his article is me, he needs to keep a temporary distance. So his pure vision of the story won't be contaminated by a personal relationship. He's writing a feature about business, about what happens businesswise to the businesswoman whose chamber pot hits the jackpot for collectibles. No different from an impartial description of how a stock might take off or a conglomerate might buy up a smaller company. Sex, cocktails, conversation, any kind of contact could skewer a reporter's badge of neutrality.

Am I kidding myself?

Mistress of rationalization, I turn on the kettle for tea. I want wine. Too early. I deserve champagne. Too premature. I'll wait till Gus goes on *Antiques Roadshow* and hears the official report. Then I'll splurge on a case of Bollinger. I'll buy myself some cut crystal flutes. I'll invite everyone at work to share a glass, not just the elite. I'll pass around French cheeses on an English ironstone platter. I'll fill Rose Medallion bowls with salted almonds and macadamia nuts. Just the prospect of all this activity sends me to the sofa. I plump the pillows. I lie down flat. I do some stretching exercises. I decide to sign up for yoga. All my bones and joints and muscles ache—from excitement, from fear, from life.

The kettle whistles. I force myself upright. My knees creak. Before I sign up for yoga, however, I'll have to get into better shape. I totter toward the kitchen. My peripheral vision registers a flickering light. The answering machine on my desk is blinking. I stare at it. I must be suffering from some kind of traumatic shock to have changed such ingrained habits. This is the first time since I left Ned's house and moved into this Inman Square flat that I have not checked my messages the instant I came through the door.

Is this lapse a sign of dementia? Or a sign of improving mental health? Considering my mounting level of anxiety and neurotic twitching, I can hardly claim mental health. The message has to be from Todd. I'm sure of it. He's overcome his work crisis. He wants me to vet his article. He wants to take another stab at the sexual pas de deux of the Old Man of the Mountain Room.

Or—I stop—he wants to worm more secrets out of me.

I press the Play button.

"Goddammit. Abby, call me."

It's Lavinia.

I'm in no rush. I dunk the last bag of chamomile into the first mug I grab. You're not going to believe this, but the mug reads NEW HAMPSHIRE IS FOR LOVERS. It's not my mug, I swear. The previous tenant must have had a bad experience in the Granite State because besides dust bunnies, a family of roaches, an under-the-sink colony of silverfish, and a wadded Women's Studies syllabus, it was the only thing he left behind. I wrap my hands around the hot ceramic. My thumb just covers the LOV. Of all the mugs on all the shelves, *of all the gin joints in all the towns in all the world* . . . Astonished, I shake my head. It has to mean something that I picked this one.

I sit down next to the telephone. I stare at it. You'd think with our deposition looming, our disputes both legal and otherwise, our general family rift, our last heated words, Lavinia would not be eager to reach out and touch me so much. At least not through AT&T. Why wouldn't she use her hired mouthpiece, that Snodgrass lackey of a representative?

The minute I decide not to return her call, the minute I allow myself a triumphant sigh of liberation, the phone rings. I jump. I spill half the mug of tea. I ignore the burning, widening stain on my lap. And, relying on the power of signs and symbols, relying on a chipped and tacky left-behind souvenir, relying on recent lubricious thoughts, I answer it on the first ring.

"I warned you," screams Lavinia.

"I'm fine, thank you. How are you?" I chirp.

"Stop chirping," she orders. "Didn't I tell you? Didn't I predict this would happen?"

"What are you talking about?" My eyes wander to a pigeon on the windowsill. I swallow the rest of the tea. I grab a pencil. I start to compose a grocery list. *Onions,* I write. *Cornflakes. Oreos . . .*

"The newspapers. And not the tabloids." She takes a few wheezing pants. "Some reporter called from the *Globe*."

This last word might well have been the hypnotic suggestion that set off the assassin in *The Manchurian Candidate* the way it explodes in my brain. I look at my list. I am shocked to see I have written *The Globe* in the penmanship of a palsied nonagenarian. My hand must have been guided by an otherworldly spirit. I fling down my pencil. My possessed body quivers. My infiltrated head rattles. "What do you mean?"

"Your friend. Your reporter friend with the stupid name." I can hear her spit out the consonants: "Ted Turner. Tip Tucker. Tad Todd. Your *very close* reporter friend, if I can quote that slimy hack."

"Go on," I manage to get out.

"He's going to write about us. The chamber pot. Our mothers. Our dispute. Our personal, private lives." She pauses. "He's planning to write about you and Ned. He's in the midst of working on the article right now."

I clutch my chest. Lavinia has twisted that knife and stabbed me right through the phone line. "He swore—" I cry.

"Are you an idiot, Abby?"

I grab a Filene's shopping bag. I start to breathe into it.

"Your father always thought so. To think I used to defend you. *There are different kinds of intelligence,* I used to tell Uncle Griff."

The bag has a hole. I crumple it.

"Earth to planet Abby. Are you there?"

"You're wrong," I gasp. And the minute I say this, I believe it. My breath comes slower. My voice grows stronger, more confident. Didn't

Lavinia always overdramatize everything? *Sarah Bernhardt,* Henrietta used to call her. *The Divine Lavinia.* Whatever Lavinia's position on anything means I now take the opposite stance. "Look, he's writing a feature on what happens after someone's been on *Antiques Roadshow.* Just about the chamber pot itself. The show. The business end."

"And if you believe that, then I take back every good word I said about you to your father." I hear the slap of a hand against wood. "Idiot," she repeats.

"You don't have to—"

"Wake up, Abby. This turd of a reporter said you told him everything."

"I didn't—"

"He gave me a few meaty examples. The kind of stuff you can only get straight from the source. From the horse's mouth. The horse's *big* mouth."

"I can't believe—"

"And he's even read Ned's book. Thanks to your practically providing him with the ISBN."

"I—"

"Given his smarmy, insinuating tone, it's pretty clear he didn't use thumbscrews to get this out of you."

"Lavinia . . ."

"Stop sputtering, Abby. Call this asshole up and read him the riot act. Not that he sounds like the type to pay any attention to"—she stops, then hisses—"the wishes of his *very close* friend."

"I'm sure there's a misunderstanding," I offer. It's a weak response.

She knows it. She's yelling now. "It's all your fault, Abby. We could have settled. We could have been spared this humiliation. You're going to be very sorry." Her voice goes quiet. She stretches out a dramatic Sarah Bernhardt silence. She clears her throat. "Just wait till I tell Ned."

She slams down the phone before I have the chance to do it first. For my own benefit, I slam it down anyway. I lift it up and slam it down a second time. The receiver cracks. Two black chips fly off. My landlady will probably make me pay for a replacement. I stagger to the kitchen. I search for another paper bag. All I find are plastic. Once again I've made the wrong choice. This time I've failed the paper-or-plastic? checkout-counter quiz.

I open the refrigerator door. I take a swig of Chardonnay right from the bottle. I need to get hold of Todd. Is Lavinia right? She's probably been coached in brainwashing techniques. In how to torture your adversary to surrender her chamber pot. A seminar in psychological intimidation held in the paneled conference room of Messieurs Snodgrass, Drinkwater, and Crabbe, counselors-at-law. This doesn't make me feel better. Nor does the wine. It's off. Vinegary. Acidulous. It sloshes in my stomach like landfill sludge.

I am going to paste myself to the telephone until I manage to reach Todd. What's the matter with me? One minute the evidence all points to the fact that he's a cad. The next minute, I plead extenuating circumstances. I make excuses, telling myself he can't be that bad. After all, the article hasn't come out yet. We don't really know what he intends to write. One thing I'm sure of: I'd be a terrible judge; or the kind of juror all eleven of the others would grow to detest.

I dial Todd's direct line at the *Globe*. Surprise, surprise, I get his voice mail. "This is Abigail Randolph," I say after the tone. "Call me," I order, imitating a Nazi commandant cowering her prisoners. "It's an emergency."

I formulate a plan of action. I decide to check Information for all the suburbs in the Greater Boston area. One of them should be able to cough up Todd Tucker's number and tree-lined street address. I grab the phone book. I start to make an alphabetical list. I begin with Abington, move on to Arlington, Belmont, Billerica, through Mattapoisett, Newton. I stop. It occurs to me that the man who drove me alone to New Hampshire, the man I had that tryst with in the Old Man of the Mountain Room, the man I let do such remarkable things to my body, the man

I put on and took off my underwear for, the man who was as close to me as a man can ever be to a woman, at least in the physical sense—that man, well, I didn't have the slightest clue where that man lived.

It takes me over half an hour to reach the end of the list. There are suburbs of Boston I've never even heard of, I who've lived here all my life. When I get to Somerville, I hit pay dirt. Of a sort. "The number you request is unpublished," informs a dulcet-toned operator.

"Screw you!" I yell, even though I know the voice is computer-generated.

I will not be deterred. My stomach growls. Go, Abby, go! it seems to be coaching from its roiling, churning acid reflux pit. This is the new Abby, the one who gets to the bottom of things, who won't give up. I riffle through the yellow pages and find the newspaper's main number. I remember calling that number not so long ago in my due diligence attempts to find out if Todd was who he said he was.

"The *Boston Globe*. Phyllis speaking. How may I direct your call?"

"Oh, Phyllis." I sigh as if I have been reunited with my best friend after decades of tragic separation. "Just the person I've been searching for."

"How can I help you?"

"Let me count the ways. I need to get in touch with one of your reporters."

"No-brainer. If you give me his name I can put you on to his voice mail."

"That's just the problem."

"Oh?"

"I've been leaving messages on his voice mail for the last two weeks. He hasn't returned any of my calls."

"Did you try his e-mail address?"

"Endlessly. To no avail."

"Well." She pauses. I can hear wheels churning. "Our reporters are very busy. Out in the field. Checking their facts. Why don't you just leave another message."

"It seems a lost cause. I've jammed his tape already. His machine is probably out of order because otherwise I know he'd get back to me."

She offers a noncommittal *hmm.*

"His name is Todd Tucker. He writes for City and Region." I twist the telephone cord around my wrist. "I hope you can give me his home phone."

"We're not allowed to reveal that information."

"Maybe you might make an exception?" I wait. "Phyllis?" I purr.

"No exceptions."

"I completely understand. But these are special circumstances. Extraordinary ones."

"Under no circumstances are we allowed to give out home phone numbers."

My throat catches. I produce a slight choking sob. "But I'm his sister. *Tanya,*" bursts from my mouth. Where did that come from? I wonder.

Does she laugh? Maybe she's simply clearing her throat because then she asks, "His sister? Tanya Tucker? Isn't that a country singer? Grand Ole Opry, if I remember right?" She groans. "Come on, I wasn't born yesterday."

I stop. I take a deep breath. "Okay. Okay. I'll tell you the truth."

"Which won't make me budge. But tell to your heart's content. I'm just about to start my coffee break."

I think about what to say. How to preserve my Tanya anonymity. I decide to leave out *Antiques Roadshow* and the chamber pot since Phyllis, surfing channels, might turn me up one night on PBS. Besides, I wouldn't be surprised to hear she's a reporter-in-training, beginning at the receptionist's desk like those crack L.A. agents who claim their humble mail-room origins. "It started out strictly business," I explain.

"It always does."

"He was doing a story on me." I pause. "Then, later, pretty soon after, it became something more."

"What more?" She waits. "The usual?"

"I'm afraid so."

She lowers her voice. "Are you suggesting sexual harassment was involved?"

"I'd have to admit it was consensual. Though what wasn't consensual was the information he extracted from me against my will."

"In a moment of passion? When you weren't thinking straight?"

"How do you know?"

"Been there, done that," she confides. "Don't get me started." In the background a keyboard clicks. A coffee machine hisses. "And you want to find out if he's going to use it? If he's going to put it in the *Globe*?" she goes on.

"Exactly."

"Men," she says.

"Men," I say.

We sigh in solidarity, followed by a mutual sisterly silence as we both scroll through our bad-men personal histories.

"Good-looking?" she asks.

"Very," I concede. I picture the cleft in Todd's chin. As soon as I do, I want to counter it. "But he's a terrible driver," I point out. "A lot of road-rage potential."

"I hear you." She clears her throat. "Listen," she says, "I'm in this great support group, Women Addicted to Married Men."

"That's not quite my problem."

"Lucky you."

I don't feel so lucky, but I'm not about to get into a my-problems-are-worse-than-yours contest with Phyllis, who is fast becoming my new best friend. Not to mention my therapist.

"But there's another group across the hall," she proposes. "Women Who Hook Up with Men Who Treat Them Wrong. They do these amazing visualization exercises . . ."

I can only imagine. "I'll bear that in mind," I promise.

"Good." She clicks her tongue. "Okay. Just this once. In sisterhood." She rattles off some numbers.

I write them down.

"And, *Tanya* . . . ?"

"Yes?"

"You know where to reach me. If you ever want information on the group. If you ever want to talk."

Despite the warnings from my stomach, I take another gulp of Chardonnay. My nerves are more important than my guts—though I'll need strong nerves to have the guts to make this call. I slosh some more wine down my throat. I hope my words won't slur. I dial.

A woman answers. "Hullo," she says. In the background I can make out the blare of the television and the mounting excited tones of a quiz show host. *Will you choose the home entertainment system or go for the gold?* I hear him shout. Some countdown music strikes a migraine-inducing drumbeat. The audience cheers. A child starts screaming. "Where's my Cap'n Crunch?" he or she yells.

"Quiet, Chip," the woman orders.

"Excuse me?" I say.

"What do you want?" she demands.

I must have made a mistake. Maybe I dialed wrong. Or perhaps Phyllis misled me, keeping to her newspaper receptionist's oath. "Is Todd Tucker there?" I ask anyway.

I'm waiting for the woman to say, Sorry, wrong number, to say, You've reached Tom Tucker's Plumbing Supply. Instead she asks, "Who wants to know?"

"This is Tan—" I begin, then correct myself. "This is Abigail Randolph, one of Mr. Tucker's interviewees."

"He should have been here a half an hour ago. I've got a fetal ultrasound scheduled, and he promised to be home to watch Todd Junior. Wait, I think I hear his car pull in. That bum."

I fall into the chair. That bum, I second. "If you don't mind," I say. "Can I ask you a question?"

"Depends. The minute his key's in the lock, I'm out of here."

"Do you have a dog?"

"No way. Todd's allergic. Besides, he hates all animals."

I start to hyperventilate again. I drop my head to my knees, telephone still at my ear. The wails of *Cap'n Crunch* turn into *Daddy! Daddy!* Behind that I can distinguish a few spousal *you asshole*s, underscored by *terrible traffic*. There's such contrapuntal harmony I could have been listening to the Mormon Tabernacle Choir—*asshole,* sings the soprano; *Cap'n Crunch,* warbles the tenor; *traffic,* croons the alto; all voices meld, then rise toward a mutually orgasmic crash of cymbals just as the quiz show host cries out, *You've hit the ten-thousand-dollar jackpot!*

"Someone's on the phone for you," the woman snarls.

"Who now?" I hear.

"One of those ditzy space cadets you're always writing about."

A door slams. The TV switches to the child-friendly sounds of *Sesame Street*. "Hello," Todd grunts.

I take a running leap. "Is this Todd Tucker, the man who was married for two minutes, the dog lover, the owner of Wordsworth, the appreciator of Flush, the poet, the nineteenth-century English lit major, the Browning admirer, the reporter who had his way with his interviewee on a four-poster bed in a New Hampshire B and B in the Old Man of the Mountain Room?"

I hear a single, laser-sharp gasp. Then silence.

I go on. "Let me introduce myself. Abigail Randolph. The ditzy space cadet you're writing about." I wait a beat. "To quote your *wife*."

More silence.

I count to twenty. "Well?" I demand.

No sound except for the falsetto of a Muppet singing a hymn to the number eight.

"Answer me!"

"Calm down," he says.

"You have some nerve."

"Charm and betray," he answers.

"I beg your pardon?"

"Charm and betray. It's what we learn in J-school. It's the number one tool in any reporter's bag of tricks."

I open my mouth. I slam it shut.

"All in a day's work," he continues. "Nothing personal."

Nothing personal? This man's bodily fluids have seeped from between my legs. He has inserted his penis into all of my orifices. He has pressed my nipple between his lying lips. He has stuck his two-faced face into my underpants. *Nothing personal?*

"Did you tell my wife anything?" Todd asks. Faux casual.

"Wouldn't you like to know?"

"Actually, I would." His voice curdles with the milk of uxorial kindness. "We're expecting a baby. I wouldn't want her upset."

"Funny how you didn't think of that in the Granite State. In the Old Man of the Mountain Room."

He ignores my New Hampshire references. "Did you tell her anything?" he repeats.

And now, reader, here's where you'll be most proud of me. Charmed and betrayed. Seduced and abandoned. I nevertheless manage to collect myself. I harden my heart and pervert my brain cells into the dark criminal mind of the blackmailer.

"It depends."

"On what?"

"Did you write that article yet?"

Another, this time longer, silence ensues. I sense the fog of Hamlet indecision seeping through the wire. Will he settle for the home entertainment center? Will he go for the jackpot? Cap'n Crunch versus Special K? Corn shellers over the King's Arrow? Ladies and Gentlemen: In this corner lies journalistic integrity. In that corner, domestic tranquillity, however tainted by lies. Place your bets.

I've placed my bet.

Ladies and Gentlemen: We have a winner here.

He clears his throat. "Funny you should mention that article. I've just decided to trash it. The whole subject—the *Antiques Roadshow,* your Cambridge family, those sappy Brownings, a chamber pot of all the disgusting things—was bound to put my readers to sleep. To think that I slogged through that novel by your friend Bickford Potter. What a piece of junk."

"Asshole!" I scream. And for the zillionth time that day, I slam down the phone.

I must admit I take to my sofa. I must confess I shed a few tears. For old, generic breaking-up's sake. You are well rid of him, I tell myself. The signs were all there. His driving. His lying. His sex manual skills. I'm sure he was the kind of kid who drowned kittens, who pulled off the wings of butterflies. Was I so desperate that I could overlook such blatant character flaws? I picture myself in bed with him. What I see is so bad, so pathetic, I have to stuff my pillow over my eyes. I am a fool. I am a motherless girl. I am adrift without a moral compass. I shed a couple more tears. But—*big but*—the article is not coming out, I marvel. I have silenced a member of the press. Wait till I tell Lavinia.

I stop. Maybe I won't tell Lavinia. Maybe I, Abigail Elizabeth Randolph, the duped, betrayed, abandoned, can work my way to the end of my cycle of misery. I think of the six wives of Henry VIII. *Divorced, Beheaded, Died, Divorced, Beheaded, Survived.* I can certainly produce a variation on that rhyme for my own faltering relationships. Yet maybe, like Catherine Parr, wife number six, I could survive and surmount the difficulty of a not-up-to-par, not-up-to-*Parr,* consort. She outlived three husbands, including Henry, and went on to marry the man of her dreams. An inspiration I'll tuck away for future revisiting.

But for now, enough about me. Enough about men. Enough about me *and* men. A subject worthy of a doctoral thesis in sociology. Or sociopathology. Let's move on to a smaller, more manageable, less male-o-centric front. I raise my fist in a V for victory. I take a bow. Could it be possible that for once in my whole sibling-free-but-not-free-of-sibling-rivalry life, I am holding the upper hand over Lavinia?

13

This morning's the deposition. I didn't sleep all night. I tossed and turned, caught between the Scylla of the chamber pot and the Charybdis of Ned. Or should it be the other way around? *Mine mine mine,* kept running through my head like the tantrum of a toddler. The chamber pot is mine. As for Ned, he once was mine but I'd sent him away. For all the right reasons. I had no choice. Charm and betray. Did every man I ever met go to J-school? Is it a rule in the XY-chromosomes-training manual to coax what you want from a woman and then leave the dried-out hollow husk the way we girls might learn how to sew on a button and brown a roast? Oops—twenty-first-century correction—the way we girls might study how to be a titan of industry and double-cross your best friend? One thing I am sure of: I no longer want to see Ned again. And yet all night all I could see was Ned. His face. The sculpted edge of his jaw. His cockeyed smile. The little yellow glints in his irises. How his eyebrows rose in astonishment at the beauty of nature, the eloquence of a line of verse. The way the light had singled him out at St. Barnaby's Chapel haloing him like a saint.

Some saint. I know I am well rid of him. I'm positive I made the right decision when I sent him away. Proved by the silence of these last years. Proved by how well I moved on and had subsequent, however doomed, relationships. Still, if I could not care less, then why is he haunting my sleep?

Stockholm syndrome, I diagnose. I am identifying with my oppressor. Patty Hearst has nothing over me. I feel a sudden chill. Wasn't Tanya her name when she was a soldier in the Symbionese Liberation Army? A name I dredged up from my subconscious to use for my own purposes? I picture her in fatigues waving that machine gun. I see myself on TV clutching my chamber pot. Will the real Tanya please stand up? Unlike me, Patty Hearst went on to marry, have a family, act in movies, attend charity balls. She survived her legal troubles. This Tanya is just beginning hers.

My head pounds. I swallow two aspirin. If I'm suffering from Stockholm syndrome, however, there's a cure. I'm identifying with an oppressor I could avoid if I'd only give up the chamber pot. Yet here's the rub: in this case the cure is worse than the disease because I can't surrender my casus belli, this source of misery. Why? Because it's also the source of my salvation, my antiques credentials, and the foundation I can build my business on. Besides, it's mine. And so few things seem to be mine these days; I've lost so much.

Usually I try not to dwell on my losses. Not that I'm some Pollyanna who can always separate the gold from the dross, as you already know. As you also already know, I do have a tendency to whine about those who done me wrong as well as my own failings, not to mention the flaws inherent in an imperfect society. But I'm making a huge effort to improve my character. If character is destiny, then I'm determined to whip mine into better shape.

Nevertheless, dwelling on my losses this particular morning is just the fuel I need to feed my anger for the deposition. I'm coaching myself to get mad at the other team so that I can walk away victorious, hoisting a ceramic trophy that once contained the metabolic waste of a famous poetess. Let's face it, sometimes aren't life's ironies just too much?

I'm coaching myself because—frankly—I think Mary Agnes is falling a little behind in her training exercises. I showed up two days ago on the dot of three for my prep session. By the time she called me into her office it was four-fifteen. I'd read two issues of *People,* one *New Yorker,* then half a *Wall Street Journal* (someone had swiped the stock listings; not that I wanted them). I was about to ask for the bodice ripper paperback splayed open on the receptionist's desk when the buzzer sounded. This prompted the same receptionist with terrible taste in literature to announce in a hoity-toity all-rise-for-the-king voice, "Attorney Finch will see you now." I was tempted to tell her I'd seen Attorney Finch in Snoopy pajamas; I was tempted to add that I too was a high-powered, overly booked professional. There are other lawyers in the Greater Boston area, I wanted to point out. Other lawyers who don't make important clients wait. But I didn't. "Thank you so much." I bowed and scraped. I made my sheepish way to Mary Agnes's office, living proof that the meek do not inherit the earth.

Once I was inside the heavy paneled doors, it was pretty clear to me that the needs of Abigail Elizabeth Randolph—both legal and emotional—were not marked top priority on Mary Agnes Finch's daily planner. Piles of paper littered her previously pristine desk. Five phone lines blinked with pulsing red lights. In the corner a fax machine was grinding out enough paper to provide Christo and Jeanne-Claude sufficient material to wrap Faneuil Hall. Secretaries and associates rushed in and out carrying blue-backed documents. Mary Agnes's hair was askew; coffee stained her lapel. She looked at me as if she didn't know who the hell I was.

"Abby," I supplied. "Here for deposition coaching." I clicked my heels together. I added a smart salute.

She didn't smile.

"I thought you'd forgotten about me. I ran out of things to read and nearly filched the Harlequin romance from your receptionist."

No amused appreciation turned up the corners of her lips. She didn't apologize for keeping me waiting. She didn't invite me to sit down.

I sat down. Someone knocked on the door, then opened it an inch. "Ginsburg and O'Connor are waiting in the conference room," informed a disembodied voice.

"Ruth Bader? Sandra Day?" I asked.

She barely shook her head. The old Mary Agnes would have marveled over the coincidence. The Mary Agnes I-knew-when would have managed a chuckle at the least. "This won't take long," she said.

She must have noticed my disappointed body language because her face softened. "We're in the middle of a really big case," she explained.

I nodded. I waited for her to add—à la Clyde—Not that yours isn't.

She didn't.

She got right down to business. She recited from memory, rolling through the words the way you'd deliver the Pledge of Allegiance or the Preamble to the Constitution. We hold these truths to be self-evident: "This should be a civilized procedure. No need for anyone to get angry. No need for you to be anxious. The purpose of a deposition is to discover information so that lawyers can evaluate your case. Discourse should be cordial. No one will attack anybody else. You'll be interviewed by the opposing attorney. I have the power to object. You'll be under oath. Be honest. Just answer the questions. If you don't know the answer, just say you don't. Don't volunteer any information. Don't speculate. Don't fill in. Don't guess. Give short answers. You can pause before the answers to think. Make sure you listen to the questions. If you don't understand, you can ask for clarification. If I object, don't speak unless I give you the go-ahead. If you feel confused or uncomfortable, you can always request a break. Watch out for tricky questions asked in a friendly style or buried in a series of seemingly innocuous inquiries."

I straighten up. "Like what?"

"A classic example is 'Have you stopped beating your wife?' If you answer yes, you still admit to the beating."

"Oh, my God!" I exclaimed. My hands tightened into fists.

"Don't worry. You'll spot those balls coming from left field. You'll avoid the land mines. I have every faith in your intelligence."

"At least somebody has."

"We *were* in college together," she stated.

"Well, thanks for the vote of confidence."

"When this is over, I hope you'll work on your self-esteem issues, Abby." She shuffled some papers. She scribbled a note on a Post-it and stuck it on the blinking telephone. I tried to read the note upside down, to see if it had something to do with my case. *Habeas corpus,* I made out. Did that apply to a chamber pot?

There was more pounding on the door. A man wearing a janitor's uniform rolled in a trolley filled with document boxes and what I recognized as the litigation cases Sam Waterston used to lug around. "Great, Tony. Stick them over in the corner," Mary Agnes directed. She cleared her throat. "As for your deposition," she began, even before Tony had left the room.

What about client attorney privacy? What about client attorney privilege? I wanted to ask. But she was talking too fast for me to point out Tony unloading boxes in the corner, a breach of confidentiality even if he did have a Walkman on.

She continued. "As we already discussed, to save money on the stenographer and for everyone's convenience, Jim and I have agreed to depose all of you at the same time, here in my conference room. I understand there might be tensions, but you and the opposing parties are all intelligent adults, well-behaved adults . . ." She looked at her watch.

"I wouldn't be so sure."

She stood up.

"Shouldn't we role-play a few questions? Don't I need a rehearsal?"

"*Law & Order* again?" She pushed her hair off her forehead. "This isn't a criminal situation."

"From *your* point of view . . ."

She sighed. She opened a drawer. She took out a pamphlet. She handed it to me. "Here's something we made up for our clients about to be deposed. Take it home. Study it." She came around from behind her desk. She put a hand on my elbow. She led me toward the class-dismissed door. "Any other questions?"

"Yes."

She cocked her chin.

"What do I wear?"

What I'm wearing for the deposition is what Lavinia would wear. Or as close to her taste as my limited budget and closet full of left-over-from-college vintage bargains and Army/Navy store camouflage would permit. I pull on a pair of black pants. I find the black blazer I bought for my mother's memorial service, still wrapped in its dry cleaner's plastic shroud. Under the bathroom light, the blacks don't match. I put on the white blouse I ironed last night with the iron I borrowed from my neighbor across the hall. I unbutton one button more than usual. For fashion's sake, not for Ned's, let me point out. I take so much care with my makeup I could be Michelangelo painting the Sistine Chapel—if only the results were so good. I blot my lips. I gulp some coffee. My stomach turns at the prospect of cereal, even of dry toast. My stomach turns at the prospect of the day ahead.

"Looking good, girl!" exclaims a kid I pass on my way to the T stop. The bounce this puts in my step lasts until, inside the train, another kid offers me a seat. "Here, ma'am," he says, jumping up like a jack-in-the-box. *Ma'am!* Do I seem that rickety? I offer the seat, in turn, to a gray-haired woman in sneakers, a backpack slung on her osteoporosis-curved shoulder. She declines. I sink down in despair. Squeezed hip to hip with two supersized women hugging Burger King bags.

For the umpteenth time I open the pamphlet on depositions Mary Agnes handed me. I've got the classic student's panic of being unprepared, a state of terror no amount of cramming seems to dispel. I've practically memorized each page. Not hard since, truth be told, the book is written to the level of a ninth grader. Actually even lower, I decide, more Dick and Jane than *Are You There God? It's Me, Margaret*. I look through the fingerprinted window into the black subway tunnel. Are you there, God? I want to cry. It's me, Abigail. Instead, I lower my eyes to my homework. *See Dick answer a question. See Jane keep her mouth shut.* There's nothing new here that Mary Agnes didn't include in her recitation. I study the big print accompanied by line drawings of men and women in suits carrying briefcases. I clutch my floppy hobo-style shoulder bag. Someone I know must own a briefcase I could have borrowed.

Don't volunteer, I read.

Ned, I think.

Watch out for tricky questions, I read.

Ned, I groan.

What's bothering me more? The prospect of being interrogated or of seeing Ned?

"Can't I do this privately?" I asked Mary Agnes yesterday when she called to set up the time. "In another room?"

Mary Agnes sighed. Could I read into her very breath the regret that old school ties blinded her into taking me on? "Abby, as you are no doubt aware from the booklet I gave you, the parties to a lawsuit have the right to be present at all depositions. The Potters requested this. And as I've already said, to save time, the expense of the stenographer . . ."

"Okay. Okay."

"I gather Ned's got a deadline and has to take the shuttle back to New York." I heard a knock. *We're waiting, Mary Agnes,* someone in the background called.

"Okay. Okay," I repeated, ever articulate.

"You'll be fine."

I'll be fine. I'll be fine, I chant as the receptionist with bad taste in literature leads me to the conference room. I freeze at the threshold. She gives me a distinct push. She has dragon-lady scarlet fingernails, which snag my blazer sleeve. "Sorry," she says. She doesn't sound sorry to me.

Once I'm through the door, the scene in front of me hardly lives up to my Perry Mason fantasies. It doesn't even match the usual *Law & Order* interrogations, which, I realize, are overdramatized to compete for ratings and to please advertisers. What I confront now is a convivial atmosphere. A coffee urn bubbles in the corner; mugs and papers and a basket filled with bagels scatter across a not-imposing island of a table. An oleander in a Chinese pot—reproduction—is abloom with pink flowers. Mary Agnes is chatting with a rumpled, rather pudgy, pleasant-looking man, not a bony three-piece-suited WASP with an arrogant arch to his brow and a tan from a winter of skippering a Concordia yawl in the Caribbean seas. Not an Alan Dershowitz type either, bristling with so much energy you suspect attention deficit disorder. They are discussing the bouillabaisse at a just-opened restaurant. *A little floury,* Mary Agnes laments. A grandmotherly woman is setting up the stenography equipment in a corner of the table. Next to her, Lavinia, wearing a pin-striped gray suit and horn-rimmed glasses (an affectation, I'm sure), is not studying the pamphlet I have in my shoulder bag but is reading the *New York Times*. The World Business section.

"Hi, Abby," she nods at me. "Nice jacket," she remarks, as if our table unites the shared booth of a Harvard Square coffee shop rather than separates adversaries in a law firm's conference room.

Nobody rises. There's no Oyez, oyez, here cometh the deponent. Instead, Mary Agnes glances in my direction. She moves some papers from the chair next to her. She pats it. "Coffee, Abby?" she asks.

"Jim Snodgrass," says the man across from her. He reaches out his hand. The table isn't so wide that I can't shake it easily. He has nice eyes, crinkled at the corners. And a warm, slight squeeze of a grasp. An endearing daub of cream cheese dots his lower lip. "Milk? Sugar?" he asks. "I'm pretty sure a little slip of a thing like you wouldn't want a sugar substitute."

"Black," I say. I smile back. I start to loosen up. This isn't so bad, I think. Especially since there's a missing person here.

Mary Agnes reads my mind. "Ned's shuttle is delayed. We can start without him. If you're all agreed, we can get through the preliminaries."

I hope Ned's shuttle sits on the tarmac at LaGuardia for the rest of the day. "Fine," I tell my attorney in my most agreeable client's voice.

The preliminaries are a piece of cake. Name, address, Social Security number, et cetera. I won't bore you with them. They're boring anyway. The stenographer types along; red polka-dotted half glasses perch on the edge of her nose. Out the window I can look over skyscrapers to Boston Harbor. I see seagulls swoop and swirl. Lavinia continues to read the newspaper. Mary Agnes doodles in the margin of her yellow legal pad. She's drawing a child's version of a house: a pointed roof, two square windows; the chimney puffs out spirals of smoke, which she starts to turn into a snake. I lean back; I see no balls out of left field, no land mines, no snakes in the grass waiting to uncoil and spit their venom out at me.

"Anytime you want a break," Jim Snodgrass says now. Kind. Avuncular. He reminds me of Uncle Bick. In fact, this whole scene harks back to halcyon childhood days, the parental Randolphs and Potters lingering around the dining room table sipping port, discussing—not legal matters—but, oh, maybe Ingmar Bergman films, we kids scribbling with Crayolas in the corner, drinking the hot cider our mothers had just mulled. "Whenever you need the bathroom. Water; a walk down the corridor to stretch your legs . . ." Jim Snodgrass goes on.

"No thank you," I say.

"Well, then let's turn to the chamber pot," he suggests.

It's about time, I want to complain. Isn't that the reason for all of this? But I keep my mouth shut. He's the lawyer after all.

He *is* the lawyer after all. He gets down to lawyerly business. His voice sharpens. His eyes pierce. "So, tell me when your mother first acquired this chamber pot."

"I'm not sure exactly."

"Can you try to place it in time?"

"Well, after she left my father. After she set up house with Henrietta."

"Tell me what you know about the circumstances of the acquisition."

"No idea."

"Have you any idea where it came from?"

"Italy."

"How do you know that?"

"She and Henrietta traveled to Florence all the time. They bought tons of things together. I assume—"

Mary Agnes nudges me. *Don't speculate* flashes in huge letters from the deposition pamphlet drummed into my brain.

"The antiques experts say it's Italian," I offer.

"Any documentation?"

"No."

"Any sales slip?"

"No."

"Did your mother tell you when she bought it?"

"No."

"Did your mother ever notify you either in words or in letters that she wanted the chamber pot to be yours?"

"Not specifically. But of course she wanted me to have everything that was hers."

"But do you know for a fact that this was hers, as opposed to belonging to Mrs. Henrietta Potter?"

"Well, if it wasn't hers, it was half hers, as they shared everything."

Mary Agnes sighs. "I'm sorry. I don't mean to interrupt, but I really need to take a break." She turns to me. "You, Abby?"

"I don't have to," I say. Even if my backbone is sometimes made of mush, I've got a bladder of iron. "Let's get this over with."

She grabs my wrist under the table. "This would be a good time to take a break now," she demands, louder this time. "You might as well stretch your legs, too, Abby," and shoves me out into the corridor.

As soon as we are far enough away from the other leg-stretchers and restroom visitors, she ticks her mouth close to my ear. "You don't want to concede fifty percent of the chamber pot at this stage."

"But if our mothers owned everything jointly, then that proves at least half the chamber pot is mine, not the whole that Lavinia claims possession of."

"The whole that *you* claim possession of, too," Mary Agnes reminds me. "Stiffen your spine. We're going for the total enchilada, the one that Lavinia, for all intents and purposes, gave up her half to you."

Back in the conference room, Jim Snodgrass repeats the question before I'm even settled into my chair. "Do you know for a fact that the chamber pot was your mother's as opposed to belonging to Mrs. Henrietta Potter?"

"No," I say, earning Mary Agnes's good-girl! kick.

"Then, can you tell me for a fact that it was your mother herself who bought this chamber pot?"

"No." I glare at the opposing attorney. I am starting to hate Jim Snodgrass. His phony avuncular smile. His fake just-plain-folks approach.

"How would you describe your mother and Mrs. Potter's relationship?"

I'm sure you well know, I want to yell. I look over at Lavinia. Her eyes are glued to her Palm Pilot. She is scratching a stylus across its screen. What am I going to say in this room with Lavinia and Mary Agnes and the grandmotherly stenographer typing away? Their lesbian relationship? Their sex life? Did they even have a sex life? I pause. And a phrase from my nineteenth-century English literature class pops into my head. God, if I knew how useful my education would turn out to be—Literature of the Plains, Henry James—I would have not only finished but reenlisted for an extra tour of duty. "Boston marriage," I say.

"Could you clarify? For the record," he adds. God forbid I'd think he might not know what I mean.

"An intimate friendship between two women sharing a household. It came from Henry James's novel *The Bostonians,*" I instruct.

"You're very well informed." Jim Snodgrass smiles. "Yes, then isn't it possible that one could make the case that what the women shared might be shared equally by their heirs"—he pauses—"except of course for what was specifically designated."

"Yes. But in that circumstance, then, Lavinia took—"

He holds up his hand. "Just answer the question, please."

I look at my lawyer. Who nods. A fine lot of help she is.

"Yes," I mumble.

"Now then . . ." He flashes his blinding teeth at me. Are they real? Did he use those whitening strips? "Can you tell me how you came to be in possession of this chamber pot?"

"Lavinia gave it to me."

His eyebrows rise to the heights of incredulity. "So the plaintiff, Lavinia Potter-Templeton, said, 'Abigail Randolph, this is yours, I want you to have it,' and handed it over to you?"

I shift in my chair. "Not exactly."

"Then how exactly?"

I scroll through my mother's rooms. The before: rooms full of plants and food and flowers, objects of desire, the objects she and Henrietta desired, china and furniture and paintings, smells, life. And the after: empty rooms, inanimate objects no longer infused with desire but, instead, emblems of our quarrel. Sadness overwhelms me. I prop my chin on my hands to keep my head from dropping onto the mahogany. "We went to our mothers' apartment to divide their possessions. Lavinia arrived with a list of the things she said belonged to her mother, all the items she said she was entitled to; she brought red stickers to mark all her stuff."

"And you didn't do the same? You didn't prepare for this in the businesslike manner that Mrs. Potter-Templeton did?"

Why does he make Lavinia's scheming seem like a virtue?

Mary Agnes comes to life. "Objection as to form. Which question would you like her to answer?"

He scribbles a note. He clears his throat. "To continue, will you describe how you ended up with the chamber pot?"

"I asked Lavinia if Henrietta had left written instructions. She said no but she had had many conversations with her mother about what her mother intended her to keep. Not that I ever heard any of this."

"Anything else?"

"I got the chamber pot by default. It was among the things she didn't want. A few plates, a plant, a photo, and the chamber pot."

"So the chamber pot wasn't specifically left to you by your mother?"

"I've already—"

"Just answer the question." He pauses. "Please," he adds as an afterthought.

"No, but—"

"You are in the antiques business, right?"

"Yes."

"Given your experience, did you tell Lavinia the value?"

"No. I didn't know its value. It was a kind of discolored, rather uninteresting object. No one would have looked twice at it."

"But you did, didn't you?"

"Yes."

"Isn't it true you took it even though it was, as you said, uninteresting?"

"Yes."

"Are you sure that as an expert you didn't recognize its value?"

Is this a do-you-still-beat-your-wife question? I wonder. Do I say I recognized its value and show I'm a good antiques dealer, if manipulative. Or do I say it looked like the piece of junk it looked like and show I've floundered in this profession as I've floundered in every other. "No, it was only when someone who has the booth next to me told me it might be special that I wondered if maybe it did have some worth."

"And then did you notify Mrs. Lavinia Potter-Templeton of this possibility, of this object she so generously let you have as a result of her feeling a bit guilty no doubt for carrying out her mother's wishes by accepting the majority of the apartment's furnishings? Did you reveal the possibility of value to Lavinia, who would at least be part owner of this, if not the full?"

My head is rattling. Mr. Snodgrass's sentences seem to twist and turn until I sound like a conniving, selfish, greedy monster, not the victim I actually am.

"Objection as to form," Mary Agnes says. She puts her hand on my arm. "The question is argumentative. Compound. Confusing."

It's about time. I take a deep breath. I smooth my hair, which is no doubt standing up as if I've been electrified. Right now I feel electrified. Electrocuted. At least they don't have the death penalty in Massachusetts. Small consolation.

No consolation. I try to visualize the treats I'll give myself when I'm out of here. Will I ever make it out of here? I reach for my coffee; my hand trembles so much some of the coffee spills. Get a grip, I tell myself.

And while I'm trying to get a grip, there's a knock at the door. Ned pushes through. "Sorry," he says. "Fog."

I come undone. All hope of a grip loosens. I stare at Ned. My body starts reacting in all the old imprinted ways, knees weak, heart in throat, a slow melting in my groin, as if sensations long buried in a time capsule still haven't caught up with current events. I clutch my pencil. I remember what it was like to slide my hand into Ned's, to tighten my fingers around his. Just one look opens the floodgates to the rush of all those feelings. Even after all this time. Even though everything's changed. Even though I no longer care for him. How can just one look . . .

I take another look. *He* looks terrible. Slumped with exhaustion. I note the bruises beneath the eyes. Flyaway hair. A scruffy jaw as if he's shaved in patches; the pale skin—EBB ashen—of an invalid; his tie's askew; the shirt collar frayed; he's carrying a stuffed, battered briefcase, one that I recognize, one that belonged to his father. A paperback sticks out of his pocket. I squint at it. *Memoirs of a Geisha*. I'm shocked. Impossible to imagine anyone, particularly a novelist, so out of the literary zeitgeist that he's just starting to read this book.

Lavinia gets up. She flings her arms around him. "At last," she grumbles. Over her pin-striped, padded, dress-for-success shoulder, he nods at me. "Abby," he says, a whisper on a slowly exhaled breath.

"I think it's a good time to pause for a coffee break. A bathroom break," Jim Snodgrass suggests. He stands up. He pushes back his chair.

Mary Agnes checks her watch. "Five minutes, then?"

I'm first out the door. All I want is to escape. I don't know what to say to Ned. I don't know what's appropriate to say to Mary Agnes. I hope never to say anything to Ned ever again. I haven't seen him since my mother's funeral. At least in the flesh, for certainly his author's photo has smiled at me from plenty of bookstores' dusty back shelves.

The ladies' room offers five stalls and generous supplies of Kleenex and paper towels. Though I expect to run into bright young women on the partner track applying lipstick to their cross-examining mouths, I have the place to myself. I run the cold water. I blot my dripping brow. I try not to look at my tortured, celadon-colored face in the mirror. I need to deal with my standing-on-end hair. Someone has kindly left behind a comb—clean—next to a bouquet of bobby pins. I make a halfhearted attempt at taming my mop. It's a lot like antiques. Trying to fix the unfixable is as hard as gluing broken porcelain so the cracks don't show.

I inspect my watch. Only an hour and a half has gone by. You'd think I've been here for a century. Which proves Bergson's theory of time, which I studied in philosophy class. I need a shower. I need a change of clothes. I need to get out of here.

When the door swings open behind me, I expect it's Mary Agnes with a critique of my performance so far and a few tips on how to proceed before I end up in a puddle on the conference room's industrial-strength gray carpeting. But it isn't. It's Lavinia. Who steps silently into a stall and flushes the toilet so I don't hear her pee. Mary Agnes must be checking up on her bigger, more important case.

I tiptoe to the door. I try to slip away before Lavinia's high-heeled boots step out from under the stall, joined to the intimidating rest of her. No such luck. "Abby," she calls.

I pull my hand back from the doorplate. "I don't think we should talk," I say, "given our position as adversaries."

"Who are you to talk?" she demands.

I don't point out her under-the-circumstances odd phraseology.

"We are only adversaries as the end result of your stubbornness."

Though I'm tempted to retort, Correction: the end result of your selfishness, I'm a model of self-restraint. I merely shrug.

She washes her hands with the thoroughness of a surgeon about to take up her scalpel in the OR. About to take up her *knife*. "This is quite a morning you put us through."

Mute, I lean against the tampon dispenser. When in doubt, keep quiet, coaches my internalized Mary Agnes Finch, attorney-at-law.

"Not to mention poor Ned," she goes on.

She's hit the open-sesame button. My lips fly apart. "He looks horrible!" I exclaim.

"No wonder. Considering what's going on in his life, he hardly needed to bust his ass to come to Boston. He has a deadline for his next book. Part of a two-book contract. Just moved into a new apartment. Upper West Side. With his new girlfriend."

I don't ask.

Which doesn't keep her from answering. "Beautiful. Charming. Has a Ph.D. in English literature. Tenure track at Columbia. Very serious." She pauses. "I'm convinced it's his first really serious relationship."

My face is a mask. I should have gone to acting school.

"It's a wrench for him to leave her."

A wrench? Try a corn sheller to strip off nerve endings. Try a King's Arrow straight to the heart. My stomach is taking roller-coaster dives. My head pounds. Old responses, I remind myself. Old habits. Out-of-date reactions. I hate him; he charmed me; he betrayed me; what does a beautiful Ph.D. girlfriend mean to me? "It's just one day," I justify.

"A day is forever when you're in love. Even you must remember that, Abby." She runs a comb—her own, which she fishes out of her sleek, designer-initialed bag—through her sleek hair. She pulls up a flacon of perfume. She sprays her wrists. It's My Sin, I register. "Look at all this unnecessary waste of time and effort you're putting us through." She sprays behind her ears. "Add to this the public humiliation in the offing. Soon our private story will be on everyone's front doorstep, thanks to your very close reporter friend."

I cement my mouth shut. My teeth are grinding together so tightly I must be wearing down the enamel. I push open the door. I try to slam it behind me. But it swings, then hits me in the butt. *Hard.*

We resume our places like an orchestra after intermission. There's a little tuning up. New legal pads; stenographer's tape replaced; hot coffee poured. The hum of polite conversation. Mary Agnes seems distracted. She's got a new, higher pile of folders next to her. *Corporation Distribution,* I can read between the crook of her elbow and her impatient, tapping fingertips. Quick study of all things legal, I know for a fact that *Corporation Distribution* has nothing to do with my case. I sip the glass of water Jim Snodgrass has just poured for me. I won't meet Ned's eyes.

Which seem to be glued to the grain of the mahogany conference table. A lock of hair falls over his forehead. I wonder if the charming, beautiful Ph.D. Columbia tenure-track professor appreciates its silkiness.

"Shall we resume?" Jim Snodgrass asks now. A rhetorical question, since he resumes without waiting for our go-ahead. "So, why did you decide to take this chamber pot onto *Antiques Roadshow*?"

"To find out its value," I answer.

"Which, don't you agree, you could have discovered in myriad different ways. For example, by bringing it to an expert, a curator, a museum?"

"I didn't know an expert."

"Really? Don't people in the antiques business have at their fingertips a host of experts to consult?"

"The man with the booth next to me, my *colleague,* suggested I take it on TV. He knew some people who worked on the show. He could arrange to get me a ticket."

"And perhaps the prospect of publicity was an incentive?"

"Excuse me?" I cup my ear like a cartoon character.

"Did or did not your business improve after your appearance on *Antiques Roadshow*?"

"Yes."

"And as a savvy businessperson yourself, didn't you see the advantages of being on a program with such a national reputation and in seemingly continual reruns?"

"I had no expectation the chamber pot would have any value."

"Even though you're in the business? Even though your colleague suggested you bring it on the program? Even though, of all your mother and her companion's possessions, you chose to take what you called"—he checks a piece of paper—"let me quote, 'a kind of discolored, rather uninteresting object.' You must have sensed your *colleague* had a reason."

Mary Agnes holds up a hand. "Objection. Which question should she answer? Stop badgering her. Ask one question at a time."

"Did you sense your colleague had a reason to promote an appearance on *Antiques Roadshow*?"

"Actually, no." What is he making me out to be, a thief, a person who knew she had a treasure, stole it from Lavinia, went on TV to promote herself? I am appalled. I am also a little flattered that he would think so much of my business acumen.

Though Mary Agnes doesn't seem to be quite so impressed. "Jim," she cautions.

"Let's take another tack," says Jim Snodgrass in the tone of a man who is nothing if not reasonable. He runs his hand through his hair. He tugs at his ear. "Could you tell us about your relationship with the coplaintiff, Edward Bickford Potter?"

I straighten up. "What does that have—?"

"Just answer the question, please."

I look at Mary Agnes. She nods. "There's no relationship," I say. My eyes are glued to the same mahogany grain that Ned's eyes are glued to at the opposite end. Maybe the table will start rattling. Maybe ghosts from childhood past will appear. Maybe a disembodied voice will put the right words in my mouth. What are the right words?

"Was there a relationship in the past?"

"What do you mean by a relationship?" I ask. "Define the terms," I add, the Clarence Darrow that necessity has made me invent myself as.

"I won't beat around the bush. Sexual," pronounces the lawyer for the other side.

"Jim," grumbles the lawyer for my side.

Ned and I expel a gasp, a mutual gasp not half so satisfying as the alternative, the sexual alternative.

"Answer the question," Jim instructs.

"Answer the question, Abby," Mary Agnes echoes.

"Sexual?" I repeat. "I guess," I allow.

"I take that as a yes?"

"Yes," I begrudge.

"Was this a rather long-lasting relationship?"

"A few years."

"Was there talk of marriage?"

"Yes."

"Then what happened?"

"We broke up."

"What were the circumstances of that breakup?"

"The usual. We fell out of love."

"What is Mr. Bickford's profession?"

"He's a novelist."

"And did he write a novel called *The Cambridge Ladies Who Live in Furnished Souls*?"

"Yes."

"And what was that novel about?"

"I'm sure you know what that novel was about."

"Was it the story of your childhood, your love affair, both of your mothers' relationships?"

"Yes."

"And did that lead to your breakup?"

"Yes."

"Why?"

"I felt betrayed," I reply, trying to choke my anger down.

"Why?"

"Because he wrote about me. Because he revealed secrets."

"Secrets that I gather were part of pillow talk?"

I feel my eyes start to brim with tears. I will them away.

"Which might account for your wanting the chamber pot from his mother?"

"*My* mother."

"I'll let this pass for a minute. I'm curious about one thing. Why would an antiques dealer want something that"—he looks down at the same piece of paper he had consulted only minutes ago—"she describes as, let me quote again, 'a kind of discolored, rather uninteresting object' unless she knew it was valuable? And, let me add, unless it was a way to get revenge against a lover who betrayed her?"

"Objection," Mary Agnes says. She puts a hand on my arm. "Would you like another break?"

"No." I'm furious now. "I want to get this over with," I practically spit. I sneak a glance at Ned. His sad eyes overflow with such sympathy I must be the most pathetic human being he's ever sat across a table from.

"Let me rephrase. Why did you want this particular pot that you saw as uninteresting?"

"Because it was my mother's. Because Lavinia took almost all the stuff. Because it was part of my mother's life. Because I loved my mother."

"Do you love Ned?"

I stop. I wait. "*Did*," I correct.

"Speak up, please."

"Yes," I say. "Once." I sob. I drop my head on my folded arms. My eyes and nose run onto the polished wood. I smell varnish. Beeswax. Linseed oil. Mary Agnes hands me water. She pats my back.

"Break," Jim Snodgrass whispers.

I lift up my head. My nose is streaming. Mascara no doubt tracks my cheeks. I'm sure my skin is blotched, my hair wilder than ever. I must look mad, out of control. "No," I nearly yell, mad, out of control. "Lavinia can have this. Nothing, no object, is worth this torture."

"Abby . . . !" Mary Agnes starts.

Ned bolts upright. He bangs his fist like a judge's gavel. "Everybody stop. I relinquish my claim. Why I ever let Lavinia . . ." He scowls at his sister, an expression I recognize from their childhood arguments, those in which Lavinia, as usual, was clearly in the wrong. "Abby should have the damn pot. I want her to have it. She deserves it. It's only right. She has nothing else. She's all alone." His voice rises into the higher reaches of indignity. "What monster would take this away from someone in her situation? There's no reason to put any human being through this."

Jim Snodgrass jumps up from his seat. "Quiet, Ned," he commands, no longer kindly and avuncular. "Sit down. You'll get your chance to speak when you're deposed."

Ned ignores him. All eyes are now on me. Even the stenographer's. Her polka-dotted glasses steam up with tears. She sniffles, then blows her nose on a pansy-bordered handkerchief. I want to disappear. I want to be swallowed up by an earthquake in India. A tornado in Nebraska. I want to be hit by a bus, return under my rock, vanish back into the lantern some cruel magician rubbed to land me here. I want my mother. I even want my father. Has there ever been a greater object of pity? A more woebegone litigant?

"Look," Ned says. "I know Abby. She would never want this because of revenge. She would never want this for commercial reasons. She's not manipulative; she's not mean; she's naïve, maybe. But she's suffered quite enough."

"Ned," Jim Snodgrass warns. "Mr. Potter, let's take a break. Let's talk outside." Jim Snodgrass crosses over to Ned. He puts a hand on his elbow.

Ned shakes it off. "Let her have it. It's all she's got." He grabs Lavinia's shoulder. "She only wants it because it's her mother's. It's just a stroke of luck that it turned out to have value."

"*My* mother's," Lavinia begins. "Ours."

"Vinny, can it," her brother orders. "You yourself dismissed the frigging pot. Are we agreed?"

Lavinia shakes her head. "Far be it for me to torture an old friend. Even though my mother specifically wished me to have it. Even though I have right on my side."

"Lavinia . . ." Ned glares.

Lavinia smiles her faux sweet, treacherous, Megan-Parmenter-is-my-best-friend smile. "But I have to honor my brother's wishes. I want to do the right thing." She turns to me. "Abby, I hope you'll do the right thing, too. I hope you'll let the reporter at the *Globe* know how this got resolved." She raises a questioning eyebrow.

Even in my moment of utter shame and despair, I manage a duplicitous nod.

"As far as the chamber pot is concerned, then, I will give up my ownership in favor of Abby." She turns to Jim Snodgrass. "Now can we leave? I have work. My brother has a plane to catch."

"If you're sure. This is an extraordinarily generous gesture on your part. It is my duty to point out that you are forfeiting half if not the whole of seventy-five thousand dollars."

"Not to mention your legal fees for this particular miscarriage of justice . . ." Lavinia begins.

"We're sure," says Ned. "Both of us," he emphasizes, then, palm splayed against her back, he pushes Lavinia out the double doors.

Mary Agnes smiles. She caps her pens, puts the pencils back in their pencil cups. "Well, we got the result we want," she says in her all-in-a-day's-work, on-to-the-next-day's-work jaunty tone. "Good job, Abby."

Jim Snodgrass sorts his papers into his briefcase. He goes over to talk to the stenographer.

Do I tell Mary Agnes how I lied? Not under oath, but by omission. Do I tell her I neglected to inform Lavinia that the *Globe* is no longer carrying a story about the chamber pot? Do I confess to my lawyer that I blackmailed Todd Tucker by threatening to tell his wife about us? Do I admit to her that this is a criminal case after all? That her old college classmate is a criminal?

I do none of those things. "Excuse me," I say. I run to the ladies' room. I see the stalls are empty; the coast is clear. I resoundingly throw up.

I gulp water. I do the best I can with my blotched cheeks, my red eyes, tangled hair, sour breath.

Ned is just leaving the men's room when I sneak out of the ladies' into the corridor. He looks almost as bad as I do. "Abby," he says. I flatten myself against the wall. If I were Superman, I could go right through it. If only. He comes closer. He takes my hand. I gaze down at it—my hand in his. An art historian would call it a familiar motif, an iconic image, like the Mona Lisa, something you've pictured, felt, seen, over and over again but still remains fresh. "Abby," he repeats. I pull my hand away. I turn my head from his pitying eyes.

"Bye, Ned," I say.

As soon as the elevator swallows him up, I lean back against the wall. I take big relaxation-response breaths. I try to empty my mind. I try the visualization techniques that yoga teachers and fit friends and twelve-step advocates and women-who-love-the-wrong-men *Globe* receptionists are always crediting for getting them through everything from traffic jams to terminal illnesses. I picture a clear crystal lake, a shadowy grove of ancient elms, a cloudless blue sky. I focus on this. I shut out everything but water, trees, sky. I shut out banging doors, scurrying lawyers, the buzz and hum of big business, the lopsided clink of the scales of justice. Water, trees, sky. Water, trees, sky. I am just about to congratulate myself on my anesthesiology powers when, suddenly, an airplane cuts through my sky over my water between my trees. It's a Delta shuttle from Boston to New York. Carrying Ned to his new apartment, his new girl, his new book, his new life.

And on the ground, diminishing to a speck, diminishing to an atom from the past, is me, clutching an empty vessel, clutching her chamber pot, this hollow symbol of a hollow victory.

My heart races. Anxiety tightens my muscles, pounds through my veins. I am a relaxation-response failure just as I'm a failure in love.

Back in the conference room, the crime scene has been all cleaned up. Everyone, except Mary Agnes, has gone on to the next client, the next legal entanglement. Mary Agnes herself looks poised for flight. Nevertheless, I can still picture the metaphorical yellow tape that marked the spot where my blood spilled, the place where I suffered the murder of my soul, the biggest humiliation of my life. I half expect to see the silhouette of my body lying there outlined in chalk.

"I've asked Tony to bring you your chamber pot from the vault," Mary Agnes says.

"Now?" I ask. "Can't I leave it there for a while?"

"We don't have the space," she says, "And since the dispute over the property has been resolved, it's my pleasure to turn it over to you." She picks up the thick blue-jacketed folder of her bigger, more important case. "Take a cab," my lawyer advises. "You can afford it now."

14

The first thing I do when I get home is slide the chamber pot under my bed. The irony of this gesture is not lost on me. No longer positioned for its intended purpose, it now occupies the territory of dust bunnies, spilled pennies, odd socks—all for security's sake, for antitheft reasons. Even more comforting is the added benefit: the chamber pot's out of my sight and thus not the constant reminder of my collusion in perverting the law, my blackmail of an adversary, to become its lawful-by-default owner. Rest assured that my hard-earned prize is not only safely stashed but also well protected, cushioned in its coat of many layers of the finest Bubble Wrap.

I take off my deponent's shoes, my deponent's black blazer, my deponent's black pants. I unbutton my now wrung-through-the-deponent's-mill formerly ironed white blouse. I study the discarded ensemble heaped at my feet. I shudder. I hadn't thought of this before—thank goodness I hadn't thought of this before—but it's the outfit a waitress might sport at a Harvard Square restaurant. All at once, I glimpse my future. Which is not a pretty sight: a former antiques dealer uniformed in two different shades of black taking orders for veggie burgers, hash browns, a side of slaw, and the house red.

Speaking of the house red. By now you're probably ready to start sending me pamphlets marked *From a Friend of Bill.* You're right to note that all my sorrows seem accompanied by glasses of wine. There have been a lot of sorrows lately, and a lot of wine along with a lot of *whine*. For which I apologize. But believe me, I'm not about to lurch down Mass. Ave. with a brown bag concealing half a gallon of Thunderbird. I've got the drinking under control. It's my lack of control over other things that worries me.

I review the events of the day, a humiliation of such immense proportions even the wine can't soften its harsh reality. I started out okay, faltered at the middle, and by the end, even though I prevailed, nevertheless dissolved into tears. Causing everyone to flee, including myself. The story of my life. Or at least the story of my love life. The worst was seeing Ned regarding me with such pitying eyes. A close second was my position as the object of uncharitable Lavinia's charity. The let-her-have-it-she's-got-plenty-of-nothin' syndrome. *We got the result we want,* Mary Agnes had crowed. But if we won, I wonder, why do I feel as though I lost?

I try to distract myself. I look around my living room. Half the clothes from my closet lie draped across sofa and chairs and tables limp as drunken party guests. Some party. Dishes stuff the kitchen sink; the bed's unmade; there's a crack in its oak frame I keep meaning to call a carpenter in to fix. I managed to extract the name of a good one from Lavinia, back when we were on friendlier terms. You can only imagine how long ago that was. Somehow the prospect of clean sheets and an orderly household doesn't console. I reach for the basket stuffed with magazines and newspapers. I flip through a couple of catalogues. Husbands and wives cuddle on Pottery Barn sofas. They curl up together in the center of mattresses the size of a small municipality. They share a cup of cappuccino over a polished espresso machine. They embrace in matching his-and-her terry cloth robes. Ecstatic smiles mark their perfect faces.

I throw the catalogues across the room. Why not a full-color spread of a slovenly, frowning, chapped-skin ex-deponent sipping wine on her ratty couch? I ignore the challenging pile of the *New York Review of Books;* I took over my parents' subscription. It must have been for life (a Harvard professor's perk?) since the biweeklies keep coming even though I never once renewed.

For some reason, what I pick up is *Harvard Magazine,* which goes to anyone who ever sent in a first-semester tuition check. For some *perverse* reason, maybe because I feel so turned around today, I start at the back. I stop. My hand freezes on the page.

I put down my wine. I stare. In front of me is a photograph of two clasped hands against a black background. One hand is edged with a ruffle of lace at its delicate wrist. The other, slightly larger ends in the fold of a cuff. *Immortal Hands,* asserts the caption, then underneath, in smaller print, *Tiny, but iconic.*

I start to read. Every sentence sends me into deeper and deeper states of disbelief. The plaster cast belongs to Harvard's Schlesinger Library. Analysts claim to see in the bone structure of the woman signs of tuberculosis. The hands are tiny. "Yet," states the article, "these are the hands of the larger-than-life lovers Robert and Elizabeth Barrett Browning."

I read that line over and over again. Can this be possible? I force myself to go on. The cast is the work of Harriet Hosmer, a neoclassical sculptor and expatriate who met the Brownings in 1853 in Italy.

Nathaniel Hawthorne himself wrote about *Clasped Hands,* that it symbolized "the individuality and heroic union of two, high, poetic lives."

For a long time I gaze at the photograph. I think of the Brownings' joined hands, the symbol of their joined lives. I think of Ned and me just hours before, our own pulled-apart hands a signal of our own separated lives. *Bye, Ned,* I had said. And—*poof!*—he was gone.

I rush to the phone. I dial the all-purpose Harvard number, a number I have known by heart since I was five. I am put through to the Schlesinger Library. The woman who answers connects me to the reference librarian.

"I'm calling about the plaster cast of the hands of Robert and Elizabeth Barrett Browning," I explain. "I saw the photo in *Harvard Magazine.* I just want to check that the cast is still on display at the library before I make my way over there."

"Actually, it isn't," she says. "Unfortunately, it's stored off-site."

I imagine huge warehouses filled with art, ranged like the gas tanks that pimple the Southeast Expressway. Not long ago I heard a news report about a warehouse fire on the outskirts of New York. Which destroyed valuable masterpieces. *The loss is immeasurable,* declared a painter whose canvases hang in museums all over the world. I look again at the photograph. How small the cast appears. How vulnerable. "Off-site in a big art warehouse?" I ask. "In Boston? In New York?"

"No. It's here in the library. Stored in a climate-controlled vault. Off-site in this case meaning not available to the public."

I'm not the public! I want to protest. I'm a near Harvard graduate, daughter of the holder of the Epworth chair, owner of Elizabeth Barrett Browning's chamber pot, which I could conceivably donate to the Schlesinger's collection of Browningiana, now that I know it has one, if I could personally witness the Browningiana myself. "Is it possible to make private arrangements to see the hands?" I request.

She clears her throat. "Under certain circumstances." Her voice is cautionary. Is she worried about theft? A lawsuit? A Lavinia-type claim? *My great-great-aunt was a friend of Harriet Hosmer, who promised her the sculpture,* I can hear Lavinia insist. *Those hands are my inheritance.*

"What circumstances?" I ask.

"You'd need to produce a good reason. For scholarly purposes as opposed to touristy ones."

Would a layman's interest in the Brownings qualify? Would a mother's love of Italy add gravitas? What about a fascination with entwined hands—the entwined hands of lovers, of ex-lovers, of poets? The clasped hands of an antiques dealer and a betraying novelist? I consider telling the reference librarian the story of my own Browning treasure. If I can earn her sympathy, maybe a chamber pot fresh from a law firm's vault could be my ticket to another—this one off-site and climate-controlled—vault. More likely she'll just dismiss me as a crackpot with a chamber pot. "What about someone who simply wants to take a look?" I offer. "Someone in the community? With Harvard connections that go way back?"

"Sorry. I'm afraid those reasons don't fit within the parameters of our library's policy."

I hang up the phone. I have to laugh. How many times can Harvard diss you, let me count the ways. Touristy! The arrogance of the university even to those of its own, to those who teach there, who study there, who bought their houses at a reduction from University Real Estate, who send in their class dues and wave the Crimson at all the football games. A friend of my mother's, a Radcliffe alum, who had been a host family for international students coming to Harvard for thirty years, wrote an essay about her experience for a local literary magazine. So delighted was she by its publication that she sent a copy to the international student office. "I expect they'll be pleased," she told my mother. They were not amused. "What's the matter?" she called up when she realized she hadn't been assigned a student for the new term.

"Your essay," came the frosty reply. "You insinuated our office served jug wine at our get-togethers when we pride ourselves on offering very fine vintages."

"Do something," my indignant mother advised. "Write an op-ed for the *Globe*."

My mother's friend had shrugged. "You can't go up against Harvard." She sighed.

Harvard be damned, I think now. Lacking the scholarly credentials to get into the inner sanctum sanctorum, I'm not as crushed as you might predict. Do I actually have to see the hands? Maybe it's enough to know they exist. That they inhabit a resting place only one zip code away from me. Perhaps it's enough to make the connections. To marvel at the coincidence. To acknowledge how plaster can resonate with flesh. To take comfort in the possibility of the "union of two high, poetic lives." I came close to such a union, I tell myself. Maybe the next.

I lie down on my creaking, unmade bed. The room spins. I'm at sea on my lumpy mattress, crashing against wave after wave, my only anchor, my only consolation, Elizabeth Barrett Browning's chamber pot.

But the minute I think this, up seeps the old familiar guilt. Ned's pity. Lavinia's charity. What have I done? What am I going to do?

Then something happens that only proves that you need to hold on to your raft, that you should never give up on life. Because when your emotions plummet so low they have nowhere else to go but up, fate can take an unexpected, soaring turn. Not that I can recognize the truth of this maxim right away.

Here's what happens: The phone rings. I can't bear any more of anything, I plead. Besides, I am so pinned to my bed of woe by woe, so weighted down with remorse and guilt, I could never lift an arm to reach for the telephone. I manage a few tubercular-sounding coughs to underscore my invalided state and let the machine pick up.

"Abby, Abby!" Gus nearly screams. "I'm just back from *Antiques Roadshow*. Your King's Arrow is worth forty thousand bucks!"

Like a miracle at Lourdes, I throw off my shackles. In an instant I'm off the bed. In seconds I'm at the phone before Gus hangs up. "I don't believe it!" I scream.

"It's true!" Gus screams.

"Oh my God! Oh my God!" I scream.

The man upstairs pounds a broomstick on his floor. I lower my voice. "What happened? Tell me everything."

"Do I have an eye or not?" he fishes.

Far be it for me to split cherubs. "You do indeed!" I agree.

"The expert vetted it. And then a museum curator came up and offered the full estimate price on the spot. I told him I'd consult the owner."

"Accept the offer. Sell it," I order. Decisive, businesslike, I revel in the take-charge-of-your-life side of me I've never seen before.

"Done."

"I'll give you a commission. Only what you deserve."

"The result is its own reward," Gus assures. He pauses. "Though I wouldn't turn down a bottle of bubbly."

"A *bottle*? I'll send you a case."

I waltz a self-congratulatory loop around the living room. I allow myself a few yelping *yippees!* which bring the pounding of the broomstick back. Without any thought, without any waffling, I know exactly what I'm going to do. Forty thousand dollars! Thirty-seven fifty is exactly half of the seventy-five. I'll have some money left over to purchase new stock for my business. I salute my professional eye. That I first set that eye on a corn sheller instead of the King's Arrow is something I hardly bat an eyelash at. Who can fault a dealer clever enough to buy the whole lot? Hooray! The solution is so clear it's astonishing.

But first I dial the University Liquor Store. I ask for the authority on champagne. Expert to expert in our different milieus, we discuss possibilities. We decide on a single vineyard. Vintage. Brut. I supply Gus's address and the number of my Visa card.

By now it's seven-thirty, way beyond quitting time. For anyone except Mary Agnes Finch, that is. I reach her on her direct line. I explain about the King's Arrow, about its forty-thousand-dollar sale.

"Is it in dispute?" she asks. Oh, no, here we go again, her tone implies.

"Not at all," I assure her. "I want to use the money to buy back Lavinia's half of the chamber pot."

"You *what?*" She stops. "I don't think I heard you right."

"I want to use the money to buy back Lavinia's half of the chamber pot," I repeat.

Though I can tell she's making a superhuman effort to keep her voice measured, I can still detect an edge of fury. "Don't be an idiot, Abby."

"I'm not. I got a windfall. I bought something for fifteen bucks that turns out to be a little more than half of the chamber pot's worth. It has to be a sign. Manna from heaven."

"And you want to give this away?"

"It seems the right thing to do."

"Abby, the chamber pot is lawfully yours."

"How could it be lawful if I lied to Lavinia?" I wince at the killed *Globe* article. At my adultery-in-the-Old-Man-of-the-Mountain-Room threats. "I didn't tell her the *Globe* story on the chamber pot had been canceled. Because she assumed it was going to be published, she gave in."

"You didn't lie. Nobody questioned you about that putative article."

"But I withheld information, I committed the sin of omission," I confess.

"Can't you just recite a few Hail Marys?"

"An agnostic? Quaker? Unitarian? We went to college together, not parochial school."

"Oh, Abby, legally your sin of omission is irrelevant."

"How about spiritually? Emotionally? Personally? Ethically?" Romantically, I'm tempted to include. I change my mind. Romance is what's *really* irrelevant.

I hear noise in the background. Doors slamming. Bells ringing. *Miss Finch,* a voice hollers out. "Hold my calls," Mary Agnes tells someone. "*All* of them."

Mary Agnes sighs. "What is it you want me to do?"

"I want you to call up Lavinia." I hesitate. "And Ned," I add. "And tell them I plan to write out a check to guarantee I have full and sole title to the chamber pot."

"Excuse me? You already own the chamber pot."

"Technically, maybe," I concede. "But I don't feel it in my bones."

"And it's worth thirty-seven thousand five hundred dollars to you to feel it in your bones?"

I hold up my left hand. "Yes," I testify. "It will banish all my guilt."

"Guilt for what? Taking what is yours? Lavinia gave it to you. She didn't want it. Possession is nine-tenths of the law. In this case, ten-tenths. Don't be a fool, Abby," Mary Agnes says. She stops. Her tone is gentler, the kind of tone she must use with recalcitrant clients, the old, the muddled, the dumb, those suffering from Alzheimer's, the people you'd talk down from the ledge of a roof. "Look, Abby, I realize I gave you short shrift during the deposition. I apologize—"

I think of Clyde. I cut her off. "No matter."

"Yes, it does matter. I was distracted by another case, which is no excuse . . ."

"I'm well aware my chamber pot is small potatoes."

"True enough. But let me remind you that Lavinia deserves nothing from you. All those red stickers she pasted over your mother's belongings. If I brought an appraiser in to tally up the value of the load she carted away compared with yours, including the seventy-five thousand, I can guarantee you there would be an enormous disparity. I'm sure the antiques she took, she *stole,* are worth many hundreds of thousands. In fact, if you ever wanted to sue . . ."

"Never. I'd never go through this again. Nothing is worth this agony."

"The truth is she stole from you."

"But she said her mother wanted her to have those things."

"She lied."

The words shock me; the short declarative sentence feels like the come-to-your-senses slap lovers in movies give women on the verge of hysteria. "But—but—" I stammer.

"Look. You've got something worth forty thousand dollars. You own a chamber pot worth seventy-five. You have legal fees. Taxes on the sale of the King's Arrow alone will add up to almost forty percent. Even with a friends-and-family reduction, my bill will be substantial. Lavinia doesn't need the money. Ned doesn't want it. What's the issue here?" She pauses. "Except for your masochism."

"Wait a minute."

"*You* wait a minute. I've known you since freshman year, Abby. You're too scrupulous."

Not too scrupulous to jump into bed with a man I had few feelings for, a situation my lawyer, for current purposes, really doesn't need to know anything about. "I wouldn't go so far as—"

"I would. You're a wimp. Remember when you passed up free tickets for that U-2 concert you were dying to attend because you'd made some tentative coffee study date with a nerd? Who in the end didn't even show up? And remember that other time when you confessed to colluding in the trashing of the quad because you thought you might have dropped a candy wrapper on the just-seeded lawn? And it turned out that townies had practically bulldozed the grass?"

"Enough. Enough. I was eighteen. Well, twenty at the most."

"You haven't changed in—what?—thirteen years. As your lawyer, I advise strongly against this folly."

"As my lawyer, don't you have to do what your client wants?"

Mary Agnes huffs. I wonder if I'm the most challenging client she's ever had. I wonder if she'll start writing law articles about me. I wonder if my case will be assigned to first-year property law students in the lecture halls of Langdell.

"I don't believe my client *knows* what she wants. Take a few days to think this over and call me back."

"I won't change my mind."

"Just consider it," Mary Agnes orders. "Go over everything. It's a no-brainer as far as I and anyone else on the planet is concerned."

"Two days," I say, "and then you promise you'll do what I want?"

"Two days," Mary Agnes warns.

I sit back in my chair. I tuck my legs under my knees. Really, I think. Am I the last man (woman?) standing? Am I the single holdout in the jury room? Just like the Eureka! recognition of a treasure in a bunch of trash, a person can instinctively know the right thing to do in the middle of an imperfect and morally challenged universe. Wimp? Masochist? Is it so wrong to see both sides of the question? Unlike Lavinia, who was always so sure of her own point of view, who owned a monopoly on the truth. "I'm the boss of you," Lavinia used to lord over me as a kid. "Do everything the way I want."

"Don't act like such a bully," I'd venture, cowering under her instructions of what to wear, what movie to see, what teacher to choose, what game to play, why I deserved to be *it*.

"If you didn't have me to tell you what to do, you wouldn't be able to make up your mind," she'd reply.

Now I scroll through my career as Lavinia's subnumerary. Our blood sisterhood, her best-friend betrayals, the unflattering dress she picked for me for her first wedding, her red stickers dotted like measles all over our mothers' furniture. The way she threw my own clothes off my own chair. As if even those jeans and shirts weren't mine. As if her singular (self-appointed) superiority granted her the prior claim.

The phone rings. "And by the way. I forgot to tell you," Mary Agnes begins with no preliminaries, "I heard from Ned. He faxed me an instrument of release and assignment—assignment to *you*—giving up his right to ownership. He apologized for his sister. Said she could be quite the bitch. Bitch," she repeats. She pauses to let the word sink in. "Got to go. Just want you to stir that into the making-the-sensible-decision pot. The only decision. *Two days.*" And before I can answer, she hangs up.

I look around my apartment. At the clothes still strewn on the chairs, dishes stacked in the sink, the clutter of antiques and junk, everything I ever owned waiting to be sorted into piles of *to stay* or *to go*. I remember when Lavinia and I cleaned out our mothers' apartment. How reluctant I was to remove all trace of my mother, to strip the apartment to its bare walls, its bare floor. And how eagerly Lavinia went to work to dismantle it. *Let's face it, you are a bit scattered, Abby. If it were up to you, we'd never get this done,* she'd sneered. But people exist in their objects; they inhabit the walls of their rooms. Old things bear traces of lives lived; possessions provoke cherished memories. That was Grandpa's watch, a son might say. I remember when he wore it, the way it dangled just so from that chain. I picture my mother holding the chamber pot, admiring the drawing of Flush, treasuring the history contained in its discolored porcelain. I see her hands setting out pâté and cornichons on the very plates I now keep on my shelf. *You haven't changed in—what?—thirteen years,* Mary Agnes said to me.

I stand up. I straighten the legs of my jeans. It's about time. I'll start with the chamber pot that Lavinia didn't want, the chamber pot that is lawfully mine. The more I tell myself this, the more I believe it. Maybe I'll be a convert to the healing power of the mantra yet. *It's mine. It's mine,* I chant. After all, was withholding the *Globe* information a federal crime? Especially since I would have told the truth if Jim Snodgrass had asked. Especially compared to Lavinia. Lavinia had lied. She has always lied. How could I have been so dumb? How could I have thought to throw my King's Arrow earnings away? How could I have been such a wimp? Such a masochist? I stop. No more. *Former* wimp. *Ex*-masochist. I don't need any Lourdes water to declare I've been cured.

I grab the vacuum. The broom. The mop and the pail. For two hours I clean. I fill four plastic garbage bags with ragged college clothes and threadbare sweaters. I plump pillows. Put away dishes. Sponge down counters. Change the sheets. Organize my files and my jewelry trays. I wash the windows with ammonia: I polish them till the glass shines like fine Waterford. I stick things in boxes to take to my booth, other cartons I designate for Goodwill. *To go. To stay.* I wish you could sort people that easily; I wish you could decide who's to go, who's to stay, that fast.

When the apartment looks like new, the new me calls Mary Agnes at home. "I've decided you're right." I announce in my firmest, most decisive voice.

"Hip hip hooray! Justice prevails!" she shouts. "Sis boom bah," she adds, a relic from her South Boston cheerleading days. "But don't squander all your money until you get my bill . . ."

"I'm hardly a spendthrift, Mary Agnes."

"Just kidding, Abby! I am so proud of you. You've got a spine. You've stood up for yourself! You've taken charge of your life!"

"Yeah, one small step for man . . ."

"Go, Abby, go!" She pauses. "Though I must confess I had my doubts you'd come around."

"You give a pretty convincing argument."

"I didn't even enumerate all the harsh words Ned had for his sister. I was afraid of overloading the dice in case you'd balk."

"Did he have any words for me?" I ask. Regretting the question as soon as it leaves my mouth.

Mary Agnes's voice softens. "Abby, are you still in love with Ned?"

"Of course not," I protest. "No way. Impossible."

"Methinks you protest too much," she suggests.

I remain silent.

"Remember in college when I broke up with Andrew Peabody?" she asks now.

I remember *he* dumped *her* for Nancy Murphy, but I am the last person to dispute the facts when it comes to matters of the heart. "Yes . . . ?"

"You brought me tea and toast. You gave me very good advice."

"I did? What did I say? I'm really curious."

"You said 'Let him go.' " I hear her turn on a faucet. I hear dishes clatter and clank. "Abby, when I called Ned's apartment, a woman answered the phone. He's living with someone."

"I know that," I declare. "I am fully cognizant of the significant other in his life," I add, in my protesting-too-much, extra-emphatic, legal-speak, and Latinate mode.

"Let him go," she advises.

"Believe me, Mary Agnes, I already have."

15

Those who say time heals are right. I'm the perfect example. Now two months after the deposition, *après le déluge,* as I like to call it, I'm doing okay. Better than you would have thought. Last week I had my Abigail Randolph Independence Day celebration at Objects of Desire. A cocktail party after closing time. I invited everybody, all the dealers, janitorial staff, movers, refinishers, even the accountant who makes sure proper Massachusetts taxes are charged to those without a registration number. I brought in wine and beer, passed around cheese and crackers, wasabi peas, stuffed grape leaves, and roasted almonds in my old bowls and platters. Thanks to the sale of the King's Arrow, I've added some gorgeous serving pieces to my stock. I borrowed a tape deck and blasted Cole Porter. People danced in the narrow aisles to "Anything Goes," winding in and out between the armoires and recamier chaises, pier tables, garden urns, jewelry cases, old toys, Coalport pottery. It's amazing how former wallflowers can evolve into orchid centerpieces. "To you, Abby," the Currier & Ives print swindler toasted from behind his raised glass. "To Abby," seconded my guests. "What are we celebrating?" the lady who sells gently used linens asked.

"Abby's fine eye," declared Gus. "Two outstanding coups. That already brought her big bucks." What he didn't add was that he was responsible for both of those coups—the chamber pot and the King's Arrow. Without his own fine eye and network of consultants, both treasures would still be gathering dust, neglected, unnoticed beneath a pile of old quilts or a bouquet of faux greenery. What I didn't point out, eager for self-promotion and loath to steal Gus's thunder, was that after the party and the antiques replenishing, I netted very little from those big bucks. Especially when you consider the scope of my own personal national deficit as a result of Mary Agnes's bill and the big bite our government took out of the King's Arrow sale.

By the end of the party, people were in high spirits, even those who suffered some minor breakage to their inventory due to the excessively vigorous bunny hop. I must say I created a lot of goodwill. People now come into my booth to consult me about their old tools, their bits of Italian porcelain. "Will you take a look at this?" a daguerreotype collector asks. "What price should I charge?" wonders a spatterware specialist. I've been asked to contribute a few paragraphs about chamber pots to a scholarly volume on water closets and early outhouse design. After work, I often join a group of fellow dealers for drinks. We're planning field trips to auctions and flea markets and garage sales. At last I can boast of a community that has nothing to do with my ancestry, neighborhood, well-connected parents, or where I went to school. I'm receiving invitations to showers, to bar mitzvahs, to potlucks. *My colleagues*, I marvel. *My colleagues*, I gloat.

Colleagues who want to fix me up. There's always the cousin, the client, the friend of a friend who'd be perfect for me. "No way," I insist. "I'm lying low. Hibernating. I'm allergic to blind dates. Absolutely not. No!"

Saying no to Gus, however, is another story. I owe him too much. One case of vintage champagne, even Brut, can hardly begin to compensate.

"Just try it, Abby," he pleads. We're lounging in his booth sharing a pot of coffee and the crossword puzzle. He points at his mug. "A simple cup of joe. How hard is that?" He flips back the newspaper. "What's your sign?"

"Sagittarius."

He adjusts his reading glasses. He clears his throat. "Be open to new relationships. Make a coffee date with a new man."

I lunge for the paper. "Let me see that," I insist.

He pulls it away. He turns back to the crossword. "What's a four-letter word for stubborn, unreasonable?"

For days Gus had been dangling in front of me the third cousin once removed who's just arrived in Cambridge from the Midwest.

"I hate Midwesterners," I say, free to unfurl my prejudices and run them up the flagpole now that I inhabit a zip code other than 02138, a zip code that tolerates a little political incorrectness from time to time.

"He's originally from Montreal."

"I don't speak French."

"Neither does he."

"What Canadian doesn't speak French?"

"He's the spitting image of Brad Pitt," he offers.

"I hate pretty men."

He flings down the paper. He throws up his hands. "Can't I just give him your number? As a favor to me? At least to get my sister off my back?"

Can I deny the friend who gave me colleagues, legitimacy, the tools to banish old ghosts and develop self-esteem? "All right. But, for the record, I categorically refuse to marry him."

Gus works fast. No doubt out of fear that I'll change my mind and his sister will stop sending him those smelly packages of Oka cheese and Québécois pork pies. No sooner am I inside my front door, even before I have put down my keys and my Styrofoam-boxed pad Thai, than the phone rings.

"This is Emile Lambert." He pronounces it *lam-bear*. "Am I talking to Abby?"

I strain to hear his voice over a background of steady thumping and chanting. I picture tom-toms around the campfire in old westerns, Indian chiefs in beaded moccasins and feathered headdresses whooping out war cries. "Can you speak up?" I ask.

"That's the problem," he shouts. "I live across the street from the Center for Expressive Therapies. They've taken over the parking lot all hours of the day and night, banging bongos, running around, screaming out their mantras."

"Call the police."

"I did. They just shrug. Say the center's good for the neighborhood. Provides the uniforms for the police softball team. Brings in commerce. As if those carrot juice drinkers, those sprout eaters would ever spend a buck at a proper bar." The thumping gets louder. The voices are yelling now. The words sound like *This land is your land*, though I have my doubts. "Can't you shut the windows?" I suggest.

"If only. I sweat something awful. After ten minutes, I stink like you'd never believe."

What can I say? Thanks for sharing? I step back as if a sample whiff is about to be spritzed over the line.

"But I'll shut them while I talk to you," he concedes, his voice that of a martyr on the verge of one too many self-sacrifices. I hear footsteps; I hear the window slam. "There." He sighs. He gets right to the point. "So, do you have a decent apartment? Quiet? With good light?"

I think of Clyde, how fast he left his room at the Y for my decent apartment with good light. Not to mention a wall to hang a bed warmer on. Not to mention the bed that abutted that wall. At least Clyde was a man who didn't stink. In the physical sense, let me qualify. "My apartment's okay," I allow.

"I've leased a studio for the time being. Week to week. But I'm looking for a better place to live." He chuckles. A stage laugh. "Do you have an extra room you want to rent?"

"My place is pretty small."

"Not as small as mine." He pauses. "We should get together."

I take a diversionary tack. When in doubt, ask them about themselves. "What do you do?"

"I'm selling ties at Macy's for the moment. Day job. In truth I'm a writer. I came here to work on my novel."

Red flags flare. But I've been brought up to be polite. "What's it about?"

"Thanks for asking. Between you and me and the bedpost, it's dynamite. Encompassing, as it does, all the themes of love, sex, betrayal, along with a gothic element." He hesitates. He hems. He haws. "Just want to make sure you're not a writer, too. I wouldn't want anyone to steal my idea. Ha. Ha. Ha."

"Rest assured."

He lowers his voice—maybe he's afraid the expressive therapists will tap out his plot in code to the rest of their tribe—and hisses into the phone. "It's about this empathic vampire born centuries ago who moves to Cambridge and then . . ." He stops. "Whew, I'm perspiring something terrible. Can we meet for coffee? My treat. And I'll tell you all about it?"

"I'm not sure that's a good idea."

"Why not?"

"Because I'm off men."

He laughs. I hear more footsteps; then the loud thumping and chanting resume. *My land. My land.* "I get it," he shouts over the din. "I want you to know that though I'm a registered Republican, I keep an open mind. To me it's a person's private matter what they do with their sexuality."

I take my pad Thai to the kitchen; I nuke it in the microwave. I eat it straight from the box. For only the most fleeting of seconds do I wonder if Emile Lambert—*lam-bear*—really *is* the spitting image of Brad Pitt.

After I've made coffee and watched the news, I check through my mail. How did I ever get on the list for every catalogue and mail-order house in the universe? I sort notices of auctions, a collector's fortieth anniversary, an announcement of the opening of a pizza shop. I stop. I fish out a thick, cream-colored envelope. I hold it up. There's my name, street, city, zip code calligraphied on the front. On the back flap, in tinier but equally elaborate letters, is Lavinia's return address. I tear it open. *We're getting married,* it announces, and gives a date four weeks hence, Sunday noon at the Faculty Club. Why would she hold her second wedding at the same place where she had her first? Why would she invite me, her former maid of honor, her ex-friend and current legal adversary? Who is now hard pressed to find any good words to say about her.

I remember my parents once returning from the funeral of the wife of a colleague, the colleague beloved, the wife despised. She was a mean, small-minded bigot who alienated everyone, even her own children. "What did the rabbi come up with for the eulogy?" I asked.

My father smiled. "That she was a regular and loyal reader of the daily newspaper and had supper on the table every night by six."

Now I study the engraved couple-to-be: Lavinia Potter-Templeton and John Cuthbert Tompkins. Will she become Lavinia Potter-Templeton-Tompkins? I wonder. If you're known professionally in the pages of the *Wall Street Journal, Crain's*, and *Fortune* as Lavinia Potter-Templeton, you can't just up and dump part of your name. I turn over the invitation. A Post-it is attached. Though hardly your ordinary yellow Staples off-the-counter brand. This Post-it is pearl gray scripted in maroon: *From the desk of Lavinia Potter-Templeton* trails down the left side.

Dear Abby, she has inscribed in her all-too-familiar anal hand. *It would mean so much to me for you to attend. We have lost too many family members. Can't we forgive and forget for old times' sake? Our mothers would have wanted it.*

I stare at the *Dear Abby*. I need to write in to Dear Abby herself. What is my obligation to attend an ex-friend's wedding? I want to ask. A person I was tempted to pay a needless thirty-seven thousand five hundred dollars to for something that clearly belonged to me. And yet if time heals, time also tamps down the red-hot flame of rage. *Dear Puzzled in Cambridge, Do what your mother would want you to do,* I'm more than sure Dear Abby would advise.

Before I can change my mind, I check salmon on the preferred-main-course reply card and seal the envelope.

I click on the television. I flip through the channels: reality TV, *Extreme Makeover* . . . I stop. I need an extreme makeover. But not the sort documented by the bruised and bandaged woman in front of me on the screen. *Liposuction, cheek implants, nose job, eye job, chin implant, breast implants,* a voice-over reports. What about a heart implant? I want to ask, a *hard*-heart implant?

I wrap myself in my heart-appliquéd quilt. Even if time can put a distance between me and Ned, time can't stuff that once-upon-a-time rabbit back in the hat without a twinge or two. He'll be at the wedding. Holding the hand of the tenure-track Columbia Ph.D. professor who shares his apartment and—presumably—his bed. I change channels again. Another reality show. What are the signs here? Time for me to face reality? Abigail Elizabeth Randolph has a nice, full life now. Without the encumbrances of a man. Time to move on.

I move on. To a movie channel. *When Harry Met Sally . . .* A man and a woman meant for each other who don't hook up until after a lot of near misses and way too many years. I make a bowl of popcorn. I can barely eat a kernel. I am too angry. How dumb can you be, I want to scream at Harry and Sally, not to notice you belong together? Though it's pegged as a comedy, I don't laugh. Even during the I'll-have-what-she's-having scene. I pause. I ponder. Would I choose to have what the Columbia tenure-track woman is having? Is that—Ned—something I want?

No you don't, my superego weighs in. *Remember what Ned did to you.*

You're right, I agree.

I watch Harry and Sally mature and head toward wedding bells. *You're wrong,* I correct.

Forget about it.

I want this.

No you don't.

Yes I do.

No you don't.

Back and forth wages the battle with myself like the duet in the Annie Oakley musical. Finally a third voice kicks in: *Yes I do, no I don't* are both beside the point, it concludes, because *No you can't!* I dump the popcorn in the garbage and go to bed.

16

Here's Bergson's theory of time again: in the way that what you dread shows up faster than what you eagerly await, four weeks have flown right by. Today is Lavinia's wedding day. I'm getting dressed, putting on my new frock, new shoes, combing my newly shorn and for-a-small-fortune highlighted locks. Talk about extreme makeover. Along with its even more extreme cost: the sale of two ironstone pitchers, a pine blanket chest, a silver-headed walking stick, three Godey prints, and a pair of brass candlesticks. Money that should have gone for rent, health plan payments, my estimated tax, charity.

No matter. Once in a while a person needs to be frivolous. Looking good, girl, I salute myself. I went to Saks and, for the first time ever, didn't flick away those cosmetics-counter ladies who swoop down on us blank canvases like Picasso on commission, rapacious as a vulture with an unlipsticked carcass in its sights. I bought enough products that the lady, "Krystal with a *K*," threw in a paint-by-numbers manual that should have carried the warning *Hazardous: Don't try this at home*. Still, after I practiced for a week, I managed to come up with an acceptable and diluted version of Krystal's thickly applied, over-the-top transvestite mask. The last time so much gunk clogged my pores was during my appearance on *Antiques Roadshow*. And you know how that turned out. Speaking of which, I would have been better off putting my efforts into an astrological chart: *Don't make any rash purchases,* yesterday's Sagittarius report warned. From the amount of money, time, care I've put into preparing myself for Lavinia's wedding, you'd expect me to be the bride.

Now I admire my enhanced skin and scarlet lips. My spruced-up self. I adjust the collar on my bias-cut pale green silk. Have I ever looked this glittering? This glamorous?

Immediately I blush with shame. I'm a traitor to my class. The Randolphs and the Granbys are cut from the same cloth as those Boston Brahmins who, so the legend goes, never *buy* their hats, they simply *have* them. They frown on style, on fashion; as far as personal adornment is concerned, they make do. Perhaps it's a matter of geography: cold New England winters, understated New England architecture, distrust of the new.

Now that's he's in La Jolla, my father's certainly adapted to the more flamboyant scenery. Would I ever in a million years have pictured him in those garish parrot-and-palm-tree shirts, driving a red MG, a bright blue swimming pool stamped on his envelope-shaped backyard? I thought I had my father typecast: tyrannical Harvard professor. Dour New England intellectual. Set in stone. Dyed in the wool. Immutable. Immovable. And now he's turned into what? A Zelig figure who takes on the colorations of his new landscape and mouths the pop phrases of those who inhabit it.

Unlike my mother. For years my mother bought her winter coat at Max Keezer's near Harvard Square, an ordinary secondhand clothing store. She stopped when other people's discarded sweaters and skirts were upgraded to vintage, when Keezer's advertised antique attire and began to specialize in tuxedos, when rich college kids started raiding its bins and prices soared to parallel the increased cachet. And yet even with my mother, there were surprises. Hadn't I also slotted her? Hadn't I characterized and dismissed her as the Harvard professor's wife, the smart sturdy helpmate who stood by her man and never complained? Would I ever have dreamed she'd run off with Henrietta? Would Mr. Barrett ever have imagined the invalid Elizabeth would leave her bed, let alone elope to Italy with Robert, a poet six years younger?

Can you ever know anybody? Let me qualify this: Can you ever know anybody, especially when that person is under the power of a great love? Maybe it's not the landscape that changes you but love. It happened to my father. It happened to my mother. I shake my head at my mirrored self. Not that it will ever happen to me.

Still, as an homage to the past, I decide to clip on the pearl earrings my father bought my mother for their fifteenth anniversary. After the cake and champagne, he'd handed them over in their Shreve, Crump & Lowe purple velvet box. *Oh, how lovely!* my mother had exclaimed. *But much too extravagant, dear.* She snapped the box shut. As far as I can remember, she never wore them. Not even once.

After she left, my father passed them on to me. *You might as well have these,* he said, sighing, then tossed the by-default gift in my direction as you would a tennis ball to a dog.

The earrings are somewhere here in the jewelry tray I not so long ago neatened up. Though I've made an amazing assault on the clutter in the process of washing that inner wimp right out of my hair, my surroundings will never qualify for *House Beautiful.* I remember a couple from an outer suburb who, years ago, moved into our neighborhood. Painters suited up the minute the clapboard started to fleck. The wife scrubbed the front steps. Her husband washed their Mercedes every Saturday afternoon. Invited in for get-acquainted tea, we were ordered to take off our shoes. *The white carpeting,* our hostess explained. Magazines squared off at right angles; each vase contained one single perfect rose. If you dropped a crumb, a handheld vacuum appeared at your feet to suck up any trace.

Obsessive cleanliness is a sign of the lower classes, my father, back in his own cracked and stained leather chair, declaimed, *contrary to Dickens's depiction of the great unwashed.* I looked around our rambling house, our shabby rooms. I took in our threadbare rugs, our chipped china and distressed wood, the old portraits with the flaking gold leaf, the out-of-date L.L.Bean catalogues our parents ordered their wardrobes from.

Within months our disapproving neighbors sold at a loss and moved away.

And I realized I had developed a love of the old, the used, the chipped, a love of everything, if not *everyone,* I grew up with.

I have to search through three drawers before I find the earring box. It's hidden under a pile of old-fashioned black-and-white elementary-school composition books. At random, I stick my hand in and choose one. Across its cover loops my own name in my childish red-crayoned scrawl. I flip it open to the middle. *My Trip* titles the top of the page. Illustrated with a rudimentary drawing of a cow and pig. *I had fun,* I read. *I patted a reel gote.* Following this riveting account is a list of people on the trip. I study the names. Some faces rise up bright as diamonds; others have vanished into the past. *Peeple I reely like are underlined,* I wrote. *Peeple half underlined I don't hate that much.* I check the list again. I may not have been the kind of stellar student to win a spelling bee, but I was people—peeple!—smart. Ned's name is fully underlined; Lavinia's only half.

And in another fifty minutes I'll be seeing both of them. One really liked; the other, not hated that much. *Plus ça change . . .* I put on the earrings. I admire myself in the mirror. All my efforts were worth it, I decide—I wipe some lipstick off my teeth—if only to give me the confidence to get through the hours ahead.

The wedding takes place in the Faculty Club library. Which looks just as you'd expect: leather armchairs, dark paneling, twin globes flanking a fireplace, vellum-bound volumes, portraits of former college presidents, a Gilbert Stuart Washington, a seventeenth-century map of Harvard Yard, a framed page from the Gettysburg address. The guest list is tastefully second-wedding-appropriate: a small scattering of businessmen and -women in their severe, expensively cut suits. I spot the groom by the lily in his lapel. He's standing in front of the mantelpiece, a tall thin man wearing a bow tie whose skimpy patch of mousy-colored hair is receding at the temples. He's flanked by a group of other soon-to-be-middle-aged men sporting assorted variations on the same theme of blue blazer, gray flannel pants, button-down shirt, rep tie; they look like a gathering of Dartmouth fraternity brothers who've barely outgrown Animal House; they're tossing back highballs, even before the I do's.

I decline the offer of a drink; I wave away an approaching tray of white wine. I'll need to keep my wits about me. To get through the ceremony. To figure out how quickly I can escape. *I'm doing this for the sake of our mothers,* I repeat. *Our mothers would have wanted this.* Just as I'm extolling my unselfishness, my superhuman effort to fulfill duties I would never set for myself, I hear a niggling inner voice: *Cut the crap, Abby,* it says. *Our mothers wouldn't have given a damn about all the effort—on their so-called behalf—that you took to look this good.* I spy Ned over in the corner talking to an elderly couple, colleagues of Uncle Bick's and my father's, whose names have disappeared into a gray sea of ancient professorial blur. I scan the rest of the room again. I wonder which one of the enormously competent and attractive women is Ned's heart's desire.

Ned sees me. He lifts his hand. He waves. And flashes me a smile of such blinding delight I'm sure that I've inadvertently stepped inside the path of a beam directed toward somebody else. I turn to see who's standing behind me, but it's only a waiter helping old Professor Moran off with his coat.

I take a little gilded bamboo seat in the back row. The ceremony itself is appropriately short and minus frills. Lavinia, in beige, a hers-to-match-his lily tucked behind her ear, appears from a side door to stand next to her groom. I breathe a sigh of relief. I'm spared watching Ned walk her down the aisle. There are no Emily Dickinson poems or Bach études, no write-your-own vows. Faster than the speed of light, Lavinia Potter-Templeton-Tompkins and John Cuthbert Tompkins-Potter are declared bride and groom. The groom plants a kiss somewhere left of center on the bride's mouth. Everyone claps. Professor Moran snores.

A well-brought-up wedding guest can't avoid the receiving line. When I reach Lavinia, she hugs me. "Abby!" she exclaims. "I've never seen you look so good. It means so much to me that you agreed to come." She squeezes my shoulder. "I've put you between Professor Moran and Professor Lowenthal for lunch. They were such friends of your parents, I knew you'd be pleased."

John Cuthbert Tompkins-Potter pumps my hand. "A pleasure," he says. "Livvy has told me so much about you." I'm a little flattered until I hear him say the exact same thing to the man whose hand he pumps right after mine.

But when I make my way to my table (the farthest from the bridal party, the closest to the kitchen—why am I not surprised?) I find Ned in the seat where I'd expected Professor Moran to be getting more zzz's.

He pops up. He pulls out my chair. "I switched the place cards." He grins at me.

"Lavinia will be pissed."

"Screw Lavinia."

I am inordinately pleased. I sit down. It's clear table nine has been designated Faculty Club headquarters of the AARP—white hair, hearing aids, canes hooked over the backs of chairs, someone's digitalis tablets set out next to the water glass. Place setting by place setting, you'll spot nobody under seventy except Ned and me.

I look around. False teeth and partial plates and cataracts and thick lenses blink up at me. "Where's . . . ?" I begin. I don't even know her name.

"Who?"

"Your"—I pause—"significant other. Lavinia told me you were living with someone. A professor. At Columbia. That it was serious."

"Lavinia." He spits out the name like a sour lemon. "She, Juliet, has flown the coop. I must confess I'm rather relieved."

Me, too, I think, though the relief of one Abigail Randolph hardly amounts to a hill of beans. So she's Juliet, I marvel. Leaving Romeo with what? The rent? A too-big bed? A broken heart? Somehow Ned doesn't look that brokenhearted. And I know for a fact he's not the actor his sister is. But maybe I'm deluding myself. "What happened?" I ask. "Not that it's any of my business," I add with fake humility.

"When my publisher dropped me . . ." he begins.

I lean forward. "Your publisher dropped you?"

He nods. "As you are well aware, my first book bombed. Rightly so." He stops. "Abby, I feel so rotten . . ."

I steel my heart. "Go on," I order.

"I had a two-book contract, which required the publisher to look at and approve what I wrote next. I'm afraid the second book was even more of a disaster. I knew it. I didn't bother to finish it." He straightens the silverware. He lines up the salt and pepper.

I watch his graceful hands. I picture Elizabeth and Robert's "tiny, but iconic" plaster clasp. I look at my own fingers splayed across the tablecloth.

Ned clears his throat. "If, as they say, everybody has one book in him, I'm proof. I wrote *The Cambridge Ladies Who Live in Furnished Souls* as therapy. It was a young man's book, by a callow twenty-something who tried to make sense of his life, to work out his problems with his family, to record all the joy of his first love . . ." He stops. He looks away.

I hold my breath.

He turns toward me. "Abby, I'm no novelist. And when it was clear to Juliet there'd be no more books, no money, and no fame, and that I was going to leave New York for Cambridge . . ."

I clutch my fork. I dig the tines into my palm. "You're coming back?"

He nods. "With my advance for *The Cambridge Ladies,* I bought a bicycle shop in Kendall Square. You know how I love bikes, how I was always tinkering . . ."

I nod my head. I remember those bikes locked to the rails of the front porch. The derelicts ready to be rehabilitated. The shiny new ones, multicolored streamers flaring from their gleaming chrome. I see Ned with wrenches and screwdrivers making adjustments, spinning wheels. As a kid, he was always fastening bells on handlebars, attaching cards to spokes. Later, he'd hold out for himself the carrot stick of rides along the Charles after a day's writing. Then burst out the front door like a trapped animal just sprung from captivity. I can still freeze-frame the joy mapping his face when he climbed on his bike, when he set out on the path to Concord. I picture his thighs in their tight black Lycra shorts. His cute little butt. My throat closes. I make myself stop.

"I can't believe you didn't think of this sooner. In retrospect, it seems so obvious, so perfect."

"It took me a while to admit that. What son of Cambridge professors ends up in overalls, down and dirty, fixing flywheels, calibrating brake alignments . . . ?" He shakes his head. "You of all people understand."

"We both had to fight against that Harvard thing. We both had to separate from our parents, figure out what we wanted to do for ourselves."

He nods. He waits. "And who we wanted to do it with."

I turn away. I make a joke. "What would our fathers have thought? A junk dealer? A bike repairman?"

"To hell with them."

The first course is served. My stomach is in knots. How can I digest a lettuce leaf when I can barely digest this? Ned's coming back. Juliet has flown the coop. Will there be peace once more between the Montagues and the Capulets? At least between two members of the opposing tribes? I reach for the wine. Maybe I won't be getting out of here as fast as I thought. And what does he mean by *who we wanted to do it with*?

Just then, Professor Lowenthal puts his hand on my arm. "Abigail, how is your dear father these days?"

It's a welcome diversion. Breathing room. I focus my gaze on two rheumy blue eyes. I smile. "Fine," I say. "He likes La Jolla."

"How am I?" Professor Lowenthal nearly yells. "How kind of you to ask. Except for my knees, I'm the picture of health for a man my age."

"That's great," I applaud.

"What's late?" he asks. He cups his hand on his ear. "You'll have to speak up."

Fortunately the *saumon en croûte* arrives under its silver dome; the waiter distributes the sauce. He refills the wineglasses; Professor Lowenthal's attention drifts. "Nice hat," he says to the woman across the table whose feathery concoction has clearly been passed down through generations of Brahmin wives.

I turn to Ned. "I can't take this all in."

"I'm not surprised." He dips his head. "After my book came out, after all the awful repercussions, I called you. I wrote you . . ."

"But I never . . . You couldn't have."

"I did. Not that I deserved any response. But I sent so many letters, left so many plaintive apologies on your answering machine that I must have stuffed your mailbox, jammed your tape." He stops. "Abby, I understand why you'd erase the messages, throw away the letters without opening them."

Clyde, I think. *Clyde,* I curse. "I didn't get the messages. Or the letters."

"No excuses necessary. I don't blame you for not answering. I was horrible. I know you felt betrayed." He holds up his hands in an I-surrender, guilty-as-charged pose. "I was horrible," he repeats.

Was he horrible? Back then I was sure of it. And now? Has my anger faded? Have I gotten over my sense of having been used, exploited. Betrayed. Or is it this wine—I take another sip—that is responsible for my temporary inclination to forgive if not to forget.

"I have so much to say to you, Abby," he says.

I'm saved by the champagne. It's time for the toasts. Though I can barely register their words. *Wonderful wife, charming husband, marriage made in heaven, the path of true love will this time run smooth . . .*

The path of true love . . .

"Ned?" Lavinia is searching the room. She shades her eyes with her newly beringed hand. Her head bobs from table to table. "Ned, where are you?"

Ned stands up. He raises his glass.

"Whatever are you doing way over there? I distinctly planned—" She catches herself. "Ned, don't you have something to say?" She turns to her guests. "My brother, my brother the *writer,* has written a toast."

Ned reaches into his pocket. He brings out a clump of paper. He looks at it. He looks at me. He sticks the clump back into his pocket. He searches the opposite one. "Here it is," he says. He opens an envelope. "I'm going to turn to another writer—since I am no longer one—who says it better. For my sister, Lavinia, and her groom, John, on this glorious day." He clears his throat. "Elizabeth Barrett Browning—sonnet fourteen. *From the Portuguese,*" he introduces.

"If thou must love me, let it be for nought
Except for love's sake only. Do not say
'I love her for her smile—her look—her way
Of speaking gently,—for a trick of thought
That falls in well with mine, and certes brought
A sense of pleasant ease on such a day'—
For these things in themselves, Beloved, may
Be changed, or change for thee,—and love, so wrought,
May be unwrought so. Neither love me for
Thine own dear pity's wiping my cheeks dry,—
A creature might forget to weep, who bore
Thy comfort long, and lose thy love thereby!
But love me for love's sake, that evermore
Thou may'st love on, through love's eternity."

Ned hoists his glass higher.

"Hear! Hear!" the guests cry out.

He holds my eye. "Through love's eternity," he repeats.

After the cake and the groom's patently pained look when Lavinia shoves a forkful of white icing into his mouth and before the coffee, Ned grabs my hand. "Let's get out of here."

We find a love seat in the corner of the downstairs lounge, empty except for a man dozing under a crumpled copy of the *Manchester Guardian*. Our thighs touch. *Move over*, my brain relays. My leg doesn't get the message; my thigh stays locked in place. *You've been warned*, I Mirandize my stubborn, quivering flesh.

From his pocket Ned takes out the clump of paper he'd brought out earlier, then exchanged for the fourteenth sonnet of *From the Portuguese*. I gaze at it. Thin, air-weight pages as creased and folded as a fine linen handkerchief sold at the antique fabric booth at Objects of Desire. "What is this?"

He pries open my fingers. He sets the pages in my hand. Gently he closes my fist over them. "I've wanted to give this to you forever. But it was too late. It seemed unfair . . ." His voice trails off; his hand clasps mine.

"What is it?" I ask again. A lock of his hair falls across his forehead. I reach over. I brush it away. How silky it is; how silky it was; the memory seared into my fingertips. "Ned?"

"I received this after our mothers died. A long time after. My mother must have written it just before the earthquake. Maybe someone—a Good Samaritan—found it on the street. Or in the ruins of their hotel. And put it in the mail."

My hand tightens on the pages. "My God!" I turn to him. "And you never told me? Never thought to tell me?"

"I wanted to a million times. But it came too late. Seemed unfair to you after you had so clearly, and justly, decided . . ." He shakes his head. "It must have been sent on a slow boat from India. It turned up—like those letters in the movies—much too late to change the course of devastating events."

"Who can control the force of nature? Who can prevent an earthquake?"

"Not that. The devastating effect of my book. The sign of an amateur and self-involved novelist, one who can't transform fact into fiction. Who hurts the last person he'd ever want to."

"I *was* hurt. Utterly shocked. I never could have imagined when I let you in on my secrets, when I laid bare my soul . . ."

"And why should you have?"

"I told you everything. All my adolescent insecurities, how I felt about my mother and Henrietta, how I failed to live up to my father's expectations, my hopes, my dreams. You used me, Ned."

His voice is a whisper. "I know."

I shake my head. Being used by men seems to have become a recurring theme in my life. Not anymore. I'm no longer that person. I resume my litany of injustices. I can't help myself. "These were my secrets, my deepest, most private feelings, meant for you, for you alone. Not for every reader with a library card or twenty-five bucks to buy a book."

"I was an asshole, Abby. A stupid, selfish prick. You probably won't believe how rotten I've felt about this, how much I regret everything. I've changed. I'm no longer that person. Can you ever forgive me? Can I ever make it up to you?"

I stare at him. I tap the letter. "Shall I read it?"

"Please." He gets up. "Let me reenlist for a stint of brother-to-the-bride hardship duty. You'll probably want to read this by yourself." He smiles. A sad clown's smile. "But I'll be back."

"You'd better" comes out before I can even think of how to answer him.

I glance across the room. The *Manchester Guardian* rises and falls with the dozing man's every breath like a tent in full wind. Next to the window the grandfather clock ticks. A muffled sound of chatter comes from the front hall. I open the letter.

Henrietta writes:

> My dearest Ned,
>
> I've been thinking of you a lot these days. Funny how when one is in the midst of exotic places, excited, overstimulated, drunk on art and color and love, one's thoughts can surprisingly turn to home. Maybe it's my own happiness that makes me want the same for everyone I love.
>
> I worry about you. Much more than about your sister, who seems and always seemed utterly capable of taking care of herself, completely aware of what she wanted and determined to get it. Of course I'm afraid that her relationships don't measure up to the other demands she puts

on herself. But I don't think this bothers her. Introspection isn't one of her talents. She's lucky that way.

Unlike you. And me. Unlike Emily, and dare I say Abigail, too. We navel watchers. We empathetic creatures. Bleeding hearts, your father used to call us, without implying the usual political connotation—though as iconic members of our species, Cambridge academic agnostic Unitarians—we are that, also.

I worry about you. I worry that you had a misleading, unfairly eccentric, confining childhood, that you felt you had to live up to expectations and ideals that weren't your own. Perhaps you had to write that novel because, by process of elimination—law, medicine, academia, business—that was what was left and maybe the struggle to put your odd childhood down on paper was a kind of therapy.

No, Emily and I were not hurt by any revelations in your book. We are beyond that. But I understand from Emily and from your current situation that Abby was hurt. I'm sure you were surprised and at the same time I am sure you are starting to understand why. Let's blame the book on the callousness of youth, something I have no doubt you've learned from. Not to diminish the achievement of publishing a novel, I sense nevertheless that you're not really a writer in your heart and soul.

You need to decide who you are and what you want to do. If it's making doughnuts, then I'm sure you will be the best doughnut maker in the whole world. Don't let your childhood, the Harvard thing dictate your own choices. While some of your classmates have thrived, many other children of these families are unhappy, adrift, bitter, estranged from their parents. You can probably name half a dozen or more of your friends who fit this category.

Though never ever would I count you among them. You

have so many gifts. And a big, generous heart. I trust it will take you a shorter time than it took me, who finally made the leap at fifty-five, to find yourself. But you're smarter, and yours is a different generation.

Here's what's important: work you love; people you love. You need to figure out the work. Emily and I think you already have the love, if you can come around to see it for yourself. We're experts now. What we want for our children is the happiness we've found. As your mothers, as the not so neutral observers of your growing pains, we can point out that the greatest leitmotif in your and Abby's life has been each other. You may not know it, but we know it. You are meant for each other. Maybe the love is a little broken now. Fragmented by bad choices. But it can be mended. Once you find yourselves, the work you love, you'll find each other.

I know you can dismiss this letter as maternal meddling, and you'd be justified. But it seemed the right time to put this down on paper just as we are about to leave to see the Taj Mahal, that monument to love. And because it's a glorious day, beauty and color and smells and spices assault our every sense, and I want you to have this. The beauty, the joy of life, the love. I know you can—with a little motherly prod.

We'll be back in Cambridge in a week. Bearing exotic spices, saris for Abby and Lavinia, a charming miniature of a bicycle race over the hills of Calcutta for you.

With love always, your mother

For a long time I sit on the love seat. I take off my shoes. I hug my knees to my chin. I read the letter two more times. I look across the room half expecting to see my mother and Henrietta sitting there, saris on their laps, exotic spices at their feet. But I see only the sleeping man, whose newspaper has now slid to the floor. No matter. I feel their presence. They're still in the stands cheering us on. Their words are alive. *These* words are a gift. I picture them arm in arm in front of the Taj Mahal. Figures you might dismiss as dull, as nondescript. But beneath the drab gray sparkle souls as romantic as Romeo and Juliet, as Robert and Elizabeth. With wisdom earned from a never-ending journey of self-discovery. *I have at last now discovered true joy. Pure ecstasy*, my mother's postcard had said. I hold Henrietta's pages close to my heart.

All at once, there's a commotion. I turn. Wedding guests are skipping down the stairs and out the front door. The ex–fraternity brothers are throwing rice at Lavinia and John. The tastefully suited businesswomen clutch the floral centerpieces they've liberated from the wedding tables; they jump up and down. The lumbering geriatric contingent takes up the rear. Someone drops a champagne glass.

I feel a hand on my shoulder. "You read it?" Ned asks.

I nod. I pass the letter back to him. My carefully made-up eyes fill. Ned grabs me.

Right there in front of everybody, in front of his sister and his father's colleagues, in front of Ph.D.s and CEOs and M.B.A.s, in front of his new brother-in-law and his old neighbors, in front of the caterer and half the staff of the Harvard Faculty Club, he gives me the kind of kiss a groom gives a bride, the kind of kiss her own groom never gave Lavinia.

17

Ned calls me from the road. "I'm in Hartford," he announces.

I look at my watch. "Then you'll be here in an hour and a half."

"Not quite. Add another hour. I need to make a stop along the way."

"Oh," I say. I want to ask who, what, when, where, and why—the questions any good J-school student would learn in the first week of the first term. I don't. I'm working on the trust thing. Which is hard, considering my past experiences.

Ned understands. "All will be revealed when I see you. I'll tell you everything."

I skip around the living room. I actually dance cheek-to-cheek with the phone, like some hokey Hollywood musical star. In two and a half hours Ned will be ringing my bell. Ned will be walking up my stairs . . .

After Lavinia's wedding, Ned had to leave immediately for New York. To clear out his side of the apartment, to take care of his bills, to pack up his books.

"Are you renting a U-Haul?" I asked. I was standing on the steps of the Faculty Club, pulling rice out of my hair, rubbing my kiss-stung lips. Everyone had left except Professor Lowenthal, who was waiting inside the doors for his driver to pick him up.

Ned laughed. "I don't think I'll even begin to fill the old '87 Volvo wagon."

"You're kidding! You still have it? It's still running?"

"Better than ever. And I can park it on the streets of New York with no worry about theft." He shook his head. "It may be dented and rusted, missing a few knobs, but it's still there."

I smiled. I had fond memories of the Potters' stately tank; the two-family trips, the car pools. I used to stare longingly at the back of Ned's neck from the cargo area where Lavinia and I had staked out our girlie giggling territory. We could play crazy eights, wave at tailgating drivers, stick our feet flat against the rear window and admire our sparkly pearl-polished toenails. I wonder if the car still bears the remains of a vinyl purse I left in it one hot summer day. The purse melted and fused onto the backseat, a fried egg of purple and pink polka dots. *Your spoor,* Ned once called it. *For weeks that smell was terrible*, he used to tease. *It was hard not to be reminded of you, such a stench every time I opened the driver's door.*

I cradle the receiver. "Any fights?" I ask now. "Any disputes over property?"

"Are you trawling for clients for Mary Agnes Finch?"

"I wouldn't wish that experience on anyone. *Almost* anyone," I correct.

"It was an amiable parting. Most of the stuff was Juliet's anyway.

She hardly wanted my bicycle paraphernalia. Or my books. She was glad to see the back of me."

No gladder than I to see the front of him. I hear whooshing cars. The blast of a horn. The revving of an engine.

"I'd better watch the road. Abby, I'll be there soon." The phone breaks into static—not crackling enough, even so, to disguise his "I can't wait."

I sit back on the sofa and admire my spanking-clean apartment. Ned's moving in. No, he didn't ask. It was my idea. I swear. He was going to bunk with a friend while he looked for a place to live.

"I think I can make room in my closet for a few mechanic's uniforms," I told him.

"You're sure?"

I took a deep breath. "I'm sure," I said. I didn't add, Never surer of anything in my life, though that's how I felt. Far be it from Abigail Elizabeth Randolph to tempt fate.

In the usual way that what you most want to happen takes forever, I tried to fill the days waiting for Ned to wind up his life in New York. I pulled those clean and ironed sheets so tight, tucked those corners into such perfect little hospital envelopes, even the most exacting marine sergeant would find nothing to grouse about. I arranged the heap of glossy bike magazines on Ned's side of the bed—*Asphalt, Ride, Bicycling*. I bought them yesterday at the kiosk in Harvard Square. "What a bundle," the man commiserated, dividing them into two bags so I wouldn't lose my balance on the way home. I held a bag in each hand like the scales of justice. Contrary to Gladstone's quote, however, in my case, justice was delayed but not denied. I tested the weight. I hefted my load. I pictured the colonial oxen yoke hanging on the wall just as you entered Objects of Desire. I thought of burdens: the burdens of the past, the balancing acts of the present, the different ways people managed to lighten such loads throughout history. "Are you a bike lover?" the man asked.

"No, my boyfriend," I said. I must admit it gave me a thrill to roll that word off my tongue. "My boyfriend," I said again, savoring the syllables.

"Too bad." The man winked. "All the good ones are taken, I guess."

At last, after the eternity in which I could have read *War and Peace*, watched all six seasons of *Sex and the City*, knitted a scarf and matching mittens, and mastered the French subjunctive, my bell rings.

I would have fallen into his arms right then and there except for the large package he holds out in front of him. The way he's carrying it, it could be the nine-month stomach of a pregnant woman about to deliver twins. I remember, what now seems like centuries ago, my own toting of the chamber pot. Ned puts his box down. We manage a few soulful kisses, tongues and lips and bodies pressed so hard together you'd expect black and blue bruises to rise on all the squished flesh-to-flesh parts. We can't get around to doing anything else because the Volvo, three bikes lashed to its rack, Ned's worldly goods stacked inside, is double-parked on Cambridge Street. "I'll just be a minute," Ned says.

"I'm going with you." I grab his elbow. "I'm not letting you out of my sight."

We untie the bikes and chain them to the water-heater pipes in the communal basement. We lug a laundry bag of clothes, a couple of cartons of books and CDs, toolboxes, Ned's computer. It only takes four arms and two trips up my three flights of stairs. "Is that all?" I ask, incredulous. I think of the first day of my freshman year at college. How many times had my mother and I driven the five blocks from my house to my tiny two-person dormitory room, the car so crammed with my stuff that its back end nearly dragged along the street? Not even taking into consideration that half my clothes remained stored at home on a seasonal need-to-use basis.

Ned smiles. He looks around my neat but still cabinet-of-curiosities, house-of-a-collector, object-stuffed space. "Jack Sprat and his wife," he pronounces.

Though abstractly I know what he means, in reality the only word I can focus on is *wife*. But because I've adjusted my personal twelve-step program into a made-to-order one step at a time, I turn my attention to something else. To the box now sitting in the middle of my living room floor. I point. "What's that?" I ask.

"It's for you. Actually for us," he amends. "We'll have joint custody."

A phrase that for a second turns me to ice, its negative repercussions all too fresh in mind and heart, not to mention pocketbook.

Ned shakes his head. His voice is gentle. "Don't worry. I don't anticipate any disputes." He hands me his Swiss army knife, its box cutter already flipped out. "Open it," Ned orders. "It's the reason I was late."

I slice the knife through the tape. I scoop away the packing: crumpled paper from scribbled-on yellow legal pads, shredded pages from journals awash in op. cit.s, and ibid.s, recycled sections of the *New York Times Book Review*.

"Ned!" I cry out.

What I see tucked in the box, a treasure buried in its treasure chest, is Professor and Mrs. Chauncey Coolidge Thayer's pale blue china soup tureen. "Ned!" I shout again. "I don't believe it!" Gently I lift it from the box. Gently I place it on the table. I touch the dancing cupids. I trace the outline of birds and butterflies. I stroke the picturesque ruins next to the gushing waterfalls. I gape at Ned.

"They wanted us to have it," Ned explains, his voice the sort of hush-in-the-cathedral whisper you'd use to contemplate a sacred artifact.

Now is the time for a who, what, when, where, why J-school interrogation, but I am speechless. I run my hand over the fine china, over the classic contours of the tureen the just-married Thayers bought together in Italy. On their honeymoon.

Ned reads my mind. "Do you remember, they got this in Italy on their honeymoon?"

I nod my head. Tears prick my eyes.

"They called me up. They've sold their apartment; they're moving into an assisted-living home. They wanted us to have the tureen. They emphasized particularly that it was for both of us. *For you and your lovely Abigail,* were Mrs. Thayer's exact words." He pauses. "Mrs. Thayer said her husband was so grateful. Of course I told her that her thanks was more than enough, that I got more pleasure from those trips than Professor Thayer ever could. I told her I couldn't possibly . . ."

Go on, I nod.

"But she said her husband spoke often of that trip to St. Barnaby's, of how the both of us had come for sherry afterward. How we were so much in love." He stops. "I went there for tea, to pick it up."

"And how are they? Are they okay?"

"Remarkable. Chauncey just turned ninety. Mrs. Thayer is still on her bicycle. I promised to come to make some modifications. I promised I'd bring you. They're excited about their new apartment; they're going to turn it into something quite modern this time, they told me. Mrs. Thayer's already found a source for old Marimekko upholstery."

I touch the tureen. "Ned . . ." I begin.

"I know," he says.

We're both quiet for a while. It's a comfortable silence. What hovers unsaid between us is eloquent enough. Perhaps we were always on the same wavelength, even when our synapses sparked off onto anomalous detours. I lift the lid of the tureen. I move my face closer. I can almost smell the traces of thousands of lovingly prepared thin consommés, thick chowders, hearty soups. I set the lid back. Maybe I went into the antiques business because of the power of objects, their ability to connote so many things, the inanimate made animate by memory, feeling, history. Or maybe I chose my profession simply because of the way a piece of porcelain, a plaster cast, a well-used, well-cherished tool can act as a touchstone for love.

I rub my finger over a chubby cupid. I look up at Ned. "I remember bringing the cocktail things into the kitchen and seeing this there," I say now. "Mrs. Thayer was talking about her honeymoon in Italy. She said that more than sixty years later, every time she served a lobster bisque in this tureen, she remembered how happy she'd been. She said it was her madeleine."

"It could be ours, too," Ned suggests. He walks over to me. He takes my hand.

I squeeze his fingers. "What a day." I sigh.

He pulls me toward my impeccably made bed. "It's not over yet." He grins.

Here's where I draw a curtain. Please forgive a digression right at the good part, but I'll explain. I once went to a reading at the Harvard Bookstore—not *that* reading, which, as you already know, I boycotted, but the reading of someone I was slightly friendly with at college. She had just published her first novel. She talked about how hard it was to write a sex scene. "There are only so many places body parts can go, only so many positions two bodies can contort themselves into," she said. "The English language is far too limited. How many words do we have for pounding hearts, heated flesh, exchange of fluids?" She gazed out at us. "How do you find a way to describe passion, a way that's really fresh?"

I can't. I'm no writer. And Ned, who once was, is not a writer anymore. Thank God.

So, in that spirit, while I'm not about to give you details, neither am I going to obfuscate with coy train-enters-the-tunnel imagery or the corny waves-crashing-to-shore symbolism and especially not that overused Hemingway earthmoving cliché.

Just know that every second, every word, every touch, every breath—all of it is absolutely wonderful.

Now Ned and I lie postcoitally in bed, fingers laced, legs as latticed as a cherry pie. Ned is making lists, counting sugarplums. "So we'll get married at St. Barnaby's; we'll honeymoon at Casa Guidi . . ." he begins.

I put my finger to his lips. *Shhh,* I want to warn. *It's too soon. Let's stay in the present. Let's take it one day at a time.*

But I don't. Maybe you can make a case for throwing caution to the wind, for daring a risk, for tossing away your crutches and hazarding a leap, for rising from your bed and running off to Italy with the one you love. Knowing your father wouldn't approve, knowing you'd stir his wrath.

Our fathers, however—Ned's and mine—would grant us a solemn nod of endorsement. *Well done,* they might allow. Our mothers, on the other hand, would be turning cartwheels on the bridges over the Arno, along the columned arcades of the Taj Mahal. Their screams of delight would sail past red-tiled roofs, Gothic towers, ridged pagodas, across oceans and deserts and into our bedroom windows in Cambridge, Massachusetts, with no diminution in decibels. Right now I sense them looking down on us, beaming, nodding, saying we told you so. Saying we knew it all along.

"Our mothers would be so happy," Ned affirms. "I feel they're here with us." He laughs. "Well, not precisely *right* here," he qualifies.

Once more he rolls over onto me. "Darling," he whispers. "Abby." He sighs. We begin again—tunnel, waves, Hemingway—you know the routine by now.

Our bed sways and creaks. Like an old Viking boat at sea in a terrible storm. Maybe louder, maybe in a different way from before. But it's a sound that registers only in the deepest recesses, a sound we, otherwise engaged, pay no attention to.

Until there's a startling crack: the bed frame splinters apart. Our mattress and its platform of plywood slats crash to the floor. Bringing on the pounded broomstick of the man downstairs.

Dumbfounded, we just lie there, our voices stopped, our limbs frozen; victims of traumatic shock, stunned in the wake of a bomb. This explosion, this *bedwreck*, is so surprising, so sudden, that it takes me, the princess on the pea, a few seconds to realize our landing is not flat, that we have crashed on top of Elizabeth Barrett Browning's chamber pot.

We get up. We start to move, sifting through the rubble that once was our bed. We pull away the tangled, wood-stabbed sheets, we kick away spears of splintered oak; we slide the mattress to the side, pry up the broken boards.

And stare at the lopsided aftermath.

"Maybe the Bubble Wrap . . . ?" I start, trying to grab onto a raft of hope.

Ned shakes his head. His voice is gentle, the kind of tone calibrated for the delivery of bad news. "Not even a chamber pot tucked inside Mary Agnes Finch's vault would have survived this"—he bends over—"this debacle." He starts to peel off the Bubble Wrap the way a surgeon might unwind his patient's bandages, all the while fearing a the-operation-was-a-success-but-the-patient-died result.

Ned pulls me to him. We survey the ruins of the chamber pot now lying in shards against its failure-to-thrive, failed-to-protect Bubble Wrap.

"Poor Abby," Ned laments. "After what you went through for this. The fight. The money. The stress. The . . . All the plans you had for it."

I bend down. I pick up a sliced-off handle. I study the broken pieces. What were my plans? Hoard it under my bed as some kind of talisman? Sell it? Donate it to Casa Guidi? Give it to the Schlesinger Library? Agonize about its safety? Feel residual guilt over how I lied to Lavinia? Wonder forever if Henrietta really did mean for Lavinia to have it? If it really belonged to her?

"You must be devastated," Ned says now.

I start to nod. An automatic response to a natural or unnatural disaster. Then I stop. A bulb sparks. It's not devastation I feel. Only an extraordinary lightening. *Relief*. The chamber pot is no longer worth anything to anybody. Only to me. I can keep it. Nobody else will want it.

"Where's the glue?" Ned asks. "Let me try to mend it. I'm good at such things."

I touch the scar on my knee. "I know you are."

He holds up his hands. "My bike mechanic's hands. I'm pretty sure I can put this Humpty-Dumpty back together again." He pauses. "Not the same as new." He smiles. "But good enough."

"Sometimes good enough is more than enough." I reach for his bike mechanic's hands. "More than good enough."

I find the glue. Ned untangles a blanket from a knot of sheets. He spreads it across the living room floor. He sits down on it. One by one he lays out the pieces. He scrutinizes each separate porcelain bit. He shifts the fragments around like jigsaw puzzle parts. He tries one combination. Then another. Until he has set out a blueprint in mosaic of the chamber pot.

I think of antiques, of objects of desire, how the hairline crack in an old vase, the foxing in an old print, the clouded glass of an old decanter mark the passage of time, commemorate the history of people's lives. *This has age*, one of my colleagues might boast to a customer, extolling its greater value over the shiny and pristine. How much easier it is to live with flaws than perfection. How much more comfortable. Scars and nicks—Ned's novel, my bad choices, our silence and time apart—can have value in human terms, too, not just in china, glass, silver, old manuscripts. Flaws can reveal growth, authenticity. Can show that two people have lived and learned.

Now I watch Ned naked, hair falling over his forehead, forehead wrinkled in concentration, arrange the pieces to reconstruct the chamber pot. I think of the day Ned taught me how to ride my bike; "Ride to me!" he'd yelled. "You can do it," he'd cheered. I remember how I'd looked at the back of his head as he cleaned and patched up my knee. We've come full circle, I realize. I touch the old scar. I rub its faint ridge. In spite of the nicks and scratches, our diverging paths along the way, Ned's return to my life, his place in my apartment, his place in my heart, makes everything once broken now whole. I'll still have the chamber pot that belonged to Elizabeth Barrett Browning; mended, it will seem more fully mine. Mended like me and Ned. We are glued back together—in a different way perhaps, changed perhaps—but here we are.

Now Ned holds a fragment of porcelain up to the window. He turns it this way and that. He examines it. From the faint brown lines, I see that it's half of Flush's ear. Ned squeezes a coil of glue along its crooked edge. He wipes off the excess. Tenderly, carefully, he joins the broken piece to its other half, back to where it belongs.

acknowledgments

My thanks, yet again, to my wonderful, steadfast agent, Lisa Bankoff, whose firm hand and big heart, not to mention incomparable wit, continue to guide me through the geography of publishing. My editor, Lucia Macro, is a pure delight. Her boundless enthusiasm for this book has meant everything to me. Thanks also to Tina Dubois and Kelly Harms, who field questions and run interference with remarkable good humor and awesome aplomb. And to Dee Dee DeBartlo for getting the word out there.

Andrea Kramer gave me a crash course on depositions and kept this legal novice on the right side of verisimilitude. My in-house lawyers, Daniel and Howard, provided backup at every turn. As always, Jono saved me from embarrassing myself musicwise. Nikki Rosengren got me up to snuff on baton twirling. Novelists Joan Wickersham and Sara Lewis read the manuscript and offered just the right finely tuned combination of advice and encouragement. I am grateful to John Aherne for his continuing and valued friendship beyond the call of duty. To Frederick Olsen for coming up with the perfect cover. And to my sister, Robie Rogge, for cheerleading and fabulous parties. Much appreciation, as well, to Frank and Rob of Antiques on Cambridge Street.

My first reader, Elinor Lipman, is the sine qua non. She's the dearest and most exceptional of friends and the dearest and most exceptional of critics. Not a page of this novel has escaped her loving, flinty, and brilliant eye.

My friends and family and my circle of fellow writers are an endless source of comfort and joy, especially Daniel and Sharissa and Jono and Marnie. This book is dedicated to my husband, Howard, whom—as I've mentioned before but it bears repeating—I met in nursery school. In all our years together, he never once said to me, "Go get a job."